the SECRET LIFE of BECKY MILLER

*a novel*
by SHARON HINCK

# the secret Life of
# Becky Miller

**BETHANYHOUSE**
MINNEAPOLIS, MINNESOTA

Published by Bethany House Publishers
11400 Hampshire Avenue South
Bloomington, Minnesota 55438

Bethany House Publishers is a division of
Baker Publishing Group, Grand Rapids, Michigan.

Printed in the United States of America

ISBN-13:  978-0-7642-0129-5
ISBN-10:  0-7642-0129-8

**Library of Congress Cataloging-in-Publication Data**

Hinck, Sharon.
    The secret life of Becky Miller / Sharon Hinck.
        p.   cm.
    ISBN 0-7642-0129-8 (pbk.)
    1. Christian women—Fiction.  2. Wives—Fiction.  3. Mothers—Fiction.  I. Title.

PS3608.I53S43      2006
813'.6—dc22                                                              2006007826

To Ted with all my love

# ONE

*A subtle change in* air pressure was my
only warning. One millisecond later, a foot flew
out of the darkness toward my head.

I backflipped out of range and reached for my sword. The
honed blade flickered in the starlight. Determination raced through me
as air rushed into my lungs. My family had guarded the imperial treasure for generations. I wouldn't allow this attacker to get past me to the
palace.

A new shadow moved toward my left and coalesced into another
lithe warrior emerging from the bamboo forest. More silent figures melted
into the courtyard. Four men advanced now, barely visible under a cloud-
shrouded moon. If they were surprised to see a woman standing guard,
they hid it well. Their eyes drilled into me from their half-masked faces.
Each ninja brandished a sword.

My heart pounded. Stay focused. Breathe deep. I had trained for
this moment all my life. No need to let them see the fear coursing
through my veins.

One of the warriors lunged for me.

I parried and struck hard, forcing him back. All my focus zeroed
onto him. A prickle on the back of my neck warned me to duck.

A razor-sharp metal star spun past me, grazing my hair.

Panic added speed to my moves, but it wasn't enough. There were
too many of them. How could anyone fight in so many directions at
once? My strict training had failed me. Terror raced up from my toes.

*I was going to lose. The treasure would be lost forever. I would break the line of heritage. The faithful guardians of the treasure . . .*

"Mommy! Cookies now." I snapped out of my daydream. Three-year-old Kelsey grabbed my sweater and hung on. All my clothes tended to list to the right these days, having been tugged relentlessly by my preschooler.

"No, sweetie. It's suppertime." I turned to stir the ramen noodles.

Dylan sailed past on his skateboard. "What's for supper?" The last words faded as he disappeared into the living room.

"Noodle soup. And no skateboards in the house!" My scolding wasn't as stern as it should have been. At age seven, Dylan exuded bliss in everything he did. He injected a dose of joy into my unremarkable life, and I hesitated to squelch his exuberance.

"*Need* cookies." Kelsey tugged harder.

"No snacks before supper." I angled my body to get between her and the cookie jar. She was a rapid climber, and it took martial arts alertness to fend her off.

"Pleeeeeze." Her wail rose in volume. In predictable harmony, the higher-pitched screech of baby Micah joined in from the boys' room.

Great. I had hoped he'd nap until Kevin got home from work.

A hiss from the stove interrupted the chorus.

I lurched forward to turn down the heat under the kettle. Too late. Water boiled over in a mass of starchy bubbles. Somehow my cheery blue-and-white kitchen had turned into a punishing purgatory. Our modest rambler felt smaller every day as the kids grew larger.

I stretched one leg back to block Kelsey's ongoing attempts to grab some Oreos.

Another plaintive squeal sounded from the baby.

"I'm coming."

Micah's wails grew more insistent with hiccupping gasps between them. He'd been fussy all day, and it sounded like his nap hadn't helped. His passionate distress had to be dealt with fast.

*A Good Mother meets all her children's needs.*

I was generally a positive person, but lately my goal to be a Wonderful Wife and Marvelous Mom had me frayed around the edges. I loved everyone under this roof with a passion and wanted to create a warm, nurturing world for them, but my self-esteem was chipped away a little more each day when I couldn't live up to my ideals.

"Come on, Kelsey. Let's check on Micah." I swooped her up and raced into the hall. My foot landed on something that moved.

We sailed several feet along the hall, my shriek adding a descant theme over Kelsey's whine and Micah's wail, before my legs scissored into splits a gymnast would envy. The skateboard shot out from under me and continued cheerfully down the hall while I fell backward, Kelsey still in my arms.

I hit the wood floor with a thud as Kelsey's elbow impaled me. My lungs struggled to find air while gray glitter edged my vision.

"Wow, Mom! That was cool." Dylan's brown eyes stared down at me from under his Beatle-length bangs.

I tried to lift Kelsey off my ribs. "Take your sister."

He probably couldn't hear my gasped request over Micah's screams, but he seemed to get the idea and pulled Kelsey up.

She whimpered and a few tears spurted from her hazel eyes. "Hurt my ankle," she said, pointing to her elbow. We hadn't quite mastered all the body parts yet.

"Don't cry." Dylan led his sister back toward the kitchen. I had only a moment to thank God for my helpful firstborn before he continued. "Come on, I'll get you a cookie."

I struggled up to one elbow. Every bone in my thirty-year-old body ached.

Micah screamed again. A loud thud told me he was rocking his crib. He'd learned how to pull himself up on the crib rail and heft his stubby weight back and forth, producing hearty thumps against his wall.

*Thump, thump.* Wail.

"Cookies! More cookies!" Kelsey's gleeful yell from the kitchen carried over pounding protests from the nursery.

I winced and eased myself back to a spread eagle flat on the floor, facing the ceiling. A few dead flies and a moth showed through the frosted white light fixture. How long since I'd cleaned it? When we bought the house years ago?

Maybe I'd stare at the ceiling until Kevin got home. Sometimes you had to concede defeat. How was I ever going to create the idyllic family life I had longed for as a child?

The phone rang from the kitchen as another crash from Micah's room propelled me to my feet and into the boys' room. One of these days he'd walk the crib straight through the wall. Dylan hadn't been thrilled when we set up the crib in his room. Sharing space with a brother might be fun one day. But a squalling, temperamental nine-month-old didn't make the best of roommates. Micah couldn't even throw a decent pitch yet, or play Nintendo.

When Micah saw me, he wriggled his padded bottom, and his cry stopped midshriek. I grabbed his sweaty body and let him wipe tears and mucus onto my shoulder as he nestled in to me. It was an old shirt anyway—like all my clothes. Why risk any quality fabric to constant spatters of spit up, leaky diapers, and mashed Cheerios?

From the answering machine, my perky voice piped an invitation to leave a message. A garbled sound carried from the kitchen, and I was tempted to step out into the hall to hear who was calling. What if Kevin was tied up in a meeting again? Or stuck in traffic? His commute wasn't usually too long from downtown, since we lived in one of the inner-ring suburbs of Minneapolis, named Richfield. A misnomer because few in our neighborhood were rich and there were no fields to be seen. Still, it was a neat, safe city with rows of small ramblers and well-kept lawns. I loved to walk to the nearby park with Micah in the stroller or watch the kids romp in the backyard.

A sour odor wafted up from Micah's sagging diaper and diverted me from heading toward the phone. Being a mother was all about triage. Three children often clamored at the same time. Various appliances screamed for my attention. I calmly and efficiently assessed the most severe trauma and tackled each crisis in order.

In my dreams.

In reality, I flailed around like my alter ego under attack by a host of speedy ninjas. My back against the wall, I lived in a state of near panic, wondering when I'd forget to duck . . . when I'd be overrun.

On top of that, I wasn't sure what I was defending any-more. Or why my efforts felt so futile. The ninjas kept coming.

I mopped up Micah's bottom and slipped a clean diaper on with an economy of movement.

Micah's wide smile pinched deep dimples into his cheeks. "Ah-boo."

"Yes, it's suppertime. Did you have a nice nap?" I blew a raspberry against his fat tummy.

He chortled. "Boo. Ah-boo." Fat legs thumped against his changing table, and he twisted.

"Whoa. Hold on." I snapped his overalls closed as he tried to dive off the table and caught him with my free arm to ease him to the ground. The rapid ballet of the diaper change. Move too slowly and the cleanup became a battle of wills. This time I'd been quick enough, and I felt a wave of satisfaction.

Micah scooted out the door in a wiggly crawl. The marines could use a few good babies like him. I sprinted past him to get to the kitchen first. Dylan and Kelsey had disappeared, but a trail of Oreo crumbs led to the basement stairs. I hit Play on the answering machine and turned to salvage the soup. A few frozen vegetables tossed into the mix might mellow the taste of burnt noodles.

*BEEP!* "Hi, Becky. It's Doreen. Listen, I know I said I'd be there to set up for the fall bake sale, but Josh has chicken pox. Sorry. Hope you find someone else."

Tension throbbed in my temples. I couldn't find another helper by tomorrow. I'd have to leave at daybreak to set up the school fundraiser alone. I'd be gluing red maple leaves and orange-tinged oak leaves to the tablecloths for hours.

Micah pulled open the cupboard next to the stove and grabbed his favorite lids. The clash of metal drove shards of pain behind my eyes.

"Micah, stop that!" I snatched the kettles away from him as the front door squeaked open.

Kevin bounded in and dropped his briefcase. He sniffed the air. "Something's burning. Oh, and I heard you yelling from the front porch. Are you all right?"

I bit back a sarcastic reply. He wasn't trying to be critical. He simply observed and commented, the way he always did. I wondered how that played out at his job. "Mrs. Smith, I see this is your third traffic accident in two years. Your premiums will be going up." Then he'd add the sympathetic smile, and she'd forgive him for his bluntness and sign up for the deluxe insurance package. Kevin had that effect on people. Good thing he didn't realize how much charisma charged through him. His genial unawareness added to his charm.

Kevin's crisp shirt had surrendered to a few wrinkles after a long day. His hair was the rich, dark color of walnut fudge. His buzz cut provided a bristly-soft cap that I loved to rub. A dusting of stubble edged his jawline. Thick lashes framed dark caramel eyes—as inviting as his open arms.

I ran to hug him. A few seconds of stolen comfort. "I'm so glad you're home." Every day I prompted myself to let Kevin decompress after work. Every day I failed in my good intentions and gave in to the urge to talk to the first adult I'd seen in hours. "Micah's still fussy. It might be a new tooth. Doreen's son has chicken pox, and I'll have to get to school early to set up. And Dylan left his skateboard in the house and I fell, but I'm okay, and I'm sorry about the noodles, they got away from me, but supper is almost ready—could you call Dylan and Kelsey?"

Micah pulled three more pots out of the cupboard and put one on his head. Kevin laughed and scooped him up, taking time to play peek-a-boo a few times before removing the saucepan.

Affection rose inside me like the steam from the soup. Kevin's buoyancy made him an incredible dad.

He deposited Micah into the high chair. "Suppertime!" he bellowed in the general direction of the stairs.

I rolled my eyes. "I could have done that."

He grinned. "You told me to call them."

A stampede pounded up the stairs. "Daddy's home!" Our two oldest danced around Kevin, bestowing hugs, kisses, and tickles.

What was I? Strained spinach? I nurtured them all day, but the instant Kevin walked through the door, he became the hero.

My thoughts softened as I watched them tussle. Why not? He was my hero, too.

Herding Dylan and Kelsey toward the kitchen table, Kevin grabbed the stack of mail off the corner desk. "Hey, did you see this one?"

"Hmm?" I rummaged in a drawer for a clean bib for Micah. "Never got a chance to sort the mail out, sorry."

"Here. Check it out." He tugged the bib from my hand and swapped it with a long blue envelope.

I squinted at the return address. *Women of Vision.* Navy script cut a diagonal across the bottom corner—*The magazine for successful women of the Twin Cities.* Probably just looking for subscriptions. I'd seen a few editions at Doreen's house. Glossy photos with improbable success stories. Inspirational features bookended by how-to columns. If I had the time to read their articles on how to save time, I wouldn't need them in the first place.

I tossed the envelope on the counter, hefted the kettle of soup onto a hot-pad on the table, and chased everyone to their chairs. Little heads bowed. Kelsey's blond curls almost touched her soup bowl. Dylan's eyes squeezed shut in earnest devotion under his dark mop of hair. Even Micah stopped pounding on his high chair tray. The sweet tableau made me smile. Kevin winked at me and led us in saying grace.

The frenzied attack of my day eased back. Family life wasn't so bad . . . once reinforcements arrived. We all dug into the simple supper of scorched noodles, and I managed to sneak in a few spoonfuls between helping the kids and asking Kevin about his day. After a litany of "She's kicking my chair," "He took the last piece of bread," and "Oops, Micah spilled his juice again," the children relaxed into momentary contentment while Kevin got out the devotion book.

I passed sugar cookies around the table. We had decided to

link spiritual enlightenment with dessert, in hopes of forging a Pavlovian connection for our children.

Kelsey beamed as she nibbled the blue-frosted cookie. She had helped me make them and applied food coloring with enthusiasm.

Dylan chewed, eyes fixed on Kevin with rapt attention.

Finally, one of our children was getting into the spirit of the "Little Journeys with Jesus" devotions. My husband threw himself into the roles of the master distributing talents, the whiny man who buried his single talent in the ground, and the diligent men who put their talents to good use. His animated voices made the kids giggle.

I squirmed. I should feel encouraged to invest my God-given resources. Instead, a blanket of condemnation smothered me. What were my talents? How did I invest them? I dreamed of caring for lepers like Mother Teresa or preaching to huge crowds like Billy Graham. Instead, I changed diapers, scrubbed sticky floors, and struggled to take an occasional night class to finish my teaching degree.

Scanning the faces around the table, I gave myself the traditional moms' pep talk. My children were my mission field. Raising them was a worthy calling. My efforts would make a difference, even if I couldn't see it yet.

*Then why do I feel like I'm falling short?*

Kevin finished the story. He noticed Dylan's concentration. "What do you think about that, big guy?"

I held my breath. Hope set my heart pounding under my stained T-shirt. My seven-year-old would share a gem of spiritual insight, and I would feel vindicated in my value as a parent.

Dylan leaned forward. "If I put food coloring in my eyes, would I cry blue?"

And there you had it. The extent of our spiritual influence.

I sank lower in my chair. My life had become a theatre of the absurd. Non sequiturs. Random entrances and exits by the actors. Snappy dialogue with an esoteric meaning that escaped me.

One day the master would come and ask what I did with my meager talent. I didn't bury it. I waved it in a hundred directions like lightning-fast parries with a sword. Yet somehow none of the strokes seemed to land on my target. Or the target kept moving. And so far, the ninjas always got past and stole the treasure.

# TWO

*"Hold back those* scurvy dogs!*" I*
*gripped the rope and slid down from the yardarm,*
*landing on the planks of the deck. The three-masted clipper*
*ship,* Forthright, *lurched beneath me. Years of serving in the*
*queen's navy had given me amazing balance, even on rough seas and*
*under fire.*

I'd led my crew in fighting off pirate attacks before, but this time we were outgunned. I ran to the nearest cannon to help load.

An explosion rocked the ship. Our topsail burst into flame. A grappling hook sailed out of the smoke to our port side.

"Side arms!" I shouted the order with feigned confidence. Waves sloshed over the listing deck. Anger surged through my veins as I drew my pistol. The Forthright was a fine ship. Agile in high seas, and well armed. But the Dark Storm had twice the cannons and a host of vicious mercenaries ready to dredge the seas for bounty while our corpses fed the sharks.

I sprang to the rail, grabbing the tattered jib for support. From here I could see past clouds of smoke to the Dark Storm in all its might. Envy shot through my blood like hot rum. She was magnificent. Fierce. Should've been named Undaunted.

I jumped back to the deck and wove through my men, offering words of encouragement that we all knew were words of farewell. My pride hung in tatters. Outgunned, outclassed. The massive ship glided closer, dwarfing our vessel. Seawater sloshed around my ankles. Another crash of cannon fire rocked my eardrums. We were going down. . . .

"Mommy! The washer's walking!" Kelsey's strident voice echoed in the dingy basement.

I blinked and looked up from the pile of clean laundry on the counter, where I had been matching socks one-handed. Micah straddled my hip in his normal position. Why were my crew socks squishy and wet?

A grind of gears and a lurching timpani rhythm warned me. The washing machine was throwing another tantrum. Our home matched my age—thirty. The house still had many original appliances. Was it a bad sign for my body's warranty that everything in our house was falling apart?

I took a step toward the washer in frustration, my foot landing squarely in a puddle. Gray water baptized my ankles and crept toward the basket of folded laundry. I sloshed through the mess and hit the control button.

A final crash and shudder halted the renegade advance of the washer.

Micah shrieked in my ear. Kelsey screeched in pretend terror and raced for the stairs, giggling.

I lunged for the basket of clean laundry and hefted it up to the counter. Water scattered in a wide arc. The bottom third of the contents had already soaked up dirty water.

Great. I had been two loads away from catching up on the laundry. My one domestic goal for the day. And I'd been so close to reaching it. If I had time, I would collapse onto the wet floor and cry. I'd survived Saturday's bake sale at the school, even without Doreen's help decorating. Church and a potluck dinner had filled our Sunday. Over the weekend while I wasn't looking, dust bunnies, scattered toys, and dirty laundry had commandeered the house.

*I will not call Kevin to whine. I will not call Kevin.*

I peeled off my wet socks and dropped them into one of the

puddles. I tossed a few old towels around the floor to contain the mess and plodded up the stairs.

The phone on the kitchen counter lured me with the same power as a chocolate doughnut. Micah's shrieks faded to sniffles, and I set him down next to his ice cream bucket of chubby plastic farm animals. He ignored those and crawled toward the cupboard with the kettles.

I grabbed the phone and hit the number one speed dial.

"Anderson Life and Home—this is Kevin." The voice was calm, in control, warm. The regional manager ready to calm troubled waters.

"Hi, honey. The washing machine is possessed again. It walked across the floor and there's water everywhere and I can't finish the laundry and I don't have time to deal with this. I'm supposed to head over to church for a meeting about the women's retreat."

I pictured Kevin rubbing his temple as he caught on this wasn't an agent from his branch office calling. "Just leave it. I'll look at it when I get home. I thought I had that pump fixed. I'm sorry." To his credit, his voice lost none of its warmth.

"It's okay." Grateful for his sympathy, I didn't mention I'd been skeptical about his repair attempts all along. My elbow bumped the growing pile of mail. I really ought to sort it. If the papers inched any closer to our slow cooker they would become a fire hazard. "I'll see you at suppertime. I've got spaghetti sauce in the slow cooker."

His pause lasted a second too long. "Oh, I forgot. A big client's coming in, and the boss wants us to take him out to dinner. I'll be late tonight."

This man was my husband. I loved him. He offered me comfort in the midst of life's chaos. I would not descend into attack mode.

Yet the words slipped from my mouth. "You couldn't have told me in advance? Why did I bother making spaghetti sauce if it's just the kids and me? Dylan doesn't even like it." My sigh layered on disapproval, frustration, self-pity, and all the other negative emotions I had determined to hide.

Kevin cut in before I escalated into complaints about his work hours, the state of our home appliances, and the cost of milk. "I can't really talk now. I'm sorry I forgot to call you sooner."

I didn't hear enough contrition in his voice. In fact, I suspected there was a hint of relief that he had a valid excuse for staying away from home a few more hours.

"Never mind. I'll handle things. I always do." I couldn't believe those sarcastic words shot past my lips. I dropped the phone and rubbed my eyes. What was my problem today?

Last night, I'd read a few pages of a book from the church library with some implausible title like *The Joys of the Supportive Wife*. This morning I had resolved to focus on that holy calling and be the most warm, helpful wife any husband had ever seen. I'd even remembered to brush my teeth before giving Kevin his good-bye kiss. Just a few hours later, and I'd transformed into a complete harpy.

I shrugged the guilt off my shoulders—the only weight-training exercise I found time for these days. Unless you counted two hundred reps of the baby bench press and the dozen or so lateral pull downs of closing the van's back hatch on errand runs.

Kelsey had disappeared into her room. I left Micah to dent our pots and pans and tiptoed down the hallway to check on her. She chattered in the chirping voice she assumed when playing with Barbies.

Not that I approved of giving overendowed fashion figures to a three-year-old girl. My sister, Judy, showered my kids with inappropriate gifts. She was single and the vice-president of marketing for a big toy company. My children adored her.

Judy couldn't absorb the fact that Kevin and I didn't appreciate the constant stream of gifts—gadgets that burned through expensive batteries, electronic gizmos that hypnotized Dylan and kept him from playing outside, construction sets with thousands of tiny pieces that had to be kept out of Micah's reach, or dolls modeling sleazy clothes that made Kelsey want to show her belly button at Sunday School. Judy meant well, but my efforts to explain my spiritual values didn't track with her.

"No, no." Kelsey's voice carried from her room, her impression of me dead-on. "Tell God thank-you first."

Maternal pride raced through my bloodstream faster than caffeine from my morning coffee. She was admonishing her dolls to say grace at her tea party. My smile grew so wide that my cheeks hurt. Maybe I was a good parent, after all.

"Let's have 'votions. God gave you stuff to do. Don't put it in the ground."

Joy made me wriggle. I wanted to stand outside and eavesdrop forever, but the women's ministry meeting started in twenty minutes. I stepped around the doorjamb.

Tiny clumps of golden Barbie hair scattered her floor. Kelsey's safety scissors rested nearby. A stuffed turtle and two bunnies had joined the tea party—a sacred circle on the floor with Kelsey overseeing. One Barbie fell over and Kelsey adjusted its joints and braced it up. All three dolls had new haircuts. Random hunks jutted out of the overall stubble. I had a feeling this Barbie fashion wouldn't catch on.

My warm glow dimmed, but I was too happy with Kelsey's signs of spiritual growth to lose my temper over some illicit haircuts. "Sweetie, it's time to go to church. Put your shoes on."

Kelsey looked up and grinned.

I shrieked.

Her blond bangs were gone. A jagged hairline weaved drunkenly across the top of her forehead.

"Kelsey!" I admit the gasp of shock and outrage in my voice should have been reserved for train wrecks and heart attacks, or at least major neighborhood vandalism. But I loved my little girl's hair. She had the blond curls I'd always dreamed of. My attempts to alter my own dark, coarse locks into a California surfer look had wasted long Saturday nights and all my spare dollars. No box of smelly dye had done the trick, and I'd given up long before Kelsey's birth. Her golden curls had been my surrogate pleasure.

"Kelsey, what have you done?" My voice rose two octaves.

She ignored the histrionics and heaved a very mature sigh. "Haircut."

How had she perfected the teenage eye-roll at the age of three? The one that said "Duh! Like, what is your problem? Get a grip, Mom."

No time to fix her now. Not that there were many bangs left to even out. I wedged one of Dylan's baseball caps onto her head. "Where are your shoes? We have to go to church."

Maybe God felt I'd had enough trouble for one morning. For once, the getting-out-of-the-house chaos stayed to a minimum. We found Kelsey's shoes, and she didn't fight me when I tied them. I kissed her nose and induced the kind of giggles that sprinkle fairy dust through the room. I laughed with her and tugged the brim of her baseball cap. I found my keys on the hook by the entry and only had to search a few minutes for the bag with the women's ministry notebook.

Never mind that the basement was full of soggy towels, smelly laundry, and a broken washing machine. Never mind that my sweet daughter had a haircut that would make even a punk rocker cringe. Never mind that I'd snapped at my husband and faced another supper alone with the kids.

I was about to revel in the world of Grown-up People with Grown-up Purpose.

Whistling along to a VeggieTales tape, I steered the van past a Big Wheel, a skateboard, and a bucket of sidewalk chalk.

When we joined our church five years ago, I pointed out the need for a women's Bible study, a well-staffed nursery, retreats, and other ministries for young moms. Somehow the agreeable church staff thought I was volunteering to organize it all.

I knew how to purse my lips to form the word *no*. I could have run the other direction. In truth, the challenge appealed to me. I'd been immersed in the world of maternity clothes, nursing, diapers, and sleep deprivation for years. The thought of having a job where I could interact with adults was a thrill. The volunteer status didn't lessen my enthusiasm. We squeaked by on Kevin's salary. Besides, developing a women's ministry assuaged a little of the ever-present pressure to do Big Things for God.

I'm not sure where I picked up that compulsion. It wasn't from my parents. And it wasn't from my sister, who excelled at doing Big Things but never worried about doing them for God. Maybe the idea took hold in college, when I got involved in a campus ministry that fired my spiritual fervor. Maybe our church's classes on "Lives of Christian Heroes" spurred my aspirations. Martyred missionaries, Bible smugglers, and folks who befriended violent gang members gave me a lot to measure up to. Suddenly our family devotions around the supper table had seemed like a lukewarm excuse for our way to serve God.

Throwing myself into the women's ministry provided an element of relief. As the program grew, I felt closer to achieving my Big Thing for God.

We pulled into the church parking lot, and I unlatched Kelsey and Micah from their car seats. Kelsey proudly carried my bag for me while I wrestled with Micah, who squirmed like a twenty-five-pound bass.

Sally, my friend in spite of her perfect blond hair, gave me a warm smile. "Pastor Roger is in a counseling appointment. He'll be ready soon. The retreat committee gals are in the library." She was the perfect church secretary—bubbly and reassuring, with an uncanny knowledge of everything that went on at church.

"Thanks." I set Micah on the floor to readjust my blouse. "I'm running a little late."

"Don't worry." She glanced around and leaned forward, plump arms resting on her desk. "I heard that the Board of Elders finally decided the women's ministry is important." Her voice dropped to a whisper. "They're talking about putting a salary in the budget for the director."

A flush of satisfaction warmed my skin, and I barely stopped myself from jumping up and down. "That would be amazing."

"And that's not all." Sally pulled a blue envelope out of her tidy desk tray and fluttered it under my nose. "Congratulations."

"For what?"

"Didn't you get yours? They chose you. I knew they would. I outdid myself on the nomination form, if I do say so myself. Of course it wasn't hard. You've done such a great job for this church. . . ." She finally noticed my blank stare and slowed down. "Hel-*lo*? *Women of Vision*? The magazine?"

Micah started his marine crawl toward the pastor's office, so I grabbed him and settled him back onto my hip. What was Sally twittering on about?

She squirmed her chair closer to the desk. "They took nominations for interesting women in the Twin Cities. They're going to feature one each month and show how they balance family life and work and personal growth. I said they should include someone in religious work. I knew you'd be perfect."

Confusion sent my brain into spin cycle. "Me? But I'm not in religious work. I just volunteer here." Did I want my life paraded in a public report? On the other hand, what better time than now, when I was about to morph my efforts at the church into a meaningful career?

"It'll be a great way to share your faith. You can thank me later. You better get into the meeting."

I glowed through the committee discussion. Validation did that to me. Arguments about how to decorate the fellowship hall, fussing about bringing in an outside speaker from a different denomination, disagreement on the need to expand the nursery—none of it fazed me. My efforts had been recognized. Even the Board of Elders believed the program was valuable. And on top of that I was going to be featured in *Women of Vision*.

Still beaming two hours later, I boosted the kids into their car seats and settled into the van. Maybe when I started bringing in a salary, Kevin and I could get new furniture for the living room.

My cell phone jangled from somewhere under the front seat.

Probably Kevin touching base. I pulled out granola bar wrappers, a half-eaten lollipop that stuck to my sleeve, and a school permission slip that Dylan should have turned in a week ago. Finally, my fingers grasped the phone and pulled it out. Wait until Kevin heard that they might put me on staff. He'd be so proud. And the magazine article would probably be good for his business. They'd be sure to mention him.

I flipped my cell phone open, still grinning. "Hello."

"Where have you been?" My sister's voice made my stomach clench and my smile tighten. "I've been calling for the last hour. Why did I buy you that cell phone when you never keep it with you?"

"I was in a meeting." I loved how that sounded. So professional. So important.

Judy didn't seem impressed. "Whatever. Listen, I have great news. The trade convention was super. And get this. I'm going to be on the *Today* show next week to talk about our new line of dolls. Can you believe it?"

I fought to muster enthusiasm for her. What twisted part of my spirit felt diminished by her success? I should be proud of her. Happy for her.

"That's so exciting." I managed a bit of a high school squeal to convince her I was on board. "The kids will love seeing their aunt Judy on television."

She didn't seem to notice my forced tone because she raced on. "I know. And I mailed off another package. I know it's not Dylan's birthday yet, but we just came out with the best video game, and I knew he had to have it. It's a little violent, but he's not a baby anymore." She laughed as if she understood the power she had to charm my children. "How are the kids? Ooh, gotta run. They're calling my flight. See ya."

All my sense of accomplishment sank like a barnacle-covered ship with cannon holes in the side. My sister, Judy, was a glorious frigate. Clean lines—after all, she had no stretch marks from giving birth three times—and smooth sailing. She had the advanced degree I coveted. She even had the blond hair in the family. She had the high-powered job. Not just any job, either. Marketing for a major toy company made Aunt Judy the biggest hero in the world. She pirated the affection of my children, just as she had pirated the admiration of my parents when we were young.

My life seemed a battered hull next to hers. Barely afloat. Now my pending position at the church tasted like salt water in my mouth. And how could being featured in a local magazine compete with the *Today* show?

Somehow, Judy had the power to make me see my life through her eyes. She had never criticized when I left college to marry Kevin. She didn't have to. Every arched eyebrow, every polite yawn spoke for her. I was a wimp and a loser, a throwback to a 1950s mom with nothing but PTA and Sunday school to get me out of the house and no higher goal than a shiny kitchen—which I never achieved anyway.

My shoulders slumped as I wrenched the car into gear. The VeggieTales tape mocked me from the speakers. Kelsey sang along to her favorite song.

"We are the pirates, who don't do anything. . . ."

# THREE

**Lights beat down** with a fierce heat.
The makeup girl flicked her brush over my skin for
a last touch-up.

I sneezed.

"Becky! Watch the volume," the audio engineer complained into my
earpiece.

I saluted an apology in the general direction of the control booth.
Gotta keep everyone happy.

The producer fretted across the studio shouting last directions to the
audience.

The show's voice-over intro sounded in my ear. "Family meals can
be an occasion—a celebration. Join our lifestyle expert, Becky Miller,
and learn how to put the super in supper, the delight in dinner, and even
the breakthrough in breakfast."

The floor director pantomimed his countdown. The small red light
of camera one winked companionably, and I turned on my million-watt
smile. The one that had leveraged my cooking and entertainment skills
into a mega-industry.

Applause washed over me from the studio audience.

I grabbed a parrot piñata and held it over my head. "Never settle
for ordinary . . ."

"When you can have extraordinary!" The audience responded with
zest.

"That's right, folks. Instead of serving your family a boring meal—
create a theme. Tonight's theme is 'South of the Border.' I'll show you

*how to create homemade tortilla shells after grinding your own corn with my patented mortar and pestle set. All that and more after these messages."*

*I let my cheek muscles sag as we cut to commercial. If our ratings didn't improve soon, our show would be bumped to some loser time slot. I wouldn't let that happen. My message was important. I had to make this work. Keep smiling. Never let 'em see ya sweat.*

*The lights flared. I reached for the bowl of cornmeal.*

My hand brushed something hot.

"Ow!" I jerked back from the slow cooker of spaghetti sauce. The ladle dipped, plopping a deep red puddle next to the plate of garlic bread.

"Mommy spilled." Kelsey had the enthusiastic delivery of a television announcer.

I scrunched a paper napkin and blotted up the mess. "Eat your bread, honey."

"Can't."

"Why not?"

"It's touching."

I glared at Kelsey's plate. Sure enough, the spaghetti sauce had migrated toward her bread. Kelsey was traumatized by foods having physical contact with each other.

Kevin usually distracted her from this sort of crisis. But he was eating with grown-ups at some fancy restaurant. He would come home and pretend he hadn't enjoyed himself. I knew better.

Desperate to get this "super supper" back on track, I tried a bright smile. "Did you know spaghetti is an Italian food? Dylan, what do you know about Italy?"

He shrugged and pushed his naked noodles around his plate. "I know I don't like their food."

Micah banged his tray. I scooped up a precise dollop of rice cereal and aimed it toward his mouth.

He worried it around inside his cheeks a few times, then pushed it out with his tongue.

Gooey rice and saliva rolled down his chin. I scraped it with the spoon and pushed it back in while checking the progress of the other kids.

"Dylan, don't tie knots in your noodles. What would you do if the president invited you to his house one day? Let's work on manners."

"Please pass bread." Kelsey sat up tall on her booster seat.

I smiled and lifted the bread. "Wait. You already have bread."

She shrugged. "I'm doing manners."

After coaxing some food into each of the kids, my own food had congealed. No wonder I'd lost my pregnancy weight so fast. Moms have to shovel, tease, mop, stir, serve, pass, wipe, and watch the unappetizing process of their children eating. I had no time or inclination to eat my own food.

I almost skipped family devotions. I wanted to throw the leftovers in the fridge, stow the plates in the dishwasher, and collapse in front of a mindless sitcom—the kind I would never tell my church friends that I watched. The blue envelope was wooing me from the pile on the kitchen counter. I needed to read the letter from *Women of Vision* and find out what Sally had gotten me into.

But Kelsey handed me the devotion book with a beatific smile, so I opened it.

No one told me how being a mother would multiply the influence and effect of each of my decisions. Three pairs of eyes followed everything I did. Little voices mimicked my words even when they didn't grasp the content. Slight ripples in my mood spread in widening circles as my brood absorbed the vibrations and broadcast them in their own ways.

Before having children, I didn't mind skipping church on a rare occasion. Now if I overslept and suggested staying home "just this once," Dylan would stare at me in virtuous shock. Kelsey's lip would quiver at the thought of missing her Sunday school sticker for the week. I'd be overwhelmed with the certainty that one day my kids would lose their faith because of my laziness.

And before children, my conscience kindly looked away when I tossed an occasional soup can into the regular garbage. Now, Dylan acted as the recycling patrol. "Mom, *someone* made a mistake." He'd hold up a dripping can. "Americans make too much garbage." Then he'd give me the glare that said the entire collapse of society rested on my shoulders. He'd ignore the alphabet soup bits plopping onto the linoleum and wave the can around while delivering a lecture from his latest *Weekly Reader,* complete with statistics.

Why didn't the parenting books warn me what it would be like when my seven-year-old developed a social conscience?

Tonight, rather than stir up the murky swamp of guilt in my heart, I opened the devotion book. Micah sucked on a bottle of apple juice. Of course, I'd heard a doctor on the radio yesterday say juice hurt babies' teeth, but life was about trade-offs. A bottle assured a few minutes of quiet.

Dylan and Kelsey listened through the story, and I plunged into the questions. Dylan jumped in to answer three in a row, and Kelsey squawked. "My turn."

"How do you think the disciples felt when the net filled with fish?" I held my palm up to remind Dylan to give his sister a turn.

Kelsey gave us all a confident smile. "Jesus!"

During past devotions, she had decided the answer to every question was Jesus. Not a bad theology when you thought about it.

Dylan kicked Kelsey's chair. "No, silly. They felt smelly.

Remember when Dad took me fishing and it was hot driving home?"

Kelsey nodded sagely, even though she hadn't been born when Kevin and Dylan made that trip.

"I opened the cooler and left the lid off. Fish are smelly." My son turned back to me with a firm jut of his chin. "So that's how the disciples felt."

Oh, to be in second grade and know all the right answers with utter confidence.

Perhaps I should have explained the awe the disciples felt at the miracle, the confusion and questions about Christ's identity. But maybe Dylan had a point.

I saw God's miracles every day. And sometimes I just felt smelly.

Kevin lingered over his business dinner until after the kids' bedtime. I helped Dylan with his spelling words, endured Kelsey's screams while I washed her hair, and read *Runaway Bunny* three times. Somehow I squeezed in a moment to open the blue envelope and read about the *Women of Vision* feature. Apparently there had been hundreds of entries and the editors only chose twelve. One for each month—a diverse representation of successful women in the Twin Cities. I would be profiled in April. Well, at least that gave me five months to get my life on track. My new official position at church would be a great start. And maybe I should try a new haircut.

After tucking in Dylan and Kelsey, I drooped into the living room rocker to nurse Micah.

He squirmed and rubbed his eyes, then rooted briefly and splayed his chubby hand possessively against my chest. With a sigh, he relaxed into a warm, needy bundle.

Contentment rolled through me as sweet and comforting as melting chocolate. I felt the familiar tingle as my milk let down.

These precious interludes would taper off soon, and I savored every sensation.

When I nursed my baby, everything in the world made sense. I was nourishing another life, giving comfort and tangible love. Existential angst was banished for those minutes. I was doing exactly what I was made to do.

I stroked the fuzz on Micah's head, still damp from his bath. I inhaled the scent of baby shampoo and the indefinable aroma of newness that babies carry. Maybe this was the same way men felt about the new-car smell: Protective, admiring, and torn with a longing to stop time—to make it last.

The door creaked open and Kevin tiptoed into the entry and set his briefcase down with exaggerated care, not wanting to wake the kids. Considerate down to his bones. How could I stay irritated with a man like that?

He stepped into the soft lamplight of the living room and smiled, but his fingers drummed an uneasy pattern against his leg as he sought to read my mood.

I smiled what I hoped looked like the dreamy smile of a Madonna in a Renaissance painting . . . and not the exhausted smile of a mom who'd had a brutal day.

Kevin stepped closer and leaned down to kiss me, letting his lips linger. "I'm really sorry I had to stay late."

I adjusted Micah's blanket. "It's okay. How was the meeting?"

He shrugged and pulled off his tie. "Fine."

"Guess what I found out today." I kept my voice soft, so Micah wouldn't jerk his head up in surprise. Last time he'd done that, he'd forgotten to let go, and the tooth marks lasted for a week. "The church plans to allocate some salary for the women's ministry director."

He managed a tired smile. "That's terrific. You deserve it.

You've built a great program, and it's about time they recognized it."

"And you know the Twin Cities women's magazine that Doreen and Sally like? They chose me to be one of their featured women. I haven't had time to read all the details, but I guess it's a big honor."

He tried to ramp his enthusiasm up a notch. "Wow. I'm married to someone famous." He sank onto the couch and stretched. "Are you sure you know what you're getting into? How much time will it take?"

I felt a bit deflated. I wasn't expecting a standing ovation, but he could at least muster a little excitement. "I'm sure it'll be fun. I just have to fill out some questionnaires, and later they'll come and interview me and take some pictures."

He gave a noncommittal grunt. Thin lines of tension creased the smooth skin of his temples, where I loved to kiss him. He sagged with something beyond typical workday weariness.

My radar kicked in with a sharp mental blip. Exhausted and lulled by Micah's peaceful drowsing, the red alert still demanded my attention. "Honey, what's wrong?"

He shifted from his sprawl to lean forward, arms resting on his thighs. His back curved forward as if he'd been lugging bricks all day instead of processing paper work. He stared at the plastic craft table that had replaced our glass coffee table after Dylan's birth. Kelsey's latest Play-Doh sculpture stared back at him with fluorescent orange eyes.

The fine hair on my arms prickled. "Kevin?"

His gaze dropped lower, to his shoes. "The numbers aren't looking good at work again this quarter. They're talking about restructuring. And layoffs."

Blame the bliss of nursing hormones, but I still didn't catch on. "That's too bad. Who are they thinking of letting go?"

Kevin's face turned hard and angry. "Me." Maybe he thought

I had intended to be cruel by making him say it. He propelled himself from the couch and pounded down the stairs.

Fear kept me frozen to the rocking chair. This couldn't be happening. With three kids and one income, we ran out of money before the end of each month. But we laughed about it and made a game of scraping by. What would we do if he were laid off?

In a minute, I heard Kevin clanging his wrench against the washing machine pump. When jarred by trouble, his instinct drove him to fix something. But there was something tightly wound in him tonight. Maybe something beyond the bad news at work.

I decided to finish nursing Micah and give my husband a little time to work out his frustrations. Much better to let him tinker with a machine for a while. I didn't understand the appeal. I would have chosen a Snickers bar and potato chips to soothe stress, but whatever rotored his motor was fine with me.

I shivered and held Micah more closely. A heavy weight of responsibility pushed me deeper into the rocker. I didn't have a studio audience, like the lifestyle experts on television, but I felt the eyes of friends and family observing my efforts. A mom had to inspire, motivate, and make life fun for everyone in the house. I was in charge of morale. How could I boost Kevin's morale when I feared our show had plummeted in the ratings and might be canceled?

# FOUR

*My leather gloves* gave me a firm grip on the wire as I rappelled straight down the elevator shaft. Dangling ten stories above solid ground didn't worry me. Keeping the access code straight in my mind concerned me more. A covert ops expert had risked his life getting the password.

My private top-secret security company rivaled all the major government agencies for information gathering. But this was the most vital mission we had taken on.

Tension coiled beneath my ultrathin Kevlar vest, and I willed my pulse to slow. No margin for error. No time for nerves.

My rubber-soled shoes touched the rim of the third-floor threshold to stop my descent. I pried the doors open, leapt into the hall, and unclipped my carabiner.

I sprinted north down the hall, then east at the first corridor. This section of the building shouldn't be heavily patrolled. Around the next corner, the door appeared exactly where our schematics had indicated. I pulled a 3X.02 electronic decryptor from my belt and connected it to the keypad on the wall. A few quiet blips and the lock disabled. So far, so good.

After scanning the hall in both directions, I slipped into the room. Gray walls surrounded a few bare desks with ergonomic chairs and computer monitors. An unimpressive office, considering the secrets it contained.

*My watch glowed a harsh green number. Five minutes. I had five minutes to slip into the system and capture the data that threatened the safety of the entire free world. I dropped into a chair and opened the screen.*

*Bling. "You've got mail."*

I dissolved out of my high-tech daydream. My computer always took forever to boot up, giving my mind time to wander. I clicked on the icon and picked up my third cup of coffee of the morning. My fuzzy pink bathrobe nestled around my shoulders. Our house was chilly, and I hadn't yet found a moment to get dressed since sending Dylan off on the school bus.

The clock on the screen warned me—only five quiet minutes before Kelsey finished watching *Sesame Street* and Micah woke up from his brief morning nap.

I cherished every moment with my e-mail. Kevin called it an addiction. He claimed I couldn't walk past the corner desk in the kitchen without clicking on to check for messages. The way I saw it, e-mail provided the new community. Our town had no village well where women drew water and chatted. Instead, I found comfort sending short notes to friends. Exchanging news. Gathering information. My e-mails provided a portal into the world beyond Fisher-Price toys and baby talk.

I browsed a few posts on the board for the college where I hovered 28 credits shy of a degree. One night class per semester made a very small dent in the requirements—but it entitled me to join the discussion loop.

This morning a debate raged about Professor Radnick, who had refused to pass several students after their final teaching practicum. At my pace, Radnick would be retired before I had to worry about that. I skimmed the titles of posts and deleted aggressively.

Next I attacked all the forwarded jokes, warnings, and sentimental pap. I kept telling my friends not to send these to me. Each one began the same way. "I know you don't want forwarded messages, but I had to send you just this one." Sigh.

Finally, I moved on to the best. Personal e-mails.

*From: Sally@sj.communitychurch.org*
*Subject: Hi Becky!*
 *How are retreat plans coming along? I overheard Pastor talking to John. They're looking forward to adding to the staff. See ya tonight! Sally*

I keyed in a quick answer:

 *Thanks for the heads up! Oh, and that magazine feature sounds really exciting . . . and kinda scary. I can't believe you did that. You should have nominated Lori instead. She would have been perfect. Can't wait for tonight. Although I'm behind in my lesson again. Did you read the chapter on suffering for doing good? Becky*

I hit Send and jumped to the next e-mail.

*From: JudyH@vp.zoopertoys.net*
*Subject: Your sister the TV star*
 *Just got back from a meeting in St. Louis and have to fly to New York. Zoom zoom. The TV spot is Friday morning. You'll be watching, right? What am I thinking? You're always home! You don't have anywhere to go. LOL! Judy*

I winced and passed over that one. I didn't have it in me to reply to my sister without going into a rant about the hard role of stay-at-home mom.

*From: Doreen@fam.village.net*
*Subject: More spots*
  *Josh's chicken pox spread to Rachel and Aaron. I'm hoping to make it to our Bible study tonight, but it depends on if Jim is up for three itchy kids. Hugs, Doreen*

Pity made it easier to forgive her for ditching me before the big bake sale last Saturday. She was the one woman in our Bible study group that I struggled to feel comfortable around. Maybe it was because her polished look reminded me too much of my sister, Judy. Doreen had been a high-powered financial advisor before choosing to spend a few years at home with her baby. When two more children followed, she got sidetracked on her plan to return to her career. Now she approached child rearing like a corporate executive—and always met her goals. I would have disliked her more, except Jim was a selfish, unsupportive husband who didn't seem to do anything but snarl at her. He couldn't blame his moods on financial pressure. They were already by far the wealthiest family in our circle. Even after three kids, Doreen carried a Gucci diaper bag, wore Banana Republic faux-casual fashions, and drove a shiny maroon SUV.

I sent a quick reply.

  *Bummer about the pox. Do you need anything? I'm praying Jim will watch the kids so you can come. Big hugs, Becky*

The next e-mail had a familiar address.

*From: KevinMiller@andersonlifeandhome.com*
*Subject: Hi Hon!*
  *Caught you checking your e-mail again! Heh, heh. Hope you have a good day. See you tonight. Kevin*

I grinned. Kevin might tease, but he would never make me feel guilty for a night out, even if the kids had chicken pox. His mood had lightened by this morning, and he had joked with the kids as usual. He even volunteered to take all three to the mall tonight since it was my turn to host the Bible study. As I stared at my computer screen, my smile morphed into a worried frown. How could I keep his spirits up when he had to spend each day under the frightening cloud of possible layoffs? And could I draw out the dark tensions I had sensed last night? Should I? Or should I play along with his cheery confidence and ignore my instincts?

I hit Reply.

*Subject: Re: Hi Hon!*
   *And I caught you writing personal e-mails at the office. So there. Micah is actually napping this morning. I think the teething is bothering him less, so he should be cheerful for the mall tonight. Have I told you that you are the sexiest man in the world? Not many men can fix a washing machine, take the kids to the mall, AND have dreamy eyes. XOXO!*

There. That should give him a smile. I moved on to an e-mail from Heather, my granola-head friend. About my age, with nine-year-old twins, she was an anachronism. Her long mane of uncombed hair, peasant blouses, and tie-dyed skirts flowing around her ankles would have fit well into a 1960s commune. I was surprised she embraced the world of e-mails, considering that she still baked bread by hand and canned her own jam.

*Subject: Tonight . . .*
   *See you tonight. Can I bring anything? I'm baking muffins today.*

My fingers flew.

*Subject: Re: Tonight . . .*
  *No, Lori's bringing some snacks. Thanks anyway!*


Close call. Last time Heather brought wheat germ and bran brownies, and I almost broke a tooth. She sprinkled compassion on all her friends like aromatherapy, and I'd trust her with my life, but that didn't mean I'd encourage her organic nutrition attempts.

Blond, bubbly Sally. Organized, sleek Doreen. Warm, other-worldly Heather. That left one more of our circle to hear from.

Sure enough, the next e-mail came from Lori.

*From: homeschoolmomtoo@protectfamilies.org*
*Subject: First Peter and Apple Pie*
  *How ya doing? Wasn't the homework from 1 Peter terrific? I used the lessons with my kids this week. Can't wait to discuss it tonight. Remember, I'm bringing apple pie, so don't eat too much supper. Oh, and I'm bringing a petition for everyone to sign about the new legislation. You don't mind if I explain it at the beginning of our meeting, do you? TTFN (Ta-ta for now!) Lori*


Oh boy. Another political cause from Lori. If I didn't love her so much, I'd be tempted to tell her to put a sock in it once in a while. When I first met her, her confidence and beauty intimidated me. With her model-tall frame and the chocolate skin of a Hollywood diva, I expected her to be a flamboyant artist type or an Alvin Ailey dancer. Instead, she marched somewhere to the right of Rush Limbaugh. And she became one of my best friends. Her staunch lifestyle choices made the rest of us feel uneasy for going to movies, letting our kids attend public schools, and listening to music other than "Christian-lite FM." But when any of us needed advice, we trusted her wisdom and integrity above anyone else. In many ways, she embodied the Christian woman of influence I longed to become.

I smiled and pushed back from the desk, tugging the lapels of my bathrobe. A whiff of sweaty skin reminded me I still hadn't taken a shower today. When I peeked into the boys' room, Micah was sleeping hard, with a trickle of drool puddling under his head and his bottom hitched in the air. Downstairs, *Sesame Street* ended, and Kelsey stared at furry dancing characters. We allowed only one show a day, but it wouldn't hurt to let her watch a little longer.

She waved me away when I told her I'd be in the shower.

Lilac bath gel clashed with chamomile shampoo, but I savored every hot steamy minute. With three small children, the shower was often the only place where I could get hot and steamy these days. I indulged in the extra extravagance of conditioning my hair, then stepped out and reached for my towel. My reflection materialized in the misty mirror. For a woman of thirty, I didn't look too bad.

My stretch marks were pale and barely noticeable, and Kevin always told me they were badges of honor. My slim form looked bustier than usual because of nursing—a definite improvement over my usual boyish torso. I raked my fingers through my wet hair. The dark layers hung several inches too long to duplicate the trendy "messy" style. My look could best be described as "frumpy mom." I leaned closer to the mirror and squinted. As the fog cleared, the view wasn't as forgiving. Shadowed pouches hung under my eyes. Too many sleepless nights had taken their toll.

"'Charm is deceptive and beauty is fleeting; but a woman who fears the Lord is to be praised,'" I chanted. Lori had encouraged me to teach Kelsey that proverb when I complained about my daughter's preoccupation with fashion dolls.

I pulled on a loose sweat shirt and my jeans—the mom uniform of most of my friends. Except Lori, who always wore a denim dress—the classic choice of the homeschool moms I knew. Oh, and Doreen. After her first child arrived, she transitioned from business suits to crisp blouses and sleek Capris.

When I peeked in on Micah, he was resting on his back, clutching one set of toes in both chubby hands and pulling them toward his mouth. He delivered an ode to the bare foot in gurgling baby poetry.

Nothing charmed me more than babies in their private moments. They grasped at dust motes, stared with rapt admiration at a stain on the crib rail, or stroked a satin blanket binding against their cheeks in soothing rhythm.

The first year with a new baby contained wonders difficult to savor due to sleep deprivation and frequent chaos. One of my big gripes with God. This was the year to be fully awake, appreciating all the moments of wonder.

My yawn interrupted my thoughts, and I walked into the room to swoop Micah up for a diaper change. Even his sweat smelled sweet and appealing. I nuzzled his nearly bald head and cooed to him. He felt a bit warm, probably from sleeping hard.

After cleaning him up, I headed for the kitchen, called Kelsey, plopped Micah in his high chair, pulled food from the fridge, closed it with my hip, hooked the cabinet door and opened it with one foot, grabbed a sippy cup, and shuffled sustenance onto the table like a Las Vegas croupier.

I wolfed down a peanut butter sandwich while sweeping the floor and emptying the dishwasher, one eye on the clock.

Kelsey's afternoon preschool started in sixteen minutes. The drive took fifteen. I should have skipped the conditioner and shortened my shower time.

Kelsey knew the drill. She grabbed her school bag and jacket from her peg and skipped out the door.

I followed in a rush and buckled Micah into his seat. When I turned to adjust Kelsey's seat belt, her bare feet swung up with glee. November in the Midwest tended to require shoes—even for someone with a casual fashion sense like me.

"Kelsey! Where are your shoes?"

She grinned, unrepentant. "Basement."

I growled and ran into the house to find them. Leaving the kids belted in the car alone added another "bad mom" indictment to my long mental list.

We raced into preschool five minutes behind schedule. Then Micah and I began our usual Thursday afternoon rounds. Dry cleaners for Kevin's spare suit. He might need it if he had to go on job interviews. I snickered at the price list on the wall. Who would bring in shirts to be professionally laundered for six dollars apiece? I could buy a new shirt for that price at the local thrift store. I could buy three when prowling next summer's garage sales.

Grocery store next. Micah was getting fussy, so I opened a box of animal crackers. He mangled a few of the cookies but then contented himself with chewing on the cardboard. The cashier wrinkled her nose at my messy boy. In the lane next to mine, a young mom wearing a Laura Ashley jumper and fall-print turtleneck crooned over her two-year-old daughter in the coordinating outfit with matching hat. *Her* darling girl wasn't fussing, tugging her ear, or smearing wet cardboard and animal crackers everywhere. How did she do it? I gave my cart a shove. One day I'd have this parenting thing mastered. I'd be the gorgeous mom with the adoring and spotless children. And I had better do it in time for the magazine article.

On to the drugstore to get Kevin's allergy medicine, and then as a treat we popped into the library. I had reserved three new books on Christian parenting that promised I could pass a godly heritage on to my children, maintain discipline in the home, and discover each child's unique learning styles. Probably while standing on my head and whistling Dixie, too.

We were only five minutes late picking up Kelsey. She babbled about her afternoon and showed off her latest macaroni art. Her teacher was obsessed with projects made of food products. Froot Loops necklaces, cornstarch modeling clay, dry-bean tambourines. If our city ever had a food shortage, we could live on Kelsey's artwork.

After unloading the groceries, a check of my e-mails granted a well-earned reward. Lori had sent another message. These notes weren't mere symbols on a screen. They were mini visits. I could picture Lori's smile with vivid clarity. I once told her she must have been a Nubian princess in another life. She had frowned and told me not to joke about something as deceptive as the lie of reincarnation. I backpedaled and apologized profusely before she burst into laughter. I got back at her the next day by telling her I'd read an article about homeschooled kids having lower SAT scores. She went apoplectic until I admitted I was teasing.

*Subject: Dylan in Sunday School*

*Hi, I forgot to tell you, Dylan used THAT WORD again when he talked to Nathan before class last Sunday. I think he's doing much better, and you know he's my favorite kid in class, but you might want to ask him about it. Hugs, Lori*

Only a very dear friend would dare to say anything negative about my son. But Lori was one of the rare people who had that permission.

This further proof of my flaws as a mother made me blush.

Dylan overheard some new words on the bus and unfortunately liked them. Lori never reminded me that he would avoid that influence if we homeschooled him—but I wondered if she thought it. I loved the concept of homeschooling, and admired Lori for tackling it, but I shuddered at the thought of the actual work involved. We couldn't afford a Christian school, like Sally could. At least not until I started earning some money.

I was grateful my circle of friends gave me some backup in the daily dilemmas of parenting. Through my network of school and church friends, I operated an espionage ring that would make top information-retrieval specialists envious. With a click of my keyboard, I could learn whether Kelsey watched TV on her playdate with Doreen's daughter and what Dylan's friend from school did at his birthday party. Sally kept me up-to-the-minute on the arrival of new babies in our congregation, which marriages were having trouble, and who bought a new car. Sally once told me Marcia Timmers was moving to Chicago before Scott Timmers had even told Marcia about his transfer.

I gave my computer an affectionate pat. Without my covert operations and field agents, parenting security systems would be twice as difficult.

Dylan, Kelsey, and Micah giggled behind me. They were sprawled on the kitchen floor, shuffling pieces of a wooden puzzle. This moment of grace provided a perfect opportunity to edit my paper due next week. I opened the file marked *Teaching Techniques for the Twenty-first Century Classroom*.

The screen gave a flicker, winked, and went blank.

I gave the monitor a gentle tap, then a more assertive thump. My fingers raced over the keyboard trying to find the magic combination of commands to stop the nightmare.

Two months of work on my term paper had disappeared. My link to the outside world was severed. I gasped for breath like a coma patient with life support unplugged.

*Fatal error. File unavailable.* Other computer gibberish sneered from the screen, but I knew what it meant. The Blue Screen of Death. My system had crashed.

# FIVE

*A mortar shell* exploded fifty yards to
our left. The red-baked clay beneath us shook.
"Ma'am, we need to divert to the airport!" My military
escort shouted to be heard over the noise.

I stood my ground. "No! It took months to arrange this meeting.
I'm not leaving until I see Iru Nabi."

He grabbed my elbow and pulled me to the relative protection of a
mud hut. At least we'd avoid some of the stray bullets here in the
shadows.

"Ma'am, he's not going to show. He's pulled this before. You can't
trust him."

Something rustled in the thatch over our heads, and I shuddered.
I'd face down trigger-happy warlords with bandoleers of bullets, but I
hated bugs. Unfortunately, the famines in this part of Africa hadn't
managed to kill the insects.

"Look, you've seen the refugee camps. This war is going to destroy
both countries. If Nabi is willing to negotiate, we could finally turn
things around."

Sergeant Cynic shook his head and gestured me back while he
peered out to scan the deserted village.

A swig from my canteen fortified me. As a U.N. ambassador, and
later as a president-appointed special negotiator, I had brokered treaties
all over the world—treaties that had saved thousands of lives. Nabi had
been an elusive warlord to track down, but if I could talk with him for
thirty minutes, he'd see reason. His people suffered from the constant

*skirmishes, and trucks full of rice and medical supplies couldn't get through.*

*A chatter of machine-gun fire erupted behind our hut. I hummed "Give Peace a Chance" under my breath to still my nerves. Nothing would stop me from completing this mission.*

"Becky, what do you think?" Heather scooted closer to me on the couch.

I blinked my friends back into focus.

Lori had passed around her petition, but an argument had erupted about the most effective and Christlike ways to protect human life, and I'd tuned out somewhere between Doreen recommending a letter writing campaign to a local business that donated to an abortion clinic, Sally wanting to host a fashion show at church to raise money for a local crisis nursery, and Heather suggesting we each invite a needy pregnant girl into our homes to live.

I didn't want my living room turning into a battle zone. "How about if we move on to prayer requests?"

"I guess we better." Sally pulled out her day planner and flipped to the pages where she kept a mammoth list of needs to pray over. "You start."

"My computer died, and I lost the term paper that's due next week. And when I told Kevin, he just said, 'Did you have a backup?'"

The women murmured sympathy for his callousness. Then Doreen leaned forward. "Well, *did* you have a backup?"

"Of course I did. But yesterday Dylan put it in the toaster."

Lori pressed her lips together and then lifted her Bible to hide her face, but I could see her shoulders shake. My indignation flared, but then a muscle twitched at one corner of my lips. "Can you imagine me telling my professor?"

Heather began to giggle. "I'm sorry, teacher. My son put my homework in the toaster."

Shared laughter did more to erase my tears than an overdose of sympathy ever could. When we sobered up again, Sally jotted an entry into her prayer list. "But you still have your notes, right? You'll be able to reconstruct the research."

"No. I cleaned my office and pitched all the notes because I'd transferred everything to the computer file." I shot a glare at Lori. "Remember that book you lent me? I was getting organized and simplifying my life."

Heather wrapped one arm around me and gave me a squeeze. "What are you going to do?"

"I don't know. It took months to put that project together. I'll have to take an incomplete." The sigh slipped out, unintended. "I thought God wanted me to finish my education degree. Why would this happen?"

The group remained silent. Several eyes turned toward Lori. Her fingers stroked the cover of her Bible. "We could make all kinds of guesses and come up with our own explanations. Let's not. Let's take it to Him in prayer. Who else needs prayer?"

Heather smiled. "I'm going to visit some boutiques tomorrow with my homemade soaps."

She had started ten home businesses since I'd known her. She made amazing baskets, stationery, pressed-flower wall hangings, wind chimes, and even macrame. And she didn't mind doing the legwork to promote them. But she had the business sense of a tea rose, and such a generous heart that I knew she gave away more of her creations than she sold.

Sally's pen scratched across the page. Doreen shifted, and we all turned toward her. She kept her gaze on a crayon mark on the wood floor. "Well, pray for sanity for me. All three kids have chicken pox."

We made compassionate sounds.

She hesitated. "Keep praying for Jim and me."

Even those short words had a huge effect on her body. Her shoulders rounded in, and the spotless espadrille that had bounced from her crossed leg now drooped, lifeless. I had learned not to brag too much about Kevin to this group. Some husbands were involved in the lives of their children, emotionally connected to their wives, hardworking and dependable, fun to be around, or as cute as Hugh Jackman in a romantic comedy. But only Kevin combined all those traits. And Jim seemed to have none.

Doreen's situation hurt me. I couldn't understand the daily slights, the aloofness, the lack of basic consideration that Jim brought to Doreen's life. I knew we only heard her side of the story, but even so, I often wanted to drive over to their house and conk him over the head with my copy of *What Wives Wish Their Husbands Knew About Women*.

Sally rearranged her ample thighs and reached for her plate of pie. "Lori, this is great. I'd love a copy of the recipe."

Heather eyed the dessert with suspicion. "Does it have any sugar or processed flour in it?"

Lori stared at her straight-faced. "No. Of course not."

We all burst into laughter, even Heather.

Sally tapped her plate with the fork. "I think we need to add something to our praise reports. The church board is voting to give the women's ministry director a salary."

My face felt hot with pleasure as everyone cheered and congratulated me. "Maybe God wants me to set aside the college work for now." Pieces of a puzzle slid into place. *That's why He let my paper disappear into the computer cosmos—to send me a sign.* "I can concentrate on working at the church instead."

"You're so good at it." Doreen's shoe tip pointed up with

happiness again. "Last year's retreat was amazing. You did a super job organizing it."

It's one thing to have friends who hurt for you. Compassion comes easy, because of the secret relief that you aren't facing the same hardship. But friends who can celebrate your victories are rare gems.

Lori leaned forward. "It's great news. But even without the church job, you're a blessing to lots of people."

I nodded with pretended agreement and spiritual maturity. Easy for her to say. She already accomplished a lot for God as a homeschool mom, political activist, and spiritual mentor to the rest of us. She couldn't understand the depth of my need to feel important *somewhere*.

"And that's not all," Sally piped in. "Tell them."

I felt another blush warm my cheeks. "Our illustrious church secretary got it in her head to nominate me for a feature in *Women of Vision*. I guess I'm supposed to be the profiled woman for April's edition."

Heather shrugged, unimpressed. She probably never read anything except *Mother Earth News*.

Lori nodded. "I wrote a letter to the editor a few months ago to protest when they did a feature on lingerie models. It would be great for them to interview someone with a godly perspective for a change."

Doreen's gaze took in my modest living room. "Why on earth did they pick you?"

"Obviously, I know how to write a good nomination," Sally said. "Feel free to contact me if any of you ever want a recommendation for anything."

We moved on to a rushed prayer time. Somehow sharing the prayer requests always took up so many of our allotted minutes, we never had long to pray. After a hurried amen, we opened our Bibles to First Peter.

Heather slid off the couch and took up a comfortable position on the floor. She rarely remained on furniture for long. Doreen stood to stretch, then repositioned herself on her chair like Miss America posing. Sally ate a few more bites of pie and dabbed at her mouth with a paper napkin.

Heather always used cloth napkins, so as not to waste trees. Doreen used cloth because she had refined tastes, and her weekly maid folded laundry. What I wouldn't do for a once-a-week maid. She was so lucky.

"'Therefore, rid yourselves of all malice and all deceit, hypocrisy, envy, and slander of every kind.'"

The words jolted me, and I looked up in wonder, thinking God was responding to my envious thoughts.

Instead, the voice belonged to Lori, reading from chapter two. "I loved this part. And the contrast with the description later in the chapter, where God says He is building us into a spiritual house, and we are living stones. Anyone else? What spoke to you?"

Heather waved her hand in the air. "In chapter three it says, 'Your beauty should not come from outward adornment, such as braided hair and the wearing of gold jewelry and fine clothes.' I think women in our church focus way too much on appearance."

Doreen sniffed. "Welcome to the real world. Hey, I know you mean well, but the folks with the money to donate to all your causes won't listen to you if you don't look sharp."

Sally twirled one of her annoyingly perfect blond curls around her finger and stared at Heather's kinky mane of muddy-red hair. "And besides, if we're God's work of art, there's nothing wrong with wanting to look our best." Since Sally used enough cosmetics to single-handedly keep Max Factor in business, I could understand her jumping in on the issue.

Heather crossed her arms. Doreen lifted her chin. Tension crackled through the room.

Conflict gave me hives. The one drawback of an honest, intimate circle of women was that on any issue you could name, opinions ranged far and wide. Living stones, indeed. God was working with a pile of rocks. All different shapes, sizes, and textures.

"I don't think it's wrong to look our best," I offered. "It's just not as important as our hearts. Isn't that the point?" I flipped a few pages. "My favorite comes later in the chapter. 'Finally, all of you, live in harmony with one another; be sympathetic, love as brothers . . .' I wish everyone in the church could get along better."

The conversation veered away from dangerous disagreements. I applauded myself on my diplomacy and sat back to enjoy the evening. These women were precious to me, and I'd do all I could to keep us from hurting one another.

The next hour was an oasis. Splashing in a wealth of spiritual refreshment. A ridiculous bounty of water, compared to the miles of parched landscape beyond our cloistered evening. Enough to drink, enough to immerse ourselves in. Enough to wash over the dry places in our souls so we could face another week of trudging through hot sands.

All too soon, Kevin slipped in the kitchen door with the kids, and my friends murmured good-byes at the front door.

"My house next time," Heather called as she headed toward the sidewalk. She lived about a mile away and had walked—to save fossil fuels. I couldn't understand her compassion for fossils but figured she had her reasons.

"Do you want a ride?" Doreen clicked her key ring, and the door of her SUV unlocked. The seat probably heated itself for her, as well. Heather nodded and joined her.

I was relieved to see Doreen reaching out to Heather. Disagreements had grown a bit heated a few times during the evening. Like a U.N. ambassador, I constantly measured the tension level between the various factions in our little group in order to forestall any serious rifts.

We had different perspectives on everything.

Sally worked at the church so her family could afford a Christian school for her daughter. Lori advocated home-schooling. Heather taught her twin girls at home, but she called it "un-schooling," a completely different approach to the home-school experience and one that I'm sure made Lori shudder. Doreen and I believed our children could infuse a bit of faith into the public school.

We also came from different economic backgrounds. Doreen's gorgeous house made me afraid to touch anything. Heather dressed like a refugee from a homeless shelter, which puzzled me because I knew her husband had a lucrative job as a doctor. Lori and I swapped tips on frugal living.

Though our common bond was our Christian faith, even there we found chasms to cross. Heather and I preferred the late service with its guitars and free-form worship. Lori and Sally's families went to early service. Lori claimed the lyrics of the traditional hymns had more depth, and she found the liturgical structure soothing. Solid, unchanging, repetitive.

Our circle disagreed on the best Bible translations, the best grocery store to shop at, baths vs. showers, cloth vs. disposable diapers, breast-feeding vs. bottles, appropriate toys, movies, and recreation. Yet I loved each woman in our group.

The last to leave, Lori smoothed the aluminum foil around the edge of her pie pan and reached to give me a one-armed hug.

Another wave of gratitude made my eyes prickle. What would I do without these friends?

"Something else is wrong." Lori stepped back and studied my face.

"No way, girlfriend. It's cool."

Lori gave my arm a playful slap. "Cut that out. Have you ever heard me talk like that?"

I batted innocent eyelashes. "But I heard Oprah say it."

We giggled like preteen girls. When we sobered, she went back to the point like a guided missile. "Come on. No more kidding around. What's wrong?"

I shrugged one shoulder. "Kevin's worried about his job. They're talking layoffs." I hadn't wanted to say anything to the group yet. Like many insurance men, my husband projected a hearty, gregarious, and utterly confident personality. The first time I understood how much he loved me was when he let down a few of his cheerful barriers. During a college date one night, we sat on bleachers under a harvest moon, shivering in our jackets and holding hands. He shared a range of honest feelings—disagreements with his roommate, fear about his heavy course load, insecurities about sharing his faith.

After all these years, I remained his one safe place. He believed exposed feelings made him weak in the eyes of others, so I tried not to disclose information that he might feel could lower his status among our friends.

Lori's eyes grew large with understanding. "I'll be praying. Call if you want to talk." With a last pat, she strode down the sidewalk to her car.

I closed the front door and turned. Kevin stood right behind me, bouncing a listless baby. Had he heard me?

"We need to talk." His voice didn't seem to carry an accusation of betrayal, just worry and weariness. "I'll lock up and check on the kids."

"Sure. Meet you on the couch." I lifted Micah from his arms and carried him to the living room. I steeled myself for whatever trouble Kevin planned to share. A strange joy mixed with my concern for him. My skills at diplomacy—looking at a problem from all angles, and just plain careful listening—were vital. I loved that he needed me. Even if the news was bad.

# SIX

**Strains of Mozart** *floated from
the orchestra and swirled around me like the bias-cut
crepe of my costume. Gradient shades of blue washed over
my body as I darted through dappled pools of light then
stepped into a balanced pose.*

I could hear Madame Romanenska's voice in my head. "Even in stillness, the body continues to move. When you hold your arabesque, the arms remain alive. Reaching. Always reaching for more."

The audience breathed in with that perfect suspended moment of silence every ballerina loves to induce. Like voyeurs, the ticket holders felt the ache of the character. The loneliness. The longing.

Just when the moment could not be stretched for another second, my partner entered from upstage.

I pressed upwards onto pointe and began the rapid bourrées across the stage intended to draw his attention and begin the romantic thread of the ballet.

Wooing and coy withdrawal. Greater and longer displays of virtuosity. Exquisite tension. All built with the frenzy of the violins.

At last, we touched. Now my early movements could expand because of his arms supporting me. My initial assemblés had skimmed the floor. Now I floated for long sustained moments as his hands held my waist and pressed me upward. We revisited every step, and they blossomed into magic beyond what I could accomplish alone.

We separated, and his arms beckoned me. In a burst of exaltation, my legs ate up the Marley floor beneath my feet with a series of glissades *and a* grand jeté. *I exploded into a final leap, rotating my body to fly backwards with perfect confidence into his waiting arms. The audience gasped in appreciation for the trust and timing of our dance.*

The music stopped abruptly as Kevin turned off the classic station on the radio and settled beside me on the couch. Remnants of swirling dancers spun through my mind as his arm encircled me. I sank back against him, adjusting Micah in my outside arm for his bedtime nursing. My husband and I leaned into each other with confidence and familiarity built through ten years of marriage. Perfectly balanced.

Micah fidgeted, but I gave Kevin my full attention. My triage system demanded that at the moment, my husband's concerns came first. "What's up? Were the kids okay at the mall?"

A grin flickered across his face, and he released his arm to rub the dark bristles across the top of his head. "Yeah. Micah fussed a little, but we had fun. Of course Kelsey needed the bathroom three different times, and the family restroom was at the opposite end of the mall each time."

I gave him a sympathetic pat on the knee. "You're the world's best dad. Thanks so much for handling them. Bible study was great." I almost plunged into a full account but remembered he had something on his mind. "So how are you?"

He angled his body so he could look me in the face. With end-of-the-day shadow along his jawline, his roguish appeal made me want his arm around my shoulder again. Hope stirred that Micah would settle down fast tonight. Usually by the time Kevin and I collapsed into bed, the only desire I felt was for sleep. I was surprised and pleased to sense a stirring of romantic interest—like a visit from a favorite mischievous old friend who'd been away too long.

Kevin drew a breath in, but instead of talking, he let it out with a sigh.

Ready to pepper him with more questions, I forced myself to wait. After his second false start, I wanted to slug him. "You're getting me worried. What's wrong? Just tell me."

"Not wrong, exactly." He slumped back against the couch and crossed his arms. His gaze swept the room but avoided me. "I did some checking with City Life today."

"Good for you." My admiration was sincere. The thought of job-hunting made my nerves twist into a macrame of knots. Another reason the ready-made staff position at the church was so perfect for me. With effort I pulled my thoughts away from my own success and back to Kevin. "If they don't appreciate you at Anderson, it's smart to start looking somewhere else. What did you find out?"

The muscles of his crossed arms tightened under the fabric of his sweater. "They might have an opening."

"Woo hoo! Honey, that's super! God answers prayer fast, doesn't He?"

My whoop startled Micah. He pulled away and started crying. As I worked to soothe him, I noticed Kevin wasn't celebrating with me. "It is good, right?" I asked tentatively. "Or are you sad because you wish you could stay at Anderson? Hey, cutbacks happen everywhere. It's not your fault. Or will you miss the folks at Anderson? I know you like working with Eric, but don't worry, you'll make new friends. We can invite them to supper."

Kevin stared at me, jaw slack.

I had slipped into my Dylan pep talk about buddies at school. Oops. I shifted Micah to my shoulder and hid my face against his hot neck. "Sorry. You were saying?"

Another wry grin flashed for a moment, and then Kevin moved closer to put an arm around me again, in our couch-bound *pas de deux*. "You aren't going to like this."

Exasperated that he wasn't getting to the point, I stiffened. "Would you let me decide that? What is it? Spit it out." Honestly, men are so hard to talk to sometimes.

"The job isn't here in town."

Scenarios jolted through my mind like a video in fast forward.

Kevin working far from home and only coming back on weekends. No, that would never work. Moving. Packing up a house. New schools for the kids. Leaving my Bible study group. Never. They were my link to sanity. My best friends for the past five years.

"How would I finish my college degree? And what about the new job at church? And the magazine profile? They want to feature women in the Twin Cities."

Kevin followed my mental footwork and stepped right into synch. "I know, sweetie. I'll keep looking in town. I could go back to being an independent agent, but that would be like starting from scratch. There aren't a lot of options. Maybe it would just be for a few years."

"But by then the job at church would be gone." Tears stung my eyes. God wouldn't snatch this away, would He?

"I knew you'd be upset. I shouldn't have told you. Nothing's for sure yet."

I dashed away a few tears and tried to smile. "Of course you should have told me. This gives us time to think about options. Where would the job be?"

"Grand Marais."

I cringed. A tiny town up north along Lake Superior and five hours from our city. "They don't have a college, do they?"

Kevin shook his head. "I don't think so." He shifted again and his fingers began their nervous pattern against his leg. "You know your dreams are important to me. But we have to pay the bills. It'll be years before you have the teaching degree."

I took a deep breath, shifting into let's-brainstorm-before-I-start-hyperventilating mode. "I'll see what I can find out about the job at church. Maybe it will pay enough to tide us over. Once I know, we'll have more facts to go on. And we'll keep praying. There's still hope. And they haven't laid you off at Anderson yet, right?"

Kevin's look was pitying but affectionate. "Sure. We'll keep looking for options. I just don't want to be left high and dry."

He reached to take Micah from my arms. My upper back strained from holding him. When had my baby become such a chunky bruiser? This probably wasn't the best time to bring up my yearning for another new baby in the house. Crazy to contemplate, when our house bulged at the seams and my fatigue stretched to the limit. Yet each child amazed me, and I often wondered what a fourth one would be like.

Kevin cupped the back of Micah's head as he stood up. "He's really hot."

Micah tugged his ear and rubbed his nose into Kevin's neck with a halfhearted whimper.

Worry propelled me off the couch. "I'll get the thermometer."

Fear about our career futures disappeared for the moment. A quick check confirmed that Micah's temperature was 103 degrees. Why hadn't I noticed sooner? He'd been restless all day. Probably an ear infection.

We wrestled some baby Tylenol past his lips. Not much got into his mouth, but Micah's T-shirt wouldn't run a fever—doused in purple streaks of medicine.

Kevin sagged with exhaustion. He'd been dealing with pressures at work, and while I relaxed with my friends, he had carted our busy brood around the mall. Then he'd had to endure a serious talk—which ranked right up there with a root canal on his scale of things he enjoyed.

"Get some sleep." I gave him a hug with Micah squeezed between us. "I'll walk with him for a while."

"Are you sure?" His forehead creased in concern, but his body slumped in gratitude and the hope of some rest.

"Yeah." I pressed a soft kiss against his cheek. "I'll wake you up if I need you."

Micah continued to fuss, but without much vigor. Was that a good sign or bad? I paced the living room floor, humming lullabies, murmuring stories, and losing myself in the mental wanderings that drift alongside like a shadow in the world of not-quite-awake.

I floated back to the first time I met Kevin. I had spilled a stack of books while sliding into a chair in my math class at college. Kevin stopped in the aisle and helped pick them up, dusting them off. "Oh, you're in Philosophy and Ethics, too." He gave me the book, along with a genuine warm smile. "I'll see you later."

I nodded and mumbled my thanks for his help, and the class began. I didn't hear much of the lecture. Kevin looked so sweet with that thick, dark hair dangling too long behind his ears. And there had been no annoyance or impatience toward me for blocking the aisle. No smarmy gaze raking me up and down. I scolded myself for getting my hopes up. In philosophy class, he'd probably be sitting with a girlfriend. Or maybe he'd ask me out—but it would be to a kegger that weekend where he'd be as loutish as some of the other guys I'd met that year.

Instead, I learned that Kevin played guitar for the chapel band. He asked me out to a play on campus. We both found the script too dark and cynical. We drank cocoa and talked far into the night. And I fell in love.

Some of my friends talked about love fading, like unlined curtains after too many years of unforgiving sunlight. But nothing had faded in my love for Kevin. We made each other better. Like a prima ballerina in the arms of her partner, I took chances I could never take alone. My admiration helped him leap higher. His support allowed me to bend and recover.

The memories kept away my current anxiety about his job and warmed me as the house cooled. We tried to save money by setting our thermostat to a lower temperature at night. Kevin complained that I defeated the purpose when I snuck out of bed to crank it up. Pacing, I rocked Micah in my arms. After a few hours, I checked his temperature again. 104 degrees.

# SEVEN

**Whispers followed** me as I mounted
the steps to the orphanage. "They say no one has
cared for so many children."

With sweet humility, I paused to place a light hand of blessing on the heads of several beggars waiting for the mission to open.

Refuse from the gutters, unwashed bodies, and the pungent hint of mold ascended around the front steps. The rainy season had left the mission walls damp again.

After unlocking the door, I held it open as the poor and sick hobbled inside. I greeted our night staff and went straight to the children's ward. Dozens of babies and young children had been delivered to our steps—almost always girls. Despite our best efforts, female infanticide persisted in India because girls who grew up required large dowries one day. We were grateful for those babies who survived, even if their mothers were forced to deliver them to our doorsteps in fear and shame.

Sister Evangeline turned from massaging a girl's shoulders. "Mother Becky, why are you back so early?" she whispered. "You worked half the night. You need some rest."

I smiled at the sleeping children we had rescued. "Serving God is my strength."

Admiration and awe shone in the sister's eyes. "You never tire of sacrificing, do you?"

"'We do small things with great love,'" I quoted gently.

She shook her head. "What you've done here in Calcutta is no small thing."

*Joy mingled with the love in my heart. She was right. Our mission had made a tremendous difference. Sleepless nights were a small price to pay. I gazed down at one of the beds.*

"Kevin," I whispered, standing beside the bed. The beam of light from the hallway hit our quilt and cast enough glow for me to see his face. Curled on his side like a little boy, cheek pressed into the pillow, his lips gave a small upward twitch as if his dreams were happy.

I couldn't bear to wake him up, so I tiptoed back out to the bathroom. I could handle this on my own. Sacrificing sleep was a badge of honor for mothers. On top of that, I'd be doing something selfless for Kevin. I gave Micah another dose of Tylenol and a sponge bath. Then I set up camp on the rocking chair in the living room. I drowsed whenever Micah did, which wasn't very often.

When weak sunlight grudgingly angled through our windows, I studied Micah. He was still hot and restless.

I hurried back to the bedroom. "Kevin?" This time my voice hit full volume.

He shot up in one move. That reflex never ceased to amaze me—some primeval instinct in him to protect his home and hearth. I almost expected him to reach for a sword.

"Shhh. It's okay. I'm just worried about Micah. I think we should call the doctor."

Kevin squinted at the clock. "Were you up with him all night?"

"I rested a little in the rocker. I've tried everything, but his temp is still high."

Kevin pulled his Dockers on. "Let's take him to urgent care. We don't want to wait for the clinic to open."

I chewed my lip. Going to the urgent care would mean admitting this was urgent. Anxiety made my tired legs quiver.

Another glance at Micah in the light of day, and I didn't hesitate. "I'll call Heather."

She arrived at our house in a few minutes. "Ron can bring the twins over when he leaves for work. He said you're doing the smart thing to bring Micah in."

I nodded, hunting behind the couch cushions for Micah's pacifier. "If you want, you can take Kelsey back to your house after Dylan gets on the school bus."

Heather gave a relaxed toss of her hair. "Don't worry. I'll take care of things." I knew her reassurance was genuine. My free-spirited friend never minded disruptions to her plans for the day. Probably because she didn't make many plans. She took each day as it came and managed to pour out a lot of comfort and warmth to others along the way.

I checked the supplies in the diaper bag while Kevin pulled Micah's hooded sweatshirt over his flushed head. Kevin clipped his cell phone onto his belt—the morning ritual of a gunslinger arming up for the day. In the car, he called and left a message at work warning that he might be in late.

More proof that my husband was one a million. He might leave school issues, chore enforcement, meals, sibling quarrels, and skinned knees in my hands. But he insisted on sharing any frightening events right alongside me.

Or maybe he was leery of letting me drive Micah to urgent care on my own after so little sleep. I wasn't the world's best driver awake, and today my reactions were fatigue-fuzzed. I stumbled on a driveway crack while hurrying to the passenger side of the van.

Other bleary patients crowded the lobby at urgent care. A few night-shift workers cradled injuries and their homemade bandages seeped blood. An old man in a nearby chair hacked in moist, unending coughs.

I held Micah closer. Kevin and I took turns reading *High-*

*lights* and decade-old copies of *Better Homes and Gardens*. When a nurse finally called Micah's name, we both leapt forward, startling her. We followed her down a maze of halls to a small room. Sour and antiseptic smells clashed. Behind one of the doors, a baby screamed.

My fatigue-induced fog parted enough for me to feel the fear growing inside me.

The nurse rapid-fired questions and did a cursory exam, making a few tsking sounds.

After she scurried from the room, I met Kevin's eyes in alarm. "She looked worried."

"It's going to be okay." He rested one hand on Micah's bare chest. Micah looked tiny and lifeless on the exam table. I wrapped an arm around Kevin's waist and stroked Micah's limp hand.

*Please, God. Let him be okay.*

Kevin's head tilted forward and his eyes closed. Softly, almost shyly, he voiced his own prayer. "Lord, thank you so much for Micah. We need your strength and wisdom, and Micah needs your comfort and healing. Please help us trust you."

I blinked back tears. In spite of my anxiety, I felt a rush of appreciation. There is a mysterious strength in the presence of a man praying. I couldn't analyze the difference, but it wasn't quite the same as the easy, relaxed prayer times I had with my women's Bible study. Or the harried and distracted bursts of chatter I poured out in my own quiet times with God. Or even the deep and thoughtful prayer times I had shared with Lori.

Seeing Kevin, with his bonhomie and got-the-world-by-the-tail zest, bow his head in quiet faith and ask for help gave me goose bumps. "Amen," I whispered.

Kevin kissed the top of my head and the door opened. The round, bald man who hurried into the room looked like a cozy family doctor. But he squinted at us through smudged glasses and waved us back, approaching Micah with stooped shoulders and a permanent wince as if he had health problems of his own.

He shot off the same questions the nurse had, and I stammered to answer, feeling myself under the glare of an interrogation-room bulb.

"And when did the fever start?" He shoved the earpieces of his stethoscope into place, and I wasn't sure whether I should answer. Could he hear me with those in his ears?

He frowned in my direction. "Well? When did it start?"

I edged closer to Kevin. "I'm not sure. He felt warm all day yesterday. He'd been teething and a little fussy."

The doctor listened to Micah's chest, eyes narrowed. He reached for the folder on the desk and flipped it open. "His lungs sound a little tight. Do any of your other children have asthma?"

"N-no. At least, I don't think so."

"Hmm." He dropped the file, grabbed an instrument, and glared into Micah's ears as if personally affronted by the sight. "I can see why he was fussy. Lots of swelling. The left eardrum ruptured. Has he had a history of ear infections?"

Kevin nodded. "Yeah, he had a couple last summer."

The doctor grimaced. "There could be some permanent hearing loss. We need to keep this under better control."

I wavered on my feet, but Kevin's arm stayed firmly around my shoulders.

The doctor slid a stool out from under the small desk in the corner and began scribbling on a prescription pad. "Ventolin for the lungs, just to be sure. If you notice any wheezing, tightness of breath, or dry cough, get him back in right away. Is he allergic to any antibiotic?"

I shook my head numbly as the doctor continued scribbling.

He tore off another sheet and handed both to Kevin. "Liquid Tylenol every four hours for the pain, and give him plenty of liquids. Follow up with your regular doctor in three days, and he'll be able to do more testing for his hearing when the infection clears."

Kevin tried to thank him, but the doctor stomped toward the door. He half turned and met my eyes. Maybe he saw my distress, because his face softened and he gave me a reassuring smile. "He'll be all right. Next time bring him in sooner." Then he left.

*"Bring him in sooner."*

Offhand remarks, tossed at me with gentle professional chiding.

But they exploded in my chest like a grenade of guilt. A few of my tears hit Micah's head as I dressed him with intense gentleness. The snaps on his jammies defeated my efforts. My hands were shaking.

Kevin reached around me to help.

As soon as Micah was dressed, I lifted him and turned away, hiding my face against his cotton sweatshirt hood.

"Let's get out of here." Kevin held the door.

I slunk past him, down the long hall, and through the waiting room. Could all the patients in the chairs see my shame?

Driving home, Kevin looked at me whenever we stopped at a light. "He's going to be fine. It's just an earache."

I stared blindly out the windshield. "But I should have brought him in sooner. The doctor even said so. Why didn't I notice? What kind of mother would wait so long to get help?"

"Hey." Kevin hit the brakes with force at a stoplight and turned toward me. "Don't talk that way about my wife."

I tried to smile, but my lip quivered instead. "It's true. I'm a terrible mom. And it's not like I have an excuse. All I do is stay home, so I shouldn't make these kinds of mistakes."

The light turned green, and Kevin eased the car forward with a sigh. "Honey . . ." His words tiptoed as if he maneuvered a minefield. "You're tired. Don't beat up on yourself. We'll pick up the medicine, and maybe Heather can take Kelsey to her house for a while. You and Micah can nap, okay?"

"And what if he has permanent hearing loss? It's all my fault."

Kevin shot me a worried look. "How about if I take you home first and then go get the prescriptions? You can take a nice hot bath."

Fury flared like my stove's gas burner on ignition. I struggled to dial back the heat. Did he think I was some superficial woman whose stresses would all dissolve in a bubble bath? Calgon wasn't going to take me away today.

"I can handle this." I opened the glove compartment and rummaged for an Altoid. "You can't afford to miss too much work." I slammed the tin of mints back into its cubby and closed the glove box with force.

Kevin stiffened against the seat belt. "I'm just trying to help. I know tomorrow's a big day for you."

The retreat.

My other baby. I'd put months of work into it, and yet it had fled my mind. I had planned to be at church this morning to check on the setup committee. We wanted the whole day to be special for the women who would be attending, from the printed outline of events, to the bookmarks and name tags, to the arrangement of chairs for small group Bible study and the sound equipment for the worship team. And I had to call our guest speaker today to confirm details with her and update her on how many folks registered. How could I have blown the whole event from my mind so completely?

I looked over at Kevin's hurt face. He'd tried to offer me comfort the best way he could—even cared about my church ministry when I wasn't thinking about it. And I had snapped at him. What kind of wife was I?

I excelled at Pass the Guilt. It's like the old curbside con game with cups and a hidden nut. Keep moving those cups around and changing the location of the guilt, and you never find it. Is it hidden under Parenting? *Alakazam*. Nope, it's under Serving God. *Presto-chango*. Where did it go? It's here . . . under the cup marked Marriage. I didn't want to peek under any more cups. I suspected there would be nuts under each one.

"I'm sorry. I totally spaced out the retreat." I moved my hand across the seat, and he took one hand off the wheel to squeeze my fingers. My thumb traced circles on his palm. "If you have time to get the prescription, I could call someone from the committee and let them know I'll be late."

"Would it help if I took a personal day and stayed home with Micah?"

Did I mention he was one in a million? He probably hoped I'd refuse, but even the offer was an amazing sacrifice.

I wished I could make more cheerful, noble sacrifices.

"No, we'll manage. I just can't believe I forgot today is Friday."

*Friday! Oh no! Judy's interview.* We had missed the *Today* show. I moaned and dropped my face into my hands.

Kevin pulled into our driveway. A plastic toy crunched under a tire. "What is it, honey?" He hung on to his patient, sympathetic voice with difficulty.

"I don't suppose we know anyone who would have taped Judy's appearance on TV this morning?"

Kevin slapped his forehead. "I forgot all about it. Oh boy. We're in big trouble now." He enjoyed Judy and didn't always understand my envy of her. But he joined me in joking about her forceful personality. "Par for the course. I'm losing my job, Micah is losing his hearing, and you're about to lose your life for missing Judy's big event."

Suddenly the horror of the last hours seemed ludicrous. A

giggle burst from my throat, surprising me. "Yeah, and don't forget the retreat. I'm losing my mind, too."

Kevin laughed hard, doubling over as he released his seat belt. "And your homework."

Instead of despair, laughter tore through me. "Heather said I should tell my professor that my son put my homework in the toaster."

Kevin hooted, and I grabbed my stomach and rolled toward him, whooping with silliness. He turned and grasped my shoulders, lifting me to face him. His mood sobered and he stared deep into my semicomatose eyes. "As long as I don't lose you."

I blinked and felt something go all soggy and mushy in the region of my heart. I was too tired to pay much attention to the odd fear in his words. "You won't. We're in this together."

I carried Micah into the house, and Kevin drove off to buy the medicine. Heather had left me a note.

> *Dylan got on the bus all right, but do you really let him eat Froot Loops for breakfast? Brought Kelsey back to my house. I can keep her all day if you want. Give me a call.*

The note was signed with a smiley face.

Heather had done too much already, but I couldn't refuse her offer. I made a round of frantic calls. Sally was already at church, wondering what had delayed me. She was happy to take over leadership of the retreat setup. Heather told me that she had a great homeopathic remedy for earaches. I wasn't sure what that meant, but it sounded vaguely obscene. I reassured her that we were getting enough help from the doctor.

Kevin returned and held Micah long enough for me to take a quick shower—although his suggestion of a bubble bath had started to sound tempting.

After he headed in to work, I curled up on the couch with Micah in my arms. My poor little guy blinked his runny eyes at me, as if wanting an explanation for the painful night, the too-bright exam room, and the foul-tasting medicines he'd had to endure.

"Shhh. It's okay. Go to sleep." I stroked his back.

If I had to miss fulfilling my obligations at church, at least I could use this quiet time to pray. I hadn't been diligent in my prayer life lately.

As soon as Micah dozed off, my own eyes began to sink. Mother Teresa had prayed for hours every morning. I bet she stayed up all night nursing the sick and still served everyone the next day and managed to pray for every need in the world. I bet she never fell asleep on the couch.

# EIGHT

*My horse's neck* frothed with sweat.
Beneath me, his hooves tore up clods of dirt as we
raced through the forest. My green cloak billowed behind
me. Another arrow shot past my head. I hunched lower in the
stirrups.

We dodged around trees and across a stream before I dared to look
back. Digging in my heels, I galloped deeper into the woods. Most of
the sheriff's men had fallen behind. One stubborn soldier wove through
the underbrush, hot on my trail.

Not a problem. My men would take care of him.

As I rounded a ridge and rode deep into a bower, I heard the whinny
of the horse behind me. Two men on watch high in the trees dropped a
net and unseated my adversary. I continued toward my campsite.

Another mission fulfilled.

"Becky, when will you listen to reason?" Our friar held the reins
while I leapt from the horse. "You can't keep this up. Your skill with a
bow won't save you forever."

I gave him my best roguish grin. "Have a little faith."

He had never fully understood what drove me—my rage against the
injustice. Taxes continued to bleed the poor, while the sheriff posted
twaddle about his loyalty to the king. His only loyalty was to his own
coffers.

For my efforts to help the local villagers, I had been declared an
outlaw. Outcast. Although I put on a brave front, the rejection stung.

*These lands were once my home, but I had been forced to hide in the shadows.*

*"Becky, we're low on arrows again."* One of the men hurried to my side.

*An eager lad ran toward me. "I just got word that the sheriff evicted three families in the east village. What are we going to do?"*

*I sprang to a log. "Peace, friends! One at a time."* I hoped my confident chuckle would still the anxiety that often threatened to swell within our ranks.

"Becky, we ran out of name tags." Doreen's pen tapped a nervous rhythm on her clipboard.

Before I could answer, Sally ran up. "Victoria Spring just called. She's stuck in traffic and will be a little late."

I grinned. The fellowship hall hummed with women savoring a time of worship. The retreat was off to a fantastic start. "Sally, are there more name tags in the church office?"

She gave a bright nod. "But what about the keynote talk?"

"I'll just let the worship team know to sing a few more songs. If we have to, we can move up the small group activity until Victoria gets here."

I was in my element. Some folks would cringe at the responsibility and the dozens of questions and small crises bombarding me. I thrived on it.

After answering a few more panicked questions, I slipped into a chair in the back and lost myself in the hymn. "Let my life bring you glory, use the humble gift I bring."

My eyes closed. Yes. I finally knew where I fit in the body of Christ. My unique skills could make a difference. If only *Women of Vision* could interview me right now. Forget all the ways I fell short as a wife, mom, student, friend—today I was a hero.

The day passed in a glow of satisfaction. I cherished the thanks and warm feedback of each of the attendees when they left that night. Then I set about giving little thank-you gifts to the retreat committee members. They each basked in the success of the day.

"Victoria was a great guest speaker." Lori stacked songbooks in a neat row. "Where did you find her? I loved her passion for Christ. Although I did think the part about being women of influence slipped into some works theology."

I shrugged. "I didn't think so. But you always notice those things more. I'll ask Pastor Roger what he thought. He popped in to listen. And thanks for writing up the small-group discussion questions. No one digs into God stuff better than you."

"Thanks." Lori smiled. "It's what I care about. Do you think everyone was encouraged? There are a lot of women at this church battling some tough issues."

I gave her a quick hug. "You can't help but encourage. You have a gift for knowing the right Scripture for every need . . . but without being preachy."

Lori lit up at my compliment. Funny. I figured she was so far ahead of me on the spiritual food chain that she never needed mere human approval. I was delighted my words had touched her.

"I still think retreats should be held outdoors." Heather floated toward us, still swaying to an inner praise song. "Next year we should have it at a campground."

A shiver ran through me. "In early November? In Minnesota?"

"Oh, that's right. I forgot it's November. Hey, how's Micah?"

"He's better. I called Kevin during the lunch break, and he said all the kids are fine."

"I can't believe he took care of them all day." Doreen looked up from tallying the final head count. "I had to hire a sitter."

"We had baby-sitters here."

"I know. I organized them." She gave me a crooked smile. "But the kids are still covered in spots."

I gave her a squeeze. "Well, I'm glad you could get out today. Do you think Josh and Rachel would like some new coloring books? Dylan has more than he can use. I can drop them off tomorrow."

"Sure. Any distraction from the itching would be great. But don't let your kids in our house. They might still be contagious."

Sally hurried over holding up a bag. "Anyone else want the peanuts and butter mints? We had some left over."

Still full from the lasagna supper, I moaned. "No thanks."

"Great. I'll take them. Oh, Pastor Roger is looking for you." She gave me a wink.

Lori gasped and hugged me. "Do you think he's going to tell you about the board's decision?"

Excitement pushed aside my fatigue. "I don't know. I'd better find him."

"Go on." Sally gave me a gentle shove. "We can finish the cleanup."

I found the pastor in the sanctuary, arranging his notes on the pulpit for tomorrow's services. Anticipation propelled me toward the front with as much enthusiasm as the brides who often made this walk down the aisle. "We're just finishing the cleanup. Sally said you wanted to talk to me."

He removed his reading glasses and smiled. "Is the retreat over already?" His voice carried a bit louder than necessary, a habit I'd noticed before—as if he had preached so many sermons he forgot to turn off the booming, confident "pastor voice." He furrowed his brow in a moment of concentration, pressing his receding hairline forward. "Oh, yes. Can you come to the Board of Elders meeting on Tuesday night?" A broad smile lifted his cheeks. "We'll be discussing something that I know will interest you."

I returned his smile. "I'll be there."

"Good, good. Oh, and could you prepare a job description listing all the things you've been supervising in the past few years? That will help a lot."

A job description? How could I organize a list of all the things I managed as the women's ministry director? My computer was dead, Micah was sick, and I had class on Monday night. "Sure. No problem."

Pastor Roger patted my shoulder as he walked past me. "Fine. See you in church tomorrow."

I trailed behind him, feeling let down. Probably just exhaustion. But I had hoped he'd tell me that the board had made their decision. Looked like they wouldn't announce it until Tuesday. Still, he'd seemed upbeat. Even conspiratorially happy. He must believe the decision was a fait accompli.

I'd help by writing the best job description anyone had ever seen.

The next few days my blood pressure climbed as I scrambled to put together a complete document. The women's ministry encompassed many categories—small groups, retreats, moms' fellowship on Wednesday mornings, church nursery. I oversaw a wide range of committees. This job description was as diverse and difficult as motherhood.

In addition to my scrawled efforts for the board meeting, my other activities in the next few days turned me into a hyperactive Robin Hood with a band of unmerry men: flying arrows, galloping energy, and occasional shouting.

I scavenged nickels for Dylan's Sunday school fund-raiser, lowered the hem on Kelsey's favorite church dress that she was outgrowing but wouldn't part with, gave Kevin a back rub when his muscles were still sore a few days after his rigorous game of Friday night basketball, dished up meals with varying degrees of edibility, drove for Dylan's field trip to the zoo on Monday and comforted his carsick friend. Cleaned the van.

On Monday afternoon a much fatter blue envelope arrived from *Women of Vision* magazine, and I groaned as I looked at the detailed questionnaire and essays they expected me to complete. My gaze landed on one of the pages. *How do you balance the often conflicting roles of a contemporary woman's life in our society?* Why did they allow a full page for the answer? I could respond in two words: I don't. I tossed the papers aside, promising myself I'd find time to come up with witty and inspiring answers later.

That afternoon I took Micah in for a follow-up appointment. Our clinic doctor was kind, but I cringed at his comments. "The next few years are crucial to his language development. I want you to take him to an audiologist and consider surgery to have tubes put in his ears." Still reeling from that assessment, I attended my college class Monday night and suffered the humiliation of requesting an incomplete as other students turned in their research papers.

On Tuesday afternoon during Kelsey's preschool, I raced to Lori's house. She helped me type and print out my job description on her computer.

I took a quick inventory before entering the church library on Tuesday night, and my confidence wavered. A bit of hot-pink antibiotic stained my blouse, but as long as I kept my blazer closed, no one would see. My shoes were scuffed, but at least I had found my nice loafers and forsaken my usual tennis shoes. My hair was clean and combed, which was saying a lot. The concealer Sally loaned me masked the bags under my eyes.

All in all, a professional ready to state her case. I smiled and opened the door.

Pastor Roger greeted me in his boisterous voice and waved me to a seat. Sally perched in place with her steno pad. She gave me a wink. Noah, the only man on the board who I knew beyond brief Sunday morning handshakes, jumped up to wrap his arms around me in a quick hug. "Lori said the retreat was terrific." He settled his bulk back into his chair.

I grinned. His warmth stilled my butterflies. And if the board of elders didn't already understand the value of the women's ministry, his comment about the retreat provided great ammunition.

The men made small talk while I shuffled my copies. One last member arrived, and Pastor Roger opened the meeting with prayer.

When he looked at me, he gave me a wide smile. "No need to keep Becky in suspense. We know this is something she's been hoping for. Sally, why don't you read the minutes of our special meeting last week?"

Sally fought to hide her dimples and attempted a formal demeanor. Under her yellow Shirley Temple curls, the effort failed. She raced through preliminary parliamentary procedures from the meeting, then slowed. "Motion made to create a paid staff position of women's ministry director. Motion seconded. Further discussion involved wages, hours, questions of medical benefits, range of responsibility. Decision made to seek input from current volunteer director. Pursuant to further research, motion is carried."

I bit my lip to keep a very unprofessional whoop from bursting out of my chest. Instead, I inclined my head. "I'm delighted about the decision. I've prepared an outline of all the duties involved." I passed copies around the table and then sat back, uncertain of what was expected of me.

Pastor Roger gave an approving nod. "This will be very helpful in our understanding of all the responsibilities and skills needed. Becky, this would be a good time for the board to recognize and thank you for the time you've given to develop this ministry for the past three years."

Noah and Sally burst into applause. The others joined in with murmurs of thanks. Doesn't every person dream of those moments when all their hard work, much of it behind the scenes and unacknowledged, is suddenly praised and appreciated?

My chest inflated with love and gratitude. I basked in the commendation . . . and almost missed Pastor Roger's next words.

"Greg, you have some great news, don't you?"

Greg loosened his tie and leaned back so his jacket flopped open. No pink stains on his shirt. "I sure do. Last week after our meeting, I jumped right in on this. I talked to our district office and already have a few great candidates lined up to interview." He picked up the outline I had passed around. "Now that we have the job description, we can set up meetings this week."

A strange buzzing grew in my ears. Vertigo made me grab the edge of my chair for support. I could feel blood drain from my face as I stared at the table.

Pastor Roger smiled. "That's what I like about this board. You're men of action. Let's hear what you've got."

"Julie Henderson is a recent graduate of our denominational college in Illinois, but she has family in Minneapolis and will be in town this week. She comes highly recommended. Teresa Vogt is the adult ministries director at Faith Community Church in Woodbury, so she's already plugged in to the local churches."

Pastor Roger beamed at Greg. "Sure, sure. I know her. She even has a master's degree in education. But let's go ahead and interview this Julie, as well."

Greg nodded. "I have a few other names, but my list is short. It's hard to find someone with all the board's requirements. Especially a degree and certification from one of our denominational colleges."

There was more chatter about qualifications, but I tuned it out.

Arrows found their mark. Cruel, piercing, wooden shards drove straight into my heart and shredded my dreams. I forced my eyes up and saw Sally across the table. Her mouth gaped open in shock, eyes wide with distress as she watched me.

A small squeak escaped my throat.

Pastor Roger turned from congratulating Greg on his finds and seemed surprised I was still there. "Oh, Becky. I'm sorry. No sense in making you sit through the rest of our meeting." He waved the paper with the job description. The job I had created. Three years of my life, my vision, my work. A ministry I had built up from nothing. The paper flapped in his hand. "Thanks for bringing this in. I see from your notes that other than Moms' Time Out, the program slows down for the holidays. That'll give us a good way to make a smooth transition."

At the obvious dismissal, I rose, clutching my copy of the report to my chest. With a last shard of dignity, I managed a nod and walked to the door, numb.

Noah sprang to his feet. "Wait. Becky has been running this program for years."

A flare of hope helped me turn to look at the faces around the table. Someone would defend me—or at least point out the huge injustice of this moment.

Noah looked at Greg. "Don't you think we should invite her to be on the interview committee? She'd have good instincts on who to hire." Noah gave me his hearty smile, oblivious to the blood pouring from my mortal wound.

"I'll think about it." I managed a broken whisper, then slipped outside and closed the door behind me. My legs felt stiff and uncooperative as I aimed them toward the rest room. The last few yards were a panicked sprint. I made it to the sink before the sobs caught up with me. Ugly, unprofessional tears rolled down my face.

How could they? And other than Sally, none of them would

understand even if they saw my tears. They expected me to be delighted that they had added a staff position. It had never occurred to them to consider me for the job.

My low wail echoed around the bare bathroom walls. "Oh, God. Didn't it mean anything? All the heart and soul I poured into this? How could they toss me aside so easily?"

Humiliation shot through my stomach. How would I keep going to church here? Everyone knew that I had built up the women's program. How could I face the congregation every week after being rejected this way?

Anger threaded around my pain, fueled by the horrible injustice. I had given every ounce of my soul to serve here. Instead of thanks they offered me banishment—wrenched me from my leadership role. Pain roiled up again and overcame every other emotion.

The arrows sank deeper, and I didn't know if I would ever be able to pull them out.

# NINE

**Reptilian wings** blocked the sunlight
and rode the sky like a storm cloud. I stepped back
from the tower parapet to the shadowed doorway. I had no
desire to draw the attention of Lord Faithbane's dragon.

Smoke hissed from the monster's nostrils like steam from a wet log
on the fire. He banked in a large circle, searching the plains and forests
below. What had him so restless today? No approaching armies marched
toward the moat. And I hadn't attempted escape in weeks. Short rations
of dry bread and sour ale, along with crippling fear, had all conspired to
weaken me.

In the first weeks after Faithbane kidnapped me, I'd fought him
with fists and words and every ounce of will. I'd pledged I would never
surrender my lands to him.

Huddled in the archway of the tower, I knew my time had run out.
He had wrenched away my control over the villages, undone the progress
I'd made for the peasants under my care. Today he would force my sig-
nature on the capitulation.

Beneath me, the massive gate rose and several knights rode out,
heavily armed. I squinted to find the threat that stirred them.

A single knight rode across the plain toward the castle. Sunlight
glinted from his breastplate. He wore fine chain mail but no helmet. His
black hair flew behind him in concert with his steed's white mane.

He drew his sword as the horse's canter stretched into a full gallop,
plowing through Faithbane's advance guard as if they were mere pages
at play.

*The drawbridge creaked upward, but his mount sprang across the space. The clatter of hooves proclaimed his entry into the castle.*

*I raced down the circular stone stairs, breathless with new hope.*

*In the courtyard, the knight leapt from his horse and faced my captor—sword to sword. Soon his attack sent Faithbane's sword flying. The young knight turned his gaze to me. The fierce resolve in his face softened into a smile that lit his face.*

*Suddenly, massive wings swooped down accompanied by an evil screech of almost human rage.*

*I screamed—one long protest of terror, drowned out by the dragon.*

"Honey, what's wrong? Are you okay?" Kevin's arms held me as the nightmare lost its grip.

"The dragon. Look out."

"Shh. Just a bad dream. You had a rough day."

Trembling, I burrowed against Kevin's chest, my arms around his shoulders. "Why are we sitting up?"

Kevin's chest rumbled with a low chuckle. "You shot up first. Scared the life out of me with that scream."

"What time is it?"

A plaintive whimper sounded from the boys' room.

Kevin sighed. "Time to check on Micah." His feet hit the floor before I could offer to go. His absence allowed cool air to touch my damp skin.

A bad dream. Just a bad dream. No dungeons. No dragons.

Memory rushed back in and burned in my stomach—the board meeting. They had thanked me for building a women's ministry and then informed me they were giving it to someone else. They planned to annex my realm.

I heard Kevin rummaging in the medicine cabinet. Probably getting Tylenol for Micah. When he padded back into our bedroom, he sat on the edge of the bed and reached for me. He wrapped me in powerful, protective arms. "Are you okay?"

My shoulders began to tremble. "They didn't even consider me."

"Shh. I know. I'm sorry." Kevin's hand stroked the back of my head as if soothing one of the children.

He'd heard the same litany a dozen times that evening as I tried to process my shock and pain. His own surprise and outrage on my behalf had comforted me. I didn't feel quite as stupid for not seeing this coming.

"Honey, I think you need to talk to Pastor Roger. Let him know you want the position."

I shook my head. "I'm humiliated enough. I won't go begging."

"Well, we have to do something. This is wrong. Do you want me to talk to the board members? Write a letter? Go bang a few heads together?"

I managed a weak snort. "I'd love to see that." Another wave of emotion slammed me, and I fought hard to hold it back. "They want what's best for the church. The candidates they're interviewing have college degrees. Maybe they thought they did me a favor to free me from the responsibility since they know I'm a busy mom." None of my rationalizations helped. My voice became tiny. "Why would God do this to me? Did I do something wrong?"

Kevin grabbed my shoulders and held me away so he could see my face. "If He's the one that did this to you, after how hard you've worked for Him—" He let me go and cast a hard glance upward. "I'm not sure I like Him very much right now. Or our church."

I was tempted for a moment. Tempted to agree and rage against God's injustice. One thing held me back—fear of the dangerous ground we were treading.

Kevin's faith had been the light that drew me toward him in college. In the years since then, marriage, children, the work world, and financial stresses had pressed his spiritual life into a more subdued place, but his faith still formed the core of his heart. His trust in God was what I loved most about him. I might rage against God on my own account, but I wouldn't provoke a rift in Kevin's faith.

I lifted one hand to touch Kevin's dry cheek, my own tears forgotten. "No. We're not going to blame God, and we're not going to run away. I'm going to find the purpose in this."

A tendon flexed along his jawline. "And what if there is no purpose? What if it's just a stupid mistake, and God let it happen?"

Hearing him voice my deepest fear made me shiver. An echo in my heart added to his words.

*What if my whole life had no purpose? What if it was a bunch of random ups and downs and none of it really mattered?*

"Romans says 'All things work together for good,'" I said. The words sounded sickeningly sweet, but I tried again. "I don't like this—don't understand it. But I won't stop believing God loves us."

It wasn't until both of us had settled back under the quilt that Kevin answered, cold doubt muffled by his pillow. "Funny way of showing it."

Wednesday mornings meant Moms' Time Out. Close to thirty women attended each week, savoring a variety of guest speakers, small group discussions, and prayer times. But the main draw was the relief of having someone else chase their small children in circles for a while. Even though I facilitated everything, the meetings ran themselves. Lori coordinated the small groups. Sally was always at the church Wednesday mornings and could oversee setup and cleanup. And in a pinch, Doreen could introduce the guest speaker and get the meeting moving with her style of military precision.

They could manage.

I couldn't. Not yet. I didn't want to talk to anyone, so Kevin offered to call Doreen and ask her to cover for me and make sure everything went smoothly. I hid out at home like a captive princess in a medieval tower.

I dove into my day, grateful for the distraction of my children's needs. Micah was feeling better. Better able to fight me off when I tried to give him his medicine. Kelsey pouted when I told her we weren't going to Moms' Time Out but perked up when I promised we could play Candy Land after our chores. Dylan raced around the house after breakfast, enacting a spaceship battle complete with loud sound effects.

"Your mother ship is approaching." I had to shout to be heard over his noise as I chased him down to hand him his backpack. "Prepare for docking maneuvers."

He grinned as I hugged him and ruffled his dark mop of hair. Then he galloped out the door. As the bus pulled away, I breathed a prayer of thanks that I wasn't a bus driver.

Kelsey shadowed me all morning, like a lady in waiting. She insisted on helping me clean the bathroom, while Micah crawled nearby.

Then I caught her misting some Windex on Micah's padded bottom. His face puckered like a wrinkled sheet, and he started to wail.

"Kelsey, what are you doing?"

She turned wide eyes in my direction. "Cleaning. He smells."

I deserted the bathroom. At least I'd had time to scrub the biggest lumps of toothpaste from the counter.

My daughter did her best to entertain Micah while I changed him. He managed to fend off the clean diaper for a few minutes with aggressive wriggles, but I eventually won the wrestling match.

Worried about the effects of his latest earache, I held him on my lap, facing away from me. I whispered "cookie" behind him, and he didn't react. Not a good sign.

But Kelsey heard the magic word, and she insisted on a snack. I caved and settled Micah in his high chair and Kelsey in her booster seat, each with a few Lorna Doones. While they munched, I pulled a card from the kitchen bulletin board. Our family doctor had recommended an audiologist to do further testing with Micah. I called for an appointment.

Keeping a suspicious eye on the machine in case it decided to explode, I started a load of laundry. I scrubbed the kitchen and reorganized my spice rack. It probably would have been a good idea to use this time to fill out my *Women of Vision* questionnaire, but I didn't have the heart to look that closely at my life. No matter how hard I tried to focus on housework, my thoughts picked at the scab of my wounds. When Micah went down for his morning nap and Kelsey settled in front of *Sesame Street,* my feet carried me to my computer by habit. My fingers reached for the power button.

Shoot. I'd forgotten the computer was dead. Kevin planned to work on it this weekend. Rebuild, virus scan, defrag, or whatever strange rituals could resurrect it. No problem. I didn't need the keyboard for comfort.

Like the model Christian woman I aspired to be, I grabbed my Bible, poured a cup of coffee, and curled up on the couch.

I flipped past chapter headings. Abraham, Joseph, Moses, David, Daniel. Epic adventures where God came through in astounding ways. The stories tasted as bitter as my coffee. I almost slammed the book closed, but I had nowhere else to turn right now.

The book of First Peter fell open, dog-eared and marked with notes from our recent study. *"Humble yourselves, therefore, under God's mighty hand, that he may lift you up in due time. Cast all your anxiety on him because he cares for you."*

A strange mix of rebellion, longing, and comfort swirled around inside me like the oil and water experiment that Dylan did for science class. I bowed my head.

"Lord, you know I'm hurting. I don't understand any of this. Kevin has worked so hard, and now his job is in danger. All I've wanted to do is serve you, but I'm barely making progress with my education degree, and now . . ." I spoke the words quietly and struggled to go on. "Now you've snatched away the one thing that made me feel useful. Why aren't you helping?"

The phone rang and I indulged a fancy that it might be the Almighty himself, ready to explain His plans to me. I dropped the Bible and ran to the kitchen desk, checking the caller ID.

My sister, Judy.

I ignored the phone and let the machine get it. She was the last person I needed right now. My chipper message played, and a sharp *click* signaled Judy hanging up.

Good. I couldn't cope with her.

I needed someone to ride in on a white horse and rescue me. Even Kevin, for all his efforts, wasn't able to play the knight and save me from this latest disaster. His hugs helped, but last night when I'd told him about the meeting, he'd jumped into "solve it" mode. He prodded me to fight back and offered reams of other suggestions that I didn't have the strength to face.

At least he sympathized. Judy would probably side with the board and remind me how unqualified I was.

The phone rang again. My lips twitched. She called herself persistent. I called her stubborn. When her three corporate job choices had turned her down, she had marched into the human resources office of the first and lobbied her way up the food chain until she won an interview with the president and eventual acceptance.

After another hang-up, the phone rang yet again.

May as well get this over with. Bracing myself, I reached for the phone.

# TEN

*A gray missile* with fins slid past me in the clear waters off the eastern Mexican coastline. I blew out a startled breath, sending bubbles shooting through my regulator. A trickle of brine slipped past my lips and I bit down harder on the mouthpiece. Another sleek form glided along the ocean floor, about forty feet below.

Not sharks. Just tarpon. Big and creepy, but harmless.

My heart took a few minutes to stop tap-dancing. I shouldn't be diving alone, but I couldn't risk letting anyone know this location. During my years in archaeology, I'd unearthed a few treasures. But this promised to be the find of my life. Excitement set my blood swishing through my ears. I checked my gauge and swam deeper, stopping to clear the pressure behind my eardrums. My fins beat in a languid motion despite my eagerness. Thrashing would waste my air.

Navigating inside the ancient ship would be a challenge. I sailed past the broken spars. Barnacles coated every exposed surface, looking like moss swallowing a fallen log. Eerie tendrils of seaweed swayed in warning.

The listing, broken cabin walls seemed to close in on the light from my head lamp. My tank scraped an upper doorframe. A moray eel emerged from a crevice to give me a baleful stare. The ship may once have been the pride of Spain, but now the denizens of the Caribbean Sea floor had claimed her. Barracudas, stingray, fan coral. This was their world. They guarded the secrets of the Inca treasure.

The search pressed the limits of my air supply as I maneuvered through a hatch and deep into the bowels of the ship. Past broken kegs and a startled school of zebra fish, my beam hit a chest.

The hasp had rusted away, so with the knife from my belt, it was a simple matter to pry open the lid.

The sight dazzled me.

Reaching past heaps of coins, I lifted out the bust of an Incan god. Even buoyed by water, the weight stunned me. Pure gold.

Suddenly, a shadow passed the jagged gap in the hull above me. I scuttled back, wary of sharks. What swam toward me was worse.

A human. Decked out in wet suit and brandishing a spear gun.

The idol slipped from my hands. The sound of my rapid breaths crackled in my ears like static on a cordless phone.

"Becky? Becky! Are you listening?"

I inhaled deeply. "Sorry, I was drifting."

I'd already apologized to Judy for missing her television appearance. When I explained about Micah's ear infection, she stopped yelling. She had noticed my lackluster tone and drilled me for more information. Against my better judgment, I babbled a teary explanation of the dead computer, my temptation to give up on college, Kevin's work problems, and the recent horror of losing my dream job at the church.

She had launched into sisterly outrage on my behalf, but my thoughts wandered.

Now Judy's sigh carried over the telephone. "Pay attention this time. I *said* that you need to go talk to whoever has the power at that church of yours."

"I don't think I can. If I thought they'd consider me for the job, I'd try. But . . ." My throat clogged. I hated admitting my failure to my sister. "They acted like it never occurred to them. After all, I don't have a degree or professional experience."

Judy used one of the words I fought to purge from Dylan's vocabulary. "Sis, you've created something special. Your vision built the momentum. You need to fight for this."

Surprise and confusion made me blink. I hitched myself up

onto the kitchen desk, sitting cross-legged. "But . . . but you've always thought it was silly."

Another melodramatic sigh. "I didn't want you getting a big head. After all, your life is so perfect."

I held the phone away from me and frowned at it. Someone had replaced my sister with an alien. When I placed the receiver against my ear she was still talking.

"You've always been so sure of yourself—the meaning of life . . . all that stuff." Today her words sounded less like a sneer and more like a jealous complaint. "You act like you have an inside track with God. And don't get me started on Kevin. Do you have any idea what kind of guys I meet? And even if I found one that wasn't a creep, I'd never have time for a relationship anyway. You are so lucky."

"Lucky? At the picnic last summer you called me a Stepford wife."

Judy laughed. "Can't you take a joke? All right, maybe I've needled you a few times. You're just so smug in your perfect little life. I can't help it."

I didn't know how to answer. My jaw worked up and down, but no words came out.

She didn't wait for a response. "Becky, you're my sister and I'm proud of you. Now stick up for yourself."

Suspicion and worry spun through my mind like a school of triggerfish. "Wait a minute. Are you all right? I mean, you don't have cancer or something, do you?"

Her snort reassured me she was in fine form. "Becky Anne Hemple Miller. Can't a sister show a little concern?" She always used my full name when she scolded. When she was really angry, she forgot to add my married name.

I was tempted to point out that showing concern and support had not been the climate of our family. We never had the warmth of the Waltons or even the Simpsons. It was a wonder that our childhood home hadn't been circled with yellow police tape warning "Danger. Dysfunctional family. Enter at your own risk."

When various addictions caught up with our parents, relief mingled with my sorrow at their funerals. Judy sobbed at the graveside when Mom's liver succumbed to years of alcohol and pills. I bounced two-year-old Dylan in my arms and swallowed my regrets. I cried with wistful longing for the mom I could have had. My tears weren't about losing her. I never had her to begin with.

Dad's world of type-A, sixty-hour workweeks and explosive rages only escalated after Mom died. A year later, he died of a stroke. Again, Judy took his death harder than I did. But she had always been the favorite. She still spoke with sentiment about our childhood, while I counted my blessings that I had escaped it.

Maybe Judy did envy my life, even while I measured mine against hers. I clutched the phone. "Thanks, Judifer." I hadn't called her that in years.

Her giggle evoked the nights we sneaked books under a tent of sheets to read way past our bedtimes. I swallowed. "And I'm sorry I've acted all smug. God's love is important to me, and I hope you'll get to know Him one day, but I don't have all the answers."

For once she didn't snipe at my mention of God. We wrapped up the conversation with her promise to mail me a tape of her *Today* show appearance and my promise to talk to the pastor or the board about the job.

In spite of the humiliation that still shot through me at random moments, for most of the busy day I also felt a bit of warmth. I had never realized how much my certitude about faith had annoyed Judy. If my failures could heal our relationship, maybe God had a purpose in this after all.

I was rarely good at figuring out God's ultimate plan in a given situation. But I was addicted to the attempt. If I had a toothache, I reasoned that perhaps God wanted me to share my faith with the dentist, and that's why He allowed the pain. When the instruments in my mouth made it impossible to say more than "Mmf. Ish urts!" I searched for another explanation.

I'd already begun the analyzing process with Micah's ear problems. Perhaps God wanted me to found some terrific ministry to the deaf one day. And the computer crash. It was probably a sign to forget college until the kids were older. And the job offer in Grand Marais. Probably a temptation to run away from problems instead of trusting God to provide Kevin with work.

Once I had all of God's strategies figured out, my mood lightened. I played Candy Land with Kelsey, rolled on the floor with Micah until giggles made his pudge quiver with joy, and greeted Dylan's homecoming with a noogie to his head and a huge hug.

When Kevin arrived home, I lifted the lid from a roasting pan of chicken and gravy. The meal was a favorite, and I didn't see any reason to tell him it was the easiest in my repertoire. Throw the drumsticks and thighs into the pot and pour a huge can of cream of mushroom soup over the top. When I was feeling ambitious, I added some dill and pepper.

Supper was a success, even if the rest of my life wasn't.

Kevin kept glancing at me, gauging my mood.

I was proud of how well I was handling things, now that the initial shock had worn off. And I couldn't wait to fill Kevin in on my insights.

After bedtime cuddles with the kids, Kevin and I settled on the couch. I tucked my legs under me and leaned into him. "I've got it all figured out," I said. And in a breathless progression, I filled him in on all my theories.

"Could be," he said cautiously. "I guess we'll see how it unfolds."

"How are things at work?"

He brightened. "Crummy. But something good happened today."

I snuggled closer. "Tell me."

"Driving in this morning, I had the radio on, and they played a song about seeking God. So I shut off the music and just talked to Him. About being mad at what's happened to you. About the problems at work. I started to wonder if this was

God's way of nudging us toward a big change."

I pulled away to watch him while I listened.

"Anyway, this morning I got a call from City Life, and they wanted to interview me. I went over on my lunch break." He squeezed my hand. "They offered me the job."

I wasn't sure how I felt. Exile to Grand Marais seemed slightly more appealing after yesterday's disastrous board meeting. But I still couldn't face the thought of leaving our home and friends. Not wanting to squelch his moment, I fought off the queasy feeling that churned at the thought of leaving. "I'm proud of you." I planted a kiss on his cheek, and he turned his head and claimed my lips.

A few breathless moments pushed everything from my mind. Judy was right. I had it all.

When we broke apart, Kevin gave me a huge smile. I was surprised but delighted that the shadows haunting him in the past days seemed to have disappeared completely. He grabbed my hand. "There's one problem. They need my decision by Monday."

My happy fog blew away. "What? But what if Anderson doesn't lay you off? We'd be uprooting the whole family for nothing."

He grinned with the same confidence Dylan showed on his bicycle. "Maybe it's our chance to practice trusting God. Like I said. Be ready for change."

"But . . . but . . . maybe God wants us to persevere. You know. Wait on Him."

"Honey, it would be a step of faith to leave."

"Or maybe we're supposed to stay." As much as I wanted to be willing to step out in faith, I valued my security, too. "We need to pray about this."

He nodded. "I promised them an answer by Monday."

How can a life of chaos and stress, errands and broken appliances, car problems and sick children fit any more confusion into it? Sometimes it seemed as if God himself was standing in my way. I made a mental note to read the book of Job in my devotions tomorrow. In college I had God all figured out. Lately, He was becoming harder to understand.

# ELEVEN

**Snow bleached** the landscape and began
a restless dance. Soon huge swirls spiraled upward
as hurricane-force winds pelted me from Norton Sound.
When we had pulled out of Unalakeet that morning, the skies
were clear and my hopes sparkled like the turquoise ice floes out at sea.
We had a strong lead on most of the other mushers. I had believed it in
my bones. This would be my year.

But now visibility shrank and I could barely see my lead dog.
Worse, I had lost my tag sled. I plowed forward in the blinding cyclone
of white, completely alone. Howling wind drowned out my wail of
despair. We were so close—only a few hundred miles of coastline until
Nome.

Year after year, I had endured the torturing miles, the frostbite, the
danger. This year my dogs were strong and well trained. I was fit and
prepared for every challenge of the trail. The course followed the northern
route on this even-numbered year—my favorite.

Two weeks ago, when I pulled out of Anchorage, I had absorbed the
excitement and camaraderie in the streets. Sleds jostled, dogs yipped and
snapped. Competitors cried out greetings to friends and enemies alike.
Those of us who survived the Iditarod formed an ironic community,
united by our love of isolation.

Pitting myself and my team against every wicked attack of nature
made my blood surge. The sheer test of endurance seduced me every year.
I thrived on the exhilaration of flying along ice-coated rivers, skimming
jagged ridges, hunkering down to survive wind chills of one hundred

*degrees below zero. A primal hunger strained in my soul, like the dogs against their harnesses. One year, I'd win the Iditarod.*

*But today, as the blizzard wrapped stinging arms around me, I couldn't spot any familiar landmarks. The storm had pushed us off course. Lost and alone, the truth burned like ice: this wouldn't be my year.*

Sleet stung my cheeks. I leaned into the wind and thrust my hands into my coat pockets, welcoming the cold bite of early winter in Minnesota. Here was a tangible storm I could understand. Not like the searing cold of my failure.

The tempest pummeled the trees, rattled against the siding on homes, iced the sidewalk, and battered my face. But it wasn't personal. November strained like a teenager at college for the first time—wild with energy and freedom. I welcomed the burn of ice against my face.

I'd decided to walk to Heather's for Bible study tonight. Wrestling the elements worked off some of my tension. Besides, I dreaded facing my friends. My steps slowed, and I skidded up the sidewalk to tap on Heather's door.

She met me with a warm hug and pulled me inside. Dried herbs and flowers hung from rafters in her living room. Heather's daughter Charity (or was it Grace? I could never tell the twins apart) greeted me. "I can take your coat." Long, full hair made her a nine-year-old imitation of her mother, but her thick glasses reminded me of her dad.

I stepped farther into the room. Candles glowed on the coffee table Heather had made from an old door. A wooden bowl of apples rested on a side table. Charity's Celtic harp nosed out from one corner of the room. Grace's collection of wooden recorders hung from brackets on the wall.

Heather's home breathed creativity and cozy simplicity. Today the peace I always felt here gave me the courage to pull my gaze from the décor and face my friends.

Lori scooted to one side of the futon couch and patted the cushion next to her. "Sit here."

Sally hunched awkwardly in a beanbag chair and didn't meet my eyes.

Doreen clattered over to me in impractical but gorgeous high-heeled boots and gave me a quick hug. She rested one hand against my cheek. "You're frozen. Come in and have some cocoa." She tottered back to a bent-willow rocking chair.

Heather folded herself cross-legged beside the table and grabbed a pitcher. "It's made with soy, carob, and honey."

Lori leaned over as I settled beside her. "Don't worry. It's pretty good in spite of that."

I managed a small smile.

Heather offered me a steaming mug. "Are you okay?'

I sipped and tried to hide my grimace. "Yeah. Let's just dive into the Bible study, okay?" I glanced at Lori, begging her to move things along.

She shook her head. "Becky, we care about you."

"I know. It's just . . . I shouldn't have gotten my hopes up."

A watery sniffle came from the direction of the beanbag. Sally looked up, black smudges of mascara melting under her eyes. "I'm so sorry." Her chirpy voice had sunk to a croak. "I shouldn't have said anything to you ahead of time. But when Pastor said the board planned to move ahead on a women's ministry director, I assumed it would be you. I don't understand this obsession about one little clause in our church constitution. A degree from our denomination is no guarantee of quality. Anyone can have one if they happened to go to one of our colleges." She dabbed her eyes with a tissue. "Even I do."

Doreen sprang from her rocker again and paced the floor, kicking aside a corner of a lumpy hand-woven rug. "It should have been you. I plan to write a letter of protest. Maybe you could sue. Change the church constitution."

Heather turned worried eyes toward Doreen. "No. She needs to embrace her feelings so she can heal." She looked at me, brown eyes warm with compassion. "Maybe you should write a poem."

Doreen sniffed and settled back in her chair. Lori rested a hand on my shoulder. "What do you want to do?"

I bit my lip. "I don't know. I'm still kind of in shock. And embarrassed. And I'm worried about Kevin. He's facing some tough decisions."

"Maybe Noah can help," Lori said.

I nodded. Friday night Kevin and Noah would meet for their weekly basketball game. Noah's advice was usually as good as Lori's, although he wasn't on my list of favorite people right now. Maybe Kevin could pump Noah for info and find out why the board didn't even consider me.

Doreen set her mug on the table with a clunk and picked up her Bible. "You should at least march into the church office and h3nd them a résumé. Demand to be considered for the job. We'll all back you up."

"Thanks, guys . . . but maybe God just doesn't want me there anymore. I need to be available to Him and His leading." It was the mature, spiritual thing to say. So why did the words catch in my throat like a fish bone?

Lori gave me a hard look but quickly led us into our prayer time. With my head bowed, I allowed a few tears to slip out but pasted on a smile after the amen.

I tried to pay attention during our Bible study, but my ears felt as clogged as Micah's.

As I watched the conversation around the room, the words hummed from a distance. An inky stain spread through my thoughts.

Sure, Doreen could tell me to protest to the church. Why

wouldn't she radiate confidence? She'd had a high-powered career and still had it all together. She didn't need to worry about an empty checking account and her husband's looming unemployment. She had never had to pinch pennies.

Heather floated in the ozone somewhere, untroubled by mere human problems. I could never emulate her approach to life, even though I secretly envied it. Her talents weren't always practical, but everyone knew the warmth of her heart and the creativity that burst out of her in a hundred directions. Everyone loved her.

Sally meant well, but her teary apologies didn't soothe my pain. I'd been set up to believe the job would be mine. Not only by Sally. During the last few years, Pastor Roger had mentioned several times that I was building a terrific program and he hoped one day to give me tangible support for my efforts.

*It was a lie to keep me slaving for free. To keep me loyal and stupid while I poured myself out for the church.*

The dark voice moaned like an arctic wind.

I turned to look at Lori. Her face was alight with passion as her finger caressed a verse in her Bible. I watched her mouth move and the heads around the room nod.

What could she possibly understand about my pain? Her household ran like a well-oiled machine. Her children were polite, brilliant, and perfectly behaved. She was my best friend, yet she was so far superior to me in her depth of faith and knowledge of the Bible, I sometimes felt I was one of her "projects." A troubled soul to mentor.

Self-pity coated my thoughts, dripping envy and isolation down my heart's walls. The stain spread until every thought was covered in it.

When the Bible study wrapped up, Heather perched on the

arm of the futon. "I'm hitting the thrift stores on Saturday. Do you want to come?"

I brightened for a moment. Guilt-free shopping was a great restorative. Each treasure I unearthed made me tingle. And I loved boasting to Kevin. "This designer blouse was forty dollars retail, and I got it for four bucks. I saved us thirty-six dollars!"

Kevin usually popped my bubble by saying, "Okay, then give me the thirty-six dollars."

He just didn't get it.

I smiled at Heather. "Sure. Sounds like just what I need."

"Great! I'll pick you up around ten. And when we're done, I want to treat you to dessert at the Tea Room. When the going gets tough, the tough get tea."

I winced. "Some healthy herbal junk with no caffeine or flavor?"

Heather flicked her hair back from her face. "Well, if you insist on clogging your arteries, they also have scones and clotted cream."

"I'm there."

Heather laughed. "I thought that might win you over. And I dare you to try the rose hip, pansy, and willow blend."

Sounded more like something to plant in a garden than to drink, but I nodded.

After Grace (or was it Charity?) brought me my coat, Lori broke away from a conversation with Doreen and gave me a hug. "God has a plan in all of this. We just can't see it yet."

Out of her mouth, the words didn't sound as forced and phony as when I'd tried to recite them to myself. Emotion choked my throat. I swallowed and nodded without risking an answer. Another word from my mouth would release a torrent. I didn't want my friends to hear the bitter thoughts tearing around inside me tonight.

Lori seemed to understand. She gave one more squeeze. "Call me if you want to talk." She buttoned her coat and headed out the door.

Doreen and Sally both offered me a ride home, but I assured them I wanted the exercise. They squinted out at the wind and sleet and gave me dubious looks but didn't press the issue.

I marched home, leaning into the weather, fists swinging at my side.

None of this was fair.

Kevin worked harder than anyone at Anderson. He genuinely cared about his clients. It wasn't fair that his boss didn't appreciate him.

I'd invested myself, sometimes at great sacrifice, to the ministry of our church. It wasn't fair that they used me and then cast me aside for someone with a degree.

Most of the students in my college class had nothing on their plate except frat parties, while I juggled three kids and a household. How could I compete with that?

Doreen could shop at designer stores while I rummaged through racks at Goodwill—racks full of odd items that smelled funny.

Everyone else's life was on a clear course.

I glared up at the sleet showcased in the beam of a streetlight. I might be alone. I might be cold inside. But I was not going to give up. My agenda for my life was a good one. These obstacles weren't going to slow me down.

Tomorrow, I'd march into the pastor's office and make him see the huge mistake they were making. Then I'd go to the library and find the books I'd used for my research paper and get back to work on it. I'd double my efforts to finish my degree. If we absolutely had to move, I'd start another women's ministry up in Grand Marais. I'd build it up from the ground floor. I'd done it once. I could do it again.

My sled was in the lead. My own grit and determination had brought me this far. Even though visibility was low, I'd plow forward.

So why did the howl of the wind stir a fear in me? Why did I wonder if the dogs of my desire were pulling me off course?

# TWELVE

**"You've done enough** reps today." The physical therapist handed me a towel.

I shook my head, scattering a mist of sweat. "Not . . . quitting." I couldn't spare breath for more words. I muscled the lat pull-downs ten more times. When my last ounce of strength was spent, I allowed my head to droop forward, sagging in my wheelchair. Around the clinic's room, clatters of weights, moans of pain, and the shuffles of ambulatory patients testing new legs, raised a chorus of misery.

The therapist rested a hand on my shoulder. "I wish I had more patients like you. I've never seen anyone work harder."

I rolled my shoulders and sat tall again. "I've always believed an obstacle is just a chance to grow stronger."

My sister strode into the room, oblivious to the way her strong legs mocked the rest of us. "Guess what? Another church called and asked if you'll speak at their conference. And Joni Eareckson Tada wants to interview you on her radio show." She leaned down to hug me. "You are such an inspiration."

I smiled with satisfaction. Some folks would have crumbled after a tragedy like mine. For years, I'd been the feature bareback rider in a touring circus. A few months ago, I had faced an arena full of cheering fans. Pink sequins caught the floodlights as I leapt astride Destiny. We cantered around the ring, and I sprang to a standing position on the horse's back. Destiny's gait outclassed any horse I'd ever worked with. I positioned myself for my challenging new flip.

*Twisting, flying, and feeling for my targeted landing behind Destiny's withers, my instinct failed me. I overrotated, grazed past the horse's flank, and hit the ground head first with a crunch of bones.*

*When the doctor gave me the grim diagnosis, I didn't allow myself to cry. My mind kicked into gear immediately, formulating plans. I tapped my fist on the arm of the wheelchair. Who could say? Maybe one day I'd jump right up.*

The sound of the bus lumbering up the block propelled me out of my chair. "Dylan, the bus is here!"

After Dylan scampered out the door, I bundled Kelsey and Micah into the van and buzzed over to church. Friday mornings were generally quiet. Sally was in the back room folding bulletins for Sunday. Kelsey ran in to hug her legs.

Sally whirled to face me, one hand to her heart. Then she smiled down at Kelsey. "Whoa! You scared me."

"Is Pastor in?"

"Yeah, he's just pacing around his office practicing his sermon for Sunday. Go ahead and knock." She pursed her lips and then leaned forward as if she would say more if I gave her a bit of encouragement. She was still feeling guilty, and I wasn't in a mood to assuage it right now.

Sally turned and grabbed a stack of bulletins. "Do you want me to watch Micah and Kelsey?"

My smile was genuine. "Sure. That would help."

She reached for Micah and pulled out a stool for Kelsey. "Want to help me fold?"

Kelsey bounced her blond curls in a vigorous nod.

Sally pulled out a Kleenex to dap at Micah's runny nose, and he tossed his head in protest. "Oh, I almost forgot." She hefted Micah higher on her shoulder so she could reach into one of her desk trays and hand me a magazine. "I'm finished reading it. I figured you'd want to read it to get prepared for your turn."

I stared at the glossy issue of *Women of Vision*, aghast. A blond, coifed, airbrushed beauty smirked from the November cover. Pumpkin and chestnut fonts shouted across her doctor's smock. *Meet this month's woman of vision. Pediatric surgeon, mother of six, and on the board of the city's top charitable foundations. How does she do it all?*

Oh boy. How on earth was I going to compete with this? There was no time to produce more children before April. Certainly no time to go to medical school. I stuffed the magazine into my shoulder bag. Well, at least I could get this job situation settled. *Director of Women's Ministry* wouldn't sound too bad on the cover.

I headed down the hall and rapped firmly on Pastor Roger's door.

"Come in." His voice boomed, as if inviting a lost soul into the kingdom.

I eased the door open. "Good morning, Pastor."

Books littered his desk, and he stood midoffice with a pencil behind his ear and a wad of papers in his hand. He gave me a warm smile. "Have a seat. How are you?"

I perched on the edge of an armchair while he circled his desk and settled into his office chair with a relaxed sigh.

Now that I was here, I didn't know how to start. "I'm fine. Well, not really. That's why I wanted to talk to you."

He leaned forward and steepled his hands on the desk. He assumed a gentle concerned face. Did he practice that look in a mirror while he was in seminary? "I'm happy to help. What can I do for you?"

Judy would dominate the room with her confidence. Where was my Hemple family chutzpah? I threw my shoulders back. "Pastor, I've poured myself into the women's ministry for the last three years."

He nodded benignly, eyes squinting with a small smile.

I bit my lip. "Why didn't the board ask to interview me for the job?"

His forehead flinched with surprise, and he sat back, crossing his arms. "Are you saying you were expecting to be considered?"

My resolve crumbled. He was making me feel like a petulant child. I regretted blurting out my question, but I'd started this, so I had better see it through. "Of course. There was no Moms' Time Out program when I joined the church. No nursery on Sundays for young moms. No annual retreats or small group Bible studies. I've worked hard all this time."

I could hear the whine in my own tone, and stopped.

Pastor Roger's pastoral expression slid back over his face. "I'm confused. Wasn't it your wish to have a vibrant program for women at our church? Haven't you lobbied for a staff person for the job this past year? I don't understand why you're not happy."

"But it's my program. My baby. And everyone says I've done a great job."

He swiveled his chair slightly, leaning back and focusing on the full wall of books. Maybe he was drawing inspiration from Luther and Calvin and Chambers. "I'm sorry you're feeling upset. I thought these were things you really wanted to do."

"Of course I wanted to."

His mouth worked side to side as if he were swishing Listerine. "But now you're feeling . . . unappreciated?"

I deflected the shame that rushed in my direction. "It's not about feeling unappreciated. If everyone is happy with my work, why didn't the board consider having me continue in my position?"

"On staff?" Pastor's incredulous tone sealed my humiliation. He rotated to face me again. "It's the policy of our church to hire graduates from our denominational college. They've studied theology, and leadership, and planning, and church growth. Don't you want the best possible person in this role?"

*I'm the best possible person. It's my dream.* I drew a slow breath. "So I was good enough to do the job for free, but not to be paid?"

He had the grace to look sheepish. "I feel terrible that you didn't realize what creating a staff position would mean. Nobody denies that you've done a wonderful job." He leaned forward, resuming his fatherly demeanor. "I'm sorry, Becky. The church has mandatory qualifications for our full-time staff."

My ribs sagged inward. Can a heart shrivel, pulling the torso toward the vacuum? He understood my hurt but wasn't about to budge. Education trumped experience and heart. I sprang up, eager to run home and lick my wounds.

He stood and gave an apologetic smile. "Well, I'm glad we had this little talk."

I wanted to glare, to snarl, to throw his plaster bust of Wesley across the room. Instead, I tugged my sweater into place and forced a nod. "Thank you for your time."

I turned to leave.

He came around his desk and walked me to the door. "Don't worry. When the new director is hired, I'm sure she will be thrilled to utilize your skills. There's always room for volunteer support. God will find a way to use you."

Kelsey jogged down the hall toward me. Pastor Roger gave an awkward chuckle. "Now you'll have more time for those delightful children of yours."

I grabbed Kelsey's hand and aimed us toward Sally's desk.

"Sorry." Sally gestured to a scattered array of bulletins. "She tossed them in the air, and when I started picking them up, she got away from me." She looked at me more closely. "How did it go?"

I shrugged. "I don't have a degree. I'm not qualified. Perfectly logical." I gave a short, brittle laugh. "I should have known better."

Sally handed a crayon to Kelsey, who began scribbling on one of the bulletins. She put a hand on my arm. "Becky, I'm sorry."

"Yeah, and he thinks he's doing me a favor. Providing me more time for my kids." I sniffed, more in anger than from the threatening tears.

"Well, maybe he has a point."

I stiffened. Those words could not have come from Sally's mouth. "What?"

"I'm just saying, you've been pretty stressed lately. Juggling a lot of things. And you've told us at Bible study that you worry you're a bad mom." She gave me a reassuring smile. "Don't get me wrong. I don't know how you do it. It's all I can do to keep up with Chelsea, and you have three kids. But maybe you should quit trying to do so much while the kids are young."

Micah crawled over and tugged the cord to the telephone, toppling it from the desktop. Sally gave a gentle "I told you so" look.

I swooped him up, replaced the phone, and called to Kelsey. "Come on. Time to go."

I refused to think. To feel. To speak. Until I had them both in their car seats. My hands clenched the steering wheel, and my arms shook. PMS-level rage built with so much pressure I thought the veins in my temples would burst.

First, the board overlooked me. Then my family and friends nagged me to stick up for myself. Then Pastor acted all logical and intractable. Now Sally sided with him. All this on top of Kevin's job situation, the broken computer, my lost term paper, and Micah's ear infection.

"Are we going, Mommy?" Kelsey's legs were getting long enough to kick the back of my seat if she scrunched down enough.

"Stop that! We'll go when I'm ready." I glared into the rear-view mirror.

Her eyes turned round with surprise, and her face puckered. Some of my anger bled away. "I'm sorry, sweetie. Mommy's just a little grumpy today." I turned the key and gunned the engine, hoping Sally would hear the gravel spurt as I spun out of the parking lot.

"Whee! Go fast!" Kelsey's indignation at my outburst evaporated. "Mommy, I did pictures."

"Yes, honey, I saw you coloring on the bulletin. But remember, we only color in coloring books."

The teachable moment zoomed straight over her head. "She has candy."

"Mm-hmm."

She launched into a recitation of her favorite candies, then gave me a list of what she wanted for Christmas. I was relieved that Kelsey could chatter happily with only occasional vocalizations from me. I didn't have the energy to pay much attention. I felt ashamed by my short temper. Kevin never raised his voice with the kids. How did he always hold himself together with so much restraint?

The throbbing in my head hadn't faded as we pulled into the driveway. My emotions were a paella—a haphazard blend of ingredients. Instead of shrimp, scallops, peppers, and rice, I stirred a pan of self-doubt, righteous indignation, genuine hurt, and steely determination over a low heat.

Fine. They didn't want me. Time for Plan B.

Instead of turning off the engine, I pulled back out of the driveway. "Kelsey, we're going to the library."

She squealed. "Can I play puppets?"

The children's section in the library had a puppet theatre and a vast selection of props. "Sure, honey."

After we jogged across the cold parking lot and pushed the

wide library door open, Kelsey scooted straight to the puppets. That left only one squirmy baby to manage while I searched out the books I needed. Tonight, I'd start rewriting my term paper longhand, and beg Kevin to take our computer in. He'd diddled with it all week without success. I know he longed to be the hero and fix it, but it was time to bring in bigger guns.

After the kids were in bed, Kevin and I could pray together, and I'd tell him that he should take the job in Grand Marais. Maybe we wouldn't have to move immediately. And even if we did, maybe the *Women of Vision* magazine could expand their series to successful women in the greater Minnesota area.

Pleased with the new course, I could almost ignore the sting of my recent rejection. "A prophet is without honor in his own country," I muttered, yanking out a journal on learning-style research while rocking Micah on my hip. A woman nearby glanced at me and then edged away.

That evening, Kevin charged out of the house to meet Noah for basketball. I tucked the kids into bed, lit a few candles, and popped a CD of Mozart music into the stereo. In my education research, I'd learned that listening to Mozart increased students' math scores. Maybe it would help decision-making skills, as well.

When Kevin came home, he launched himself onto the couch.

He looked adorable and rugged in his ripped, sweaty T-shirt, and I almost forgot my agenda.

Kevin looked around the room and noticed the ambience. A slow grin curved upward.

I could tell he was misunderstanding the purpose of my setting. I shook my head and scooted to the edge of my chair. "We need to talk."

"Sure." The grin stayed in place. "But why don't you come sit over here?"

"Later." I filled him in on my futile talk with the pastor,

pushing the words out quickly, because the humiliation returned the moment I relived the conversation. "What did Noah say?"

Kevin sobered. "Pretty much the same thing Pastor Roger told you. But Noah felt really bad. He said they made the decision like a bunch of men. It never occurred to them to think about your feelings."

"No hope of them changing their minds? Even if I promise to keep working toward my degree?"

He shook his head, gentle pity in his eyes.

I'm sure my resolute nod surprised him. He was probably expecting another burst of tears. "Okay. I admit I had my heart set on this. But I've got it figured out."

Kevin's forehead wrinkled, but he waited quietly. Despite his expansive and outgoing nature, he was a great listener.

I stared at the tongue of light on one of the candles. "It's a sign. I don't know why I didn't see it sooner."

"A sign?"

"Yeah. From God. It all makes sense. The door closed on the job at the church, you find out you might get laid off. You get a great offer from City Life . . ."

"Great offer? But you don't want to pull up stakes, do you?"

"Well, I didn't at first. But that was before I figured everything out. God wants me to start a new women's program for a church up north. I'm sure of it. They don't appreciate us here. Your company, our church. Time to be like Abraham."

"Abraham?"

Why was he repeating everything I said? "Yeah. 'Leave your home and go to the land I will show you.'" I sat back, satisfied. "It's Plan B." I waited for Kevin to compliment my wisdom. Or at least to agree with me.

Instead, he shifted on the couch and eased to his feet without looking at me. "I need to take a shower."

"Hey, wait a minute. Is that all you have to say?"

"What is there to say? You have it all figured out." His voice had an edge.

My determination deflated slightly. "But you agree, don't you?"

"Maybe." He rubbed one of his shoulders. "Let's talk about it later, okay?"

"But you have to give City Life your answer on Monday."

"Did you remember to pick up some Gatorade this week? I'm parched." He hurried to the kitchen, rummaged for a bit, then clanked a glass into the sink.

I was too confused to tag after him. A minute later, he raced down the hall and into the bathroom. The shower splashed, but I didn't hear him humming to himself like he usually did.

What was eating him?

# THIRTEEN

**Clouds hid the moon.** *Maybe the darkness was a good omen. If any of the Nazi patrols
saw us, they'd shoot us in a Prussian second. A wedge of
ice settled in my chest at the thought.*

*A tug on my sleeve drew me back to the mission at hand, and I
followed the man code-named Monsieur K deeper into the woods. Our
target tonight was a radio transmission tower. Claude would meet us
there with explosives.*

*We huddled near a tree, watching the clearing.*

*"After the war," Monsieur K murmured into my ear, "we'll move
south and have a vineyard."*

*I smiled. Even though I refused to marry him until the war ended,
he spun dreams of our life together that filled me with hope.*

*Suddenly, a shadow separated itself from the trees across the clear-
ing. Claude made his way toward the tower and set down a duffel
bag.*

*"It's time." My partner's quiet words made my heart pound an
adrenaline-charged rhythm. We picked our way into the clearing.
Claude saw us coming and took a few steps to meet us. I felt cool air
against my back as K pulled away.*

*"It's them." Monsieur K's voice rang out, loud in the hushed
night.*

*Claude and I both jumped. What was he doing? Silence was our
only defense.*

*An explosion of noise near the tree line alerted me to the truth.*

*Lights flooded the clearing and German voices shouted. Soldiers charged forward. Like a stupid rabbit, I froze.*

*Claude ran toward the trees. A machine gun chattered and his body jerked again and again, like a gangster in a bad American movie. He fell.*

*I stumbled toward him and collapsed to my knees on the cold ground. I looked back at my former resistance contact. "Traitor!" The scream tore from deep in my soul—a declaration and a curse. I cradled Claude's head, ignoring the soldiers around us. The hot moisture of his blood seeped into my clothes.*

I gasped, my mind jumping from the nightmare with confusing abruptness. The clock glowed 5:30. Kevin breathed deeply beside me.

I still felt wet.

Tiny bare feet thumped against my shin. Kelsey. She had crawled into bed with us around 3:00 A.M. after her own nightmare.

Of course. If she had to wet a bed, she'd have to pick ours.

I groaned and started evacuating us all from the bed. Kevin was comfortable and dry on his side, but I finally roused him so we could change the sheets. He carried Kelsey back to her room for clean pajamas.

I padded to the kitchen to start the coffee. Not enough time left to try going back to sleep now.

The kids didn't understand Saturday time. Their internal clocks had them bouncing off the walls by 6:30.

Kevin joined me in the kitchen and sighed into a chair kitty-corner from mine. He reached for my hands. "You're a good mom."

Simple words, but more precious than a Medal of Honor. "What brought that on?"

He shrugged. "I don't tell you enough. Do you want the shower first?"

I shook my head. "Go ahead."

He stood and leaned over to kiss the top of my head. "I love you."

As he retreated from the kitchen, I pulled my brain out of my morning fog. Something felt off balance. He was acting weird. Not that he wasn't usually kind and loving. He was. But there was a funny vibe to him lately.

I stood, stretched, and aimed for the coffeepot. He was probably just struggling with the new direction God was showing us. New job, new town, new friends. I could relate. Change was tough. I made a mental note to be particularly sweet to him all weekend.

My plans got sidetracked.

Sally called after breakfast. "I'm feeling bad. I hope you didn't take anything I said yesterday in the wrong way."

*You mean your insinuation that my work at the church made me an inadequate mom?* "No. I know you're just trying to give me some perspective on this."

"So you're not upset about Pastor Roger and the board?"

"Not anymore." It was a small lie. "I think God may be opening new doors for us." *And when He does, I'll be able to stop feeling angry about everything.*

"I'm so glad." Relief crackled through the phone line. "I was afraid you'd be mad at me."

"Of course not." I forced warmth into my voice, and after a few more reassurances, we said our good-byes.

After I corralled Dylan into his morning chores, a soft tap sounded on the kitchen door. Kevin was busy disconnecting our computer, finally ready to take it in for repair. I stepped around him and pulled the door open.

Lori shivered in the gray cold and held a polka-dotted gift bag. "I found this and thought of you."

"Come in." I opened my arms.

She stepped inside and leaned down a bit to hug me, then noticed the legs jutting across her path. "Hey, Kevin. How's it going?"

My husband pulled his head out from under the kitchen desk with a fistful of cords. "Not bad. Did Noah tell you I whipped the pants off him last night?"

She laughed. "That's not quite the way he told it." She offered the bag to me. "Come on, open it."

I smiled. Brightly colored tissue paper couldn't help but cheer me. "Do you want some coffee?"

She peeled off her gloves and rubbed her hands. "I'll help myself."

I pulled away the tissue paper and lifted out a CD of instrumental praise music. My squeal was genuine. "This is awesome. But you didn't have to do this."

She grinned. "I know. But I figured you've had a lot to deal with lately and I wanted to remind you that I care."

I drew her into the living room, chasing Kelsey to her room to pick up her toys. Lori shrugged out of her coat sleeves, switching her coffee cup from hand to hand, and sank onto the couch. "So how are you holding up?"

Every brain cell urged me to give her the plastic answers. About how I had faith God was in charge, and all things worked together for good, and the church had good reasons for its decision. Instead, I sighed and met her eyes. "It really blindsided me. This was my one little special gift. The one thing I could give. My identity. You know? Like the little drummer boy."

I waited for Lori to lecture me, but instead she nodded. "I would have been really hurt."

"And confused, and angry, and discouraged. But I'm getting past it."

Lori sipped her coffee and waited.

I ran a hand through my hair. "Here's what I think. God's letting everything go wrong because He wants to get my attention. He's leading us somewhere new."

Lori's large brown eyes studied me. "Are you sure?"

"It makes as much sense as anything. God wants me to serve Him, and if this door is closed, I need to find a window, right?"

"I'm sure it brings Him joy—the way you want to serve Him. But . . ." She set her coffee cup on the table and looked out the window, where wind kicked up a volley of tiny dry snowflakes.

"What?"

Lori turned back to face me, offering a gentle smile. "I just worry sometimes. You're trying so hard. You know, sometimes even the best projects that we do for God can get in the way of *loving* God."

I stiffened, but I didn't want to start a disagreement.

"You said God is trying to get your attention," she said. "Maybe He just wants you to curl up in His arms."

Soap bubbles and butterfly wings tickled my soul. The image she painted made me yearn for that kind of rest. The responsible, driven side of my nature fought back. "Yeah, well if we all did that, who would get the work done?"

She laughed. "Okay, you have a point. But you've been feeling overwhelmed lately. Maybe it would be okay to let a few things go for now."

*Et tu,* Lori? Had everyone defected to the enemy forces?

She must have sensed my frustration, because she left soon after.

Heather arrived around ten, with Grace and Charity in tow. "The girls said they'd be happy to help watch your kiddoes while we shop. I figured Kevin might appreciate reinforcements. Ron isn't on call this weekend, so if you'd rather take the kids to our house, we can."

Kelsey was sculpting her Play-Doh in the living room. When she saw the twins, she launched across the room. "Play games!"

Grace (or was it Charity?) giggled and picked up my daughter.

Heather led me out to her battered station wagon, and we aimed it for the nearest thrift store. Our shopping spree was lackluster, but the scones and tea helped. I was grateful that she didn't try to talk to me about my traumas, failings, or need for a deeper spiritual perspective.

I had almost recovered from Lori's well-intentioned counsel by the time we got back to the house. Kevin had taken Heather up on her offer and brought all the kids to her place. Charity and Grace would be having a great time with the kids. With Dr. Ron at home, if Micah needed anything, he'd be on top of it.

"You can come and get them in a few hours." Heather pulled her wool cape around her like a character in a French film. "Take your time."

After the door closed behind her, I looked at Kevin. The silence in the house took my breath away. I threw my arms wide and twirled in a circle. "We have the house to ourselves."

Kevin gave a brief snort of laughter but didn't seem to share my enthusiasm. "Hon, sit down. We need to talk."

I stopped spinning. His jaw was tight, his forehead pinched.

Back to the real world, full of conflicts, problems, and anxieties. "Okay." I couldn't hide my sigh.

I flopped into the rocking chair.

Kevin paced circles around the plastic play table. Then he threw back his shoulders in a moment of decision and perched on the arm of the couch. "I have something to tell you."

I could almost hear the air raid siren. Incoming bad news. If he indulged a series of false starts this time, I'd scream.

He rubbed his unshaven chin. "I called City Life yesterday morning and turned them down."

Breath sucked out of me. "What?" The word came out as a gasp.

He met my eyes with firmness. "I told you I felt God was leading me to trust Him."

"But what about the layoffs? And I wanted to leave and start a ministry at a new church. And why didn't you tell me last night when I was talking about our move?"

He frowned and stood to pace again. "Hey, this was really tough for me. You have no idea—" He shook his head. "I knew you'd be upset. It didn't seem like the right time."

"You mean you felt guilty." Anger heated my skin. If I stood outside, the snow and sleet would melt with a hiss when it touched me. "We never make a big decision without talking about it."

He stopped walking, his back to me. He rubbed his neck. "I tried to talk to you about it. But you had your own agenda. You wouldn't listen."

"How could I listen when you didn't tell me?" Hot tears ran down the channels of my face. I tasted salt on my lips. "I can't believe you hid this from me."

He pivoted and glared at me. "I wasn't hiding anything. I was just waiting for the right time to talk about it."

"It's the same as lying." My chin jutted forward. "You let me babble about my ideas when you'd already made the decision for us." Pain stomped all over my already raw feelings like a unit of storm troopers.

I jumped from the chair and ran up the stairs, slamming the

bedroom door. Childish, yes. But satisfying, and as far as I was concerned, appropriate.

Sure, the church might have let me down. My friends may not have understood. Their attempts at giving me counsel made the ache worse. But this was the worst betrayal.

Kevin was a traitor to our marriage. Making arbitrary decisions. Ignoring my feelings. And worst of all, hiding them from me for the last twenty-four hours.

The last remnants of hopeful determination had just been machine-gunned to pieces by my closest ally. I hugged a pillow and sobbed. It hurt too much to be brave any longer.

# FOURTEEN

**From backstage the** rumbling applause
in the huge stadium sounded threatening instead
of supportive. I hummed low in my throat to loosen my vocal
cords.

The voice of one of the presenters echoed around the concrete hall
behind the raised platforms. From here, distortion warped her words, but
I knew she was doing a wonderful job preaching to the crowd. Our music
would be the crowning touch on the evening of "Fearless Faith for
Women."

The four other "Fearless Faith Singers" huddled with me for a
quick prayer. I squeezed the hands of the women on either side of me.
"Just think. A few years ago we were singing in church basements and
to little groups of twenty."

The alto jogged in place lightly, staying loose. "Now our music leads
hundreds to Christ every time we sing."

One of the backstage staff rolled a huge cart past us on his way out
to the entryway. Boxes of our CDs would be waiting after the show—
no, I meant the worship conference—for us to autograph.

Sure, I'd heard a few complaints about these conferences becoming
too commercial. The speakers sold their books, we sold our music, and
our promoters sold us. But it was all for God.

The stage manager beckoned us, and we waited for the applause to
signal our entrance. Then we bounded up the stairs and out to the platform.

"We'll never fail if we have faith." My soprano voice rang out clear as a chime. "Turn your small dreams into something more."

I poured my heart into the song. I wanted to convince the thousands in the stadium that their dreams would come true if they turned to Christ. Even as the canned orchestral score swelled, a sudden qualm darted through my mind. Were we selling something, just like our promoters? Were we hawking the great features of our way of life and leaving out some of the truth?

I shoved aside the thought. Undoubtedly an attack by Satan. Look at my life. I'd accomplished everything I'd ever dreamed, and they could, too. I sang even louder.

The drums pounded and the guitars thrummed as our congregation clapped and sang a chorus. Dylan and Kelsey sang along, sandwiched between Kevin and me.

Micah was playing in the church nursery. The nursery I had organized three years ago.

With effort, I brought my thoughts back into line for worship. After a few more songs and one slow, majestic hymn, we settled into our pew.

Pastor stepped into the pulpit and adjusted his glasses. For a panicked moment, I wondered if he would preach about serving God with no hope of personal gain—and use me as an object lesson. But it was worse.

He preached about forgiveness. The need to show mercy. I glanced over at Kevin. His jaw was stony, but there was a little-boy hurt in his eyes as he gazed at the front of the church. Last night we'd maneuvered around each other in cold silence as we got ready for bed. I'd been aloof all morning—still furious that he hadn't talked about his decision. We'd always been partners. My anger gave way to a deeper pain as I acknowledged the hurt and fear tussling in my heart. What else had he hidden from me?

Would I even sense it, if there was something else? I'd always been able to read him, but this time . . .

What did it mean for our marriage? He couldn't trust me enough to be open. I couldn't trust him enough to wait until he was ready to share.

Years ago, after a big fight, Kevin had held my hand, chin low, eyes peeking up like a guilty child. "You have to forgive me."

His teasing tone had made it impossible to hold on to my frustration with him.

He tugged my hand, pulling me closer. "We're Christians. It's not an option. You have to forgive me."

I rolled my eyes. "Fine. I forgive you. But I wanted at least a few hours to sulk first."

He laughed his strong, deep-chested laugh. Love danced a polka through my heart. Another false step averted. When we remembered we were on the same team, marriage was a bouncing gallop of joy, complete with oompah-pahs.

Today our commitment to each other was a dirge. Plodding step after plodding step, pulling against each other.

After the benediction and final hymn, Pastor Roger reminded the congregation of a special meeting that night. The Board of Elders would report on the building program and staff additions and give a missions report.

I ducked out to claim Micah. On our drive home, the silence was less bristly than it had been on the way to church.

"When's lunch?" Dylan piped up.

I turned to grin at him. "Not until I can get out of the car and fix it, all right?"

Kevin shot a sympathetic half smile my way. The same question hounded me every day. Did Dylan really think we'd forget to feed him? "What's for breakfast? Isn't it time for supper? Whatcha making? When are we eating?"

"Do you want to go to the meeting tonight?" Kevin rubbed his stubbly hair forward, and I felt an urge to pet it back the right direction.

"I don't know if I have the guts."

"Sweetie, you've always had more courage than anyone I know."

I blinked and sank back against the seat. "You really think that about me?" My voice was small.

He sighed. "Another thing I don't tell you enough. I'm sorry."

I knew his apology covered more ground than his wish to be a better encourager. "I forgive you." After church today, the words were easier to say without choking.

He took a deep breath, as though given a reprieve from the guillotine. "I'll be at the meeting with you."

I nodded. "I'll have to face it some time."

We pulled into the driveway and got each of the kids unbuckled. Kelsey and Dylan raced ahead to the door, and Kelsey screamed when Dylan touched the doorknob first.

"My turn. My turn!" By the time she turned two, she had figured out that she couldn't overcome Dylan in size. Now as a three-year-old, she decided volume was a good weapon. Her shrieks probably made the neighbors think we were beating her.

Kevin tossed Micah into my arms and hefted Kelsey into the air. Her screeches converted to giggles as he launched her up and caught her several times. He set her down and knelt in front of her. "It's okay to let others go first. I don't remember whose turn it was, but let's show Dylan how to be kind, okay?"

She puffed up and tossed her curls. " 'kay."

Dylan thought that was a fine idea, and when Kevin turned the key, he raced into the house shouting, "I'm first!"

Kelsey kicked one patent leather shoe against the front step, but Kevin winked at her, and she skipped into the house without further protest.

I studied his easy smile and patient, relaxed manner with the kids. "You're a great dad."

Kevin held the door while I carried Micah inside. "Easy for me. I'm not with them 24/7."

He did understand. Well, not everything. He'd never endured childbirth or monthly cramps. He'd never felt the walls close in when all the kids had stomach flu and the one other adult in the house sailed out the door to work. He didn't struggle with menu planning, Dylan's poor aim in the bathroom, lost socks in the dryer, or constant calls asking for cookies for each church and school event. But he knew the things that hurt me and did what he could to stand by my side.

I walked into the kitchen and slid Micah into his high chair. "Okay, I'll go to the meeting tonight—if you hide me when I burst into tears."

He rummaged the cupboard for saltines and handed one to Micah. "You won't." Then he reached to squeeze my ribs in their ticklish spot.

I dodged away and grabbed a spatula. "Watch it, buster."

Kelsey danced around the kitchen, leaving black skid marks on the linoleum. For once, I didn't care.

Sunday afternoons are the best. Dylan plays Scrabble with me while Micah chews his tree of stacking doughnuts. Kelsey plays Pretty Pretty Princess with Kevin. One time she had him decked out in a tiara, huge clip-on earrings, and a gaudy sapphire necklace when the doorbell rang and my macho husband sprang up to answer. The neighbor boy selling magazine subscriptions backed away, calling, "Never mind." An effective way to deal with solicitors.

As happens every Sunday afternoon, the kids eventually grew tired of us. Micah went down for his nap, clutching a motley stuffed bear. Kelsey hosted a tea party for her dolls. When fatigue hit her, she tipped over to the floor and drowsed. Once Micah was settled, Dylan scampered into their shared room to read.

Sunday afternoons are the best.

Kevin and I brewed a fresh pot of coffee and talked. He sprawled on his side of the couch. I curled up on my side and flirted with him over the top of my cup. I could still surprise a laugh out of him with perky chatter. He could still startle me with an occasional profound and sensitive observation. Judy was right. Sometimes I forgot how great my life was.

Today I gave Kevin a wry grin. "Good sermon, huh?"

"See, I'm not the only one who says you have to forgive me." His smile held all the charm that lured me to him in college. Then he sobered. "I really am sorry I didn't tell you right away. I honestly thought you'd be relieved."

I shrugged. "I would have been if I hadn't felt so eager to get away from our church."

"They aren't rejecting you, hon. They're just building on what you started."

"And tossing me aside in the meantime."

"I know. It's not fair." He sipped his coffee. "And I ruined your Plan B. What's your Plan C?"

I breathed out a wisp of a laugh. "I don't know."

Kevin set his cup between two Duplo houses on the table. "Let's pray."

After ten years, you'd think it would be natural. But I still felt a strange shyness as I took his hand and closed my eyes. Adam and Eve, we approached the throne of God together. Shamed by our mistakes, called by God's love, welcomed by His grace.

Sunday afternoons are the best.

That night, I almost felt ready to handle the church meeting. We bundled the kids into jackets and hats. The air was nippy, so I pulled the winter bin off the top shelf and handed out mittens.

The church buzzed with polite and smiling faces. We dropped both Micah and Kelsey at the nursery. Heather and her girls were on duty tonight. She had distributed chiffon scarves to all the kids and was leading them in an Isadora Duncan procession around the room.

"Can I stay, too?" Dylan stared longingly at the carts of toys.

"Sure," said Charity (or Grace). "You can help us with the toddlers."

Kevin and I waved a grateful good-bye. Some of the youngsters sobbed as their parents eased out of the room. Our kids ignored us. I turned to Kevin. "Do you think that's a bad sign?"

He threw an arm around me, following my chain of thought. "No, it means they feel secure."

We saw Doreen in the narthex. Without Jim. I stopped to give her a quick hug. Her smile was a bit too bright. Mine probably was, too.

When we settled in the back pew, Sally waved to us from across the aisle.

My only goal tonight was to keep my game face on and not let anyone see what a wounded puddle I was inside. The first part of the meeting wasn't too bad. I yawned at the inevitable reports about fundraising for a new wing, decisions about how much of our budget should go to the denominational missions, and how much to set aside for local projects. The youth pastor made a plea for more volunteers and gave an update on the growth in our Sunday school program.

When Pastor Roger moved on to the issue of hiring a women's ministry director, I sank lower into the pew. Kevin wrapped a protective arm around my shoulder, and I concentrated on pacing my breathing to his.

"The Board of Elders has voted to add a staff position to oversee all the women's ministry projects."

A murmur of agreement ran through the church like a soft wave.

"We'll be interviewing candidates this week."

A few women from the Mom's Time Out group turned to smile at me.

Greg, the oh-so-corporate elder stood up to talk about the two candidates he'd already mentioned last Tuesday. One or two friends swiveled their heads to raise their eyebrows in my direction. I forced a small smile and shrugged.

"And we've also invited one of our own staff to interview for the position."

A tingle of hope spread from my breastbone through my body. Had they changed their minds?

"She's been involved in our church for many years. Sally, why don't you stand up and give a wave?"

She pushed herself upward and beamed over the congregation. My mouth sagged open, and Kevin gave me a warning squeeze. "Just keep smiling."

I stared in shock at my friend, taking some comfort in the way the skin under her arm waggled as she waved. Sally should know better than to wear a sleeveless blouse. And why would she in November, anyway?

I banished that unworthy thought from my head.

*Lord, was she scheming to do this all along?* No, of course not. I'd reassured her that I had moved on to Plan B and wasn't upset about the elders overlooking me. She was a logical choice. She knew our church inside out, and she had a degree.

After she sat down, Sally threw a worried glance my direction. I managed to smile and nod before bending down to tie my shoe. The one that was already perfectly tied.

"Kev, I need to go out to the car. Can you get the kids?"

"Are you okay?" His concern was more than I could handle.

I nodded quickly, squeezing my lips together. I pulled on my coat at a jog and made it to the van. How many times this week could I run out of the church in tears?

I shivered in the front seat, grateful that one of the parking-lot lights had burnt out and I could huddle in the dark.

"Okay, Lord. I can't take much more humiliation. Don't you get it? I just wanted to serve you. You could show a little appreciation."

I leaned forward, resting my folded arms on the dashboard. "There's so much need in the world. I could do so much for you if you'd just let me."

I paused to pull a tissue out of the box between the seats and blow my nose. "And what about all those people you called who didn't want to go where you called them? Moses, Jonah. Aren't you glad that I *want* you to use me?"

A gust of wind rattled the car. I hunkered back in my seat to wait for Kevin and the kids. I was getting all too familiar with the confusing ache of silence.

# FIFTEEN

**"*Sparrow Two,*** *how's your com signal?"*

I sucked air within my helmet and grinned at Glen's silly designations. "Big Birdhouse, I read you just fine. Now let me get to work."

Floating in the buoyancy of space, I pulled myself along small handgrips toward the satellite dish. Space debris had dented it and knocked it out of alignment, and it was my turn for a space walk.

As I pulled a tool from a Velcroed pocket, I paused to stare at Earth. The sight never ceased to awe me. Wisps of cloud cover and huge swatches of blue and green erased all evidence of war, famine, and small acts of cruelty. From here, all I saw was paradise.

"Sparrow Two, what's it look like?"

For a moment I thought Glen was asking about Earth. Then I reeled my mind back in to my assignment. "Whoa, baby. I can see why our backup system was disrupted. It's a mess."

"Do what you can, but don't stay out too long. Confirm."

"Confirmed, Big Bird."

Glen's sigh carried through our com link. "That's Birdhouse."

I indulged an unprofessional giggle. "That's a roger, Elmo."

I edged farther along the surface to examine the dish from behind. The sight made my pulse spike. A piece of shielding on the hull curled like a jagged wound. The repair had suddenly become more difficult and more urgent.

*"Sparrow, what's the situation?"*

*"Hull damage. I've got it covered." I pulled myself past the damaged plate so I could turn and work from a new angle. Blood rushed in my ears and my breath hissed in and out.*

*I never heard the rip that severed my connecting cord, but as I rotated, I saw the frayed end.*

*Panic made me grab for any protrusion on the ship, but my frantic movements only ricocheted me off the hull.*

*I was alone. Floating in silence and doom. I twisted my head to see the Earth, feeling every mile of my distance from her. I was no longer connected to my world or to my crew mates. Spinning slowly, I watched everything in my life pull away.*

The lengthy *Women of Vision* questionnaire floated into focus. My career history looked rather sketchy on paper, and my mind had drifted as I worked on the essay about the value of being a stay-at-home mom. Frustrated, I pushed the form away.

The week after the church meeting, the level of surprise and pain had overwhelmed me. I sank into blessed numbness. Soul Novocain. I couldn't feel anymore.

Routine kept me functioning, but my mood was as flat and gray as the skies. Each day I used precious naptime minutes to reconstruct my note cards for the term paper. I had to finish before winter quarter began. I'd heard Psych of Learning was a tough class. I wouldn't be able to handle catching up on my incomplete while diving into a new class.

One thing at a time. Right now, my mission was to finish this questionnaire. Under *General Information* I struggled to fill in the generous space allotted for hobbies. I wasn't sure if bubble baths counted, but that sounded better than scraping jam off the kitchen counter or trimming chewing gum off of stuffed animals.

I waxed poetic on the page about keeping romance alive in a marriage, feeling a bit more confident on that topic. I batted my buzzings of conscience aside when I thought of how little energy I'd had for Kevin in recent months. It was the thought that counted, right?

I stalled out again on *Parenting Philosophies*. I wanted to write about how my faith influenced my parenting, but as I thought about my bouts of yelling or my martyred sighs of frustration, I shoved the forms aside again. Maybe after I'd had a few Good Mom days, I'd feel able to tackle that essay.

Kevin brought the computer home Tuesday night. After hooking up a bewildering array of cords, he led me to the chair like a king bestowing a gift on his queen. I admit that seeing the screen light up broke through some of my despair.

Until I read my e-mails. Pity from friends grated against my pride. Questions about women's ministry issues annoyed me. It shouldn't be my problem anymore. Then I opened an e-mail from Judy.

> *Hey, sis. Did you give 'em what for at that church of yours? Guess what? I got some time off and can come for Thanksgiving this year. Can't wait to see you. I need some home cooking. I'll be there Wednesday.*

My shriek drew Kevin back into the kitchen at a jog. "What? Did you see a bug?"

"Judy's coming for Thanksgiving."

Kevin was still searching the walls for a creepy-crawly. "That's nice."

"You don't get it, do you? That's only one week away. I've

got to dig out my recipes and clean the house and sew a new tablecloth and—"

"Whoa. It's just your sister." Kevin pulled me away from the chair and into a hug. "And I can help. Don't get all worked up."

A shout interrupted us from the basement. We ran downstairs. Dylan yelled, "Is not!" He tugged at an electronic game in his sister's hands and wrenched it from her grip.

Kelsey screeched. "My turn!" She fended him off with a wild dog-paddle of slaps against his arm.

Dylan jumped back and hid the game behind his back. "Mom! She's hitting. She broke the rules."

Great. Not only did I have to buy food and get the house in shape, I had one week to turn my little savages into well-behaved children for Judy's visit.

That night, my head throbbed as I tumbled into bed. Parenting books from the library rested on my nightstand. I was too busy parenting to read them. Kevin reached for me, and I snuggled against his warm flannel-clad chest but was too preoccupied to be amorous. A mental grocery list spun through my mind like an asteroid until sleep claimed me.

Thursday night I swooped trays of fish sticks and French fries from the oven, to a platter, and onto the table. Kevin finished eating first and grabbed a Bible from the kitchen desk, ignoring the devotion book. "I've got a perfect story for tonight."

His eyes sparkled as he dove into a boisterous reading of the fish and loaves story. The kids emptied their plates while watching him, wide-eyed. He closed the Bible with a flourish. "God can take little things we give Him and multiply them." His dark caramel eyes met mine over the plastic pitcher of water. "We just have to trust Him."

Dylan looked longingly at the empty platter. "Why didn't God multiply *our* fish?"

"I want Him to mullaply cookies." Kelsey bounced in her booster chair.

I jumped up to deposit the dishes into the sink. Time for my small-group Bible study. Tonight we were meeting at Lori's house, and the drive would take longer. She lived in an outer-ring suburb that still sheltered scattered farms among the developments.

Tonight would be rough, and I steeled myself. I needed to deflect any further attention and sympathy—and try to muster genuine forgiveness toward Sally so she never had to know how deeply she'd hurt me. I needed to congratulate her on being considered for the job. My job.

*God, give me strength.*

As I was kicking the dusting of snow off my shoes on Lori's front porch, she pulled the door open. Her strong hug coaxed me inside, and she led me to the kitchen. I was relieved to have a few more minutes of respite before facing our group.

Later, I carried in a tray of coffee cups and muffins, not meeting any eyes.

"Hello, Mrs. Miller." Abigail peered around the doorjamb from the hallway. Her dusky complexion was a darker shade of chocolate than Lori's. Tight black braids framed her head.

"Hi, Abby. What are you up to tonight?"

"Working on my essay about the role of government in protecting human life."

Good grief. She was just one year older than Dylan. Maybe

I should reconsider the homeschooling option. Dylan's class was reading *The Cat in the Hat*.

She tilted her head. "Dad's watching Jeffy tonight."

I nodded. Jefferson was a year younger than Kelsey. For a minute I had been afraid she'd say her little brother was studying quantum physics.

Lori's living room doubled as her classroom. Maps and hand-writing charts adorned the walls. Nature collections filled a cabinet against one wall. Yet nothing seemed out of place. Her home was orderly, calm, and polite. Just like her children.

I settled into a reupholstered wing chair. Lori had done the repair work herself, with Abigail's help. Every task was a teaching opportunity in their household.

Our group was quieter than usual, and Sally opened her day planner. "Prayer requests?"

Doreen cleared her throat. Her sweater was old and nubby, and sagged around her shoulders. Instead of glossy leather boots, she wore tennis shoes stained with the salty slush from the sidewalks.

Worry made me scoot my chair closer to hers.

She looked around the room, trying for a half smile that was really a grimace. "No sense beating around the bush." She uncrossed her legs and planted both feet on the floor, holding the chair arms as if she were on a carnival ride about to take off.

We all leaned forward.

"Jim is leaving the kids and me."

Whatever I had expected, these words floored me. I gaped at her, frozen.

"It's true. He said he doesn't love me." Another grimace. "He claims there's no other woman, but somehow that makes it even worse." Now the tears poured down her face as she held very still.

I rocketed from my chair and reached to hug her. "How could he? Oh, Doreen. I'm so sorry."

"Will he consider counseling?"

"What are you going to do?"

"How can we help?"

The questions orbited around the room.

Doreen's torso shook as I held her, but the tears poured from her in silence. I almost wanted her to scream and wail.

Lori motioned to us, and we gathered around Doreen, touching her shoulder, the top of her head, even her tennis shoe, as we prayed.

My recent arguments with Kevin rose up to frighten me. How could I have ignored the dangers of festering criticism and doubt? Our group of women was immune to this kind of tragedy, weren't we? Rambunctious children, sure. Illness, sometimes. Feeling overwhelmed by our roles, always.

But not this.

If this could happen to one of our small group, it could happen to any of us.

We prayed, and cried, and prayed some more.

Doreen's whole world was shattered. Shame welled up in my chest as I thought of my frequent sour thoughts about her luxurious life and massive talents.

I could imagine a view of her world from space as fault lines cracked deep toward the core of the planet. Huge wedges broke away and spun off into the galaxy until nothing remained except debris.

And I was helpless to call the pieces back and wrap them together. All I could do was hold Doreen and cry with her—and wonder about the strength of the safety line between Kevin and me.

# SIXTEEN

*The steamboat horn blasted.*
*Standing at the rail, I watched the waters of the*
*Mississippi churn behind us, as dark and murky as my*
*fears. New Orleans disappeared around the first bend in the river,*
*and I turned to walk toward the ballroom.*

*Although the organizers of the poker tournament had been shocked*
*to see a woman signing in with lace parasol in hand, they were glad to*
*accept my entrance fee.*

*With an ailing mother, three small children, and a husband lost*
*to the Yankees, our survival rested on my ability to win the prize*
*money.*

*The first round wasn't even a challenge. I batted my eyelashes and*
*pretended so much ignorance of the game that when I pulled the pile of*
*chips toward me, the men around the table sank back into their chairs*
*as if they'd been rifle-butted in the stomach.*

*The field quickly narrowed in further rounds. I was gifted at picking*
*up on a player's tells—the nervous stroking of a mustache, the twist of*
*a lip, a shift in the chair. I could spot a bluff a mile off.*

*After long hours of play, cigar smoke stung my eyes as I sat at the*
*final table. My true competition lounged, studying his cards with*
*casual indifference. Kevin "Ace" Miller lifted his eyes and smiled*
*into mine. A cold, confident smile. "Well, lil' lady, I do believe I'll*
*raise."*

He tossed a handful of chips into the pot. I studied him for a long moment, but he didn't flinch. Sweat trickled down my ribs.

I flashed a false tell, twisting a curl around one finger. "It's so stuffy in here. Let's move things along, shall we? I'll see y'all and raise."

His eyes narrowed, and a chill of danger stroked my spine. Rumor had it Ace once shot a man in St. Louis.

I squared my jaw.

A lazy grin took its time spreading on his handsome face. He was a predator, and he was hunting more than just a win in a game of poker.

The men crowding around us called out ribald suggestions. Coming alone to this tournament suddenly seemed like a foolhardy plan.

As if he sensed my growing panic, Ace leaned forward, his voice gentle. "Ma'am, play your cards. Win or lose, I'll see you safely off the boat."

"How does anyone know who they can trust?" I asked quietly.

Kevin's dark eyes widened in surprise. We had been sitting in a long, tired silence after I had stumbled through my report on Doreen and Jim. Kevin had seemed as shaken as me, and while my thoughts had drifted, he had bounced his fingers against his leg and stared into space. "He must have given her some explanation."

Angled toward each other on opposite sides of the couch, I hugged a throw pillow. "All he said was that he doesn't love her anymore." I bit my lip and waited for Kevin's response.

"Has he been hurting her or the kids?"

What an odd thing to ask. "You mean physically?"

He gave a curt nod.

"No. Doreen is devastated at him leaving."

Kevin crossed his arms. "What a jerk. How could he do that to her? And the kids?"

I nodded. "The thing is, it scared me."

"What do you mean?"

"None of our close friends have ever gone through a divorce. I never would have believed it . . . just like I'd never believe it could happen to us."

Kevin's frown deepened.

"Kev, what if I'm wrong about us, too?"

He launched forward, pulling the pillow from my grip and tossing it aside so he could wrap me in a secure hug. "You're not wrong. I love you. I made a promise to you, and I've never looked back."

A deep sigh relaxed me into his arms. "I love you, too." I felt as if we were speaking our wedding vows all over again.

"And we aren't in this alone." His breath tickled my ear. "I don't know about Jim and Doreen, but we've asked God to hold us to our word. To help us forgive when we drive each other crazy. To keep us true." He pulled back enough to look me in the face. "I'm not going anywhere."

The emotion behind his hoarse words overwhelmed me. "You better not. Judy's coming for Thanksgiving, and I'm gonna need your help."

His bark of laughter added glue to my renewed security in him. He jumped up and offered his hand. "Come on. Let's turn in for the night, and I'll show you how much I love you."

How could he still make me blush after all these years? I took his hand and we headed down the hall. We peeked in at our sleeping cherubs, whose sweet faces belied all the mayhem they sometimes brought into our lives. I wrapped an arm around Kevin's waist and rested my head on his shoulder as we tiptoed to our room. Peace and contentment flooded me, and I forgot about all the things I was supposed to be worrying about.

The next morning I watched Kevin sleep. The energetic lines of his face softened and his lashes provided dark awnings over his cheeks.

Tenderness seeped over me like the warmth of an electric blanket. In the past few weeks he'd battled his own demons, yet he'd held me when I cried, coaxed laughs from me, prayed with me, and assured me of his faith in my courage, and of his love for me.

The corner of Kevin's mouth twitched. Happy dreams again. I hoped this one was about me.

Out of nowhere, a sleek viper of doubt darted through my thoughts. Does anyone really completely know another person? Doreen thought she knew Jim. She could probably read his moods and guess his thoughts with a wifely radar just like mine. But somehow, Jim hid the biggest deception of all.

Can anyone ever really read another person?

Kevin's eyelids glided open, and he knuckled the corners of his eyes like a little boy. A huge yawn stretched his whole body, and he flashed me a smile preparing to bound out of bed the way he always did.

His smile faded and he reached out a finger to tweak my nose. "You look worried. What's wrong?"

I sat up and hugged my knees. "Just trying to decide if I should try the pecan cranberry stuffing when Judy comes."

He chuckled. "Sounds good to me." He sprang from bed, both feet hitting the floor in one thump.

"Yeah, everything sounds good to you." Affection chased

away my doubts. "I wish your mom could come, too. We haven't seen her in ages." Mom Miller lived in Florida, and her health made travel difficult. Kevin's dad had been killed in a car accident when Kevin was twelve, so he tried to stay connected to his mom, although distance and our finances had made it impossible for us to visit her often.

He reached forward to ruffle my hair. "Maybe next year." He jogged to the bathroom. Soon off-key humming joined the sound of spraying water.

I giggled. He was in a particularly good mood this morning.

The day steamed forward against the current, full of zigzags, interruptions, and shifting priorities. I snagged a quiet moment to call Doreen. Her voice sounded beaten down and hoarse from crying. "He packed some things this morning and left."

I made soothing sounds, feeling helpless.

"And he admitted—" A soft gasp choked her words. "It's his secretary. How plebian is that? He couldn't even be original."

Anger churned up like Mississippi mud. How dare he hurt Doreen like this? Plus, Jim's actions made all the rest of us feel uncertain and insecure. I wish I had a solution to provide, but I didn't. So instead, I offered to pray. Over the phone, I wrapped Doreen in warm words and placed her in the arms of the only One who could bring her solace.

Problems floated over my head like clouds of cigar smoke as the day moved on. Micah couldn't get in to the audiologist until mid-December, and even with the infection cleared up, he didn't seem to be hearing well. Kevin's job could end any time. The church was interviewing candidates to displace me. My term paper consisted of haphazard scratching on recipe cards. Doreen's husband was leaving her. And Judy was coming for Thanksgiving. But I was determined to bluff my way through a few bad hands.

"Lord, I haven't figured out Plan C yet, but I know you have one. Whatever I do, I'll do with all my heart."

*And one day you'll be convinced I can do Big Things for you.*

I cranked up my new worship CD and danced around with my dust rag. Soon the whole living room smelled like lemon oil. Kelsey joined me in the kitchen to pat out a piecrust while Micah spun pie tins on the floor. When Dylan got home from school, he joined the fun by skidding Hot Wheels across the linoleum.

Since I was preoccupied with my preparations for the best Thanksgiving dinner ever, I reached into the freezer for something to thaw for supper.

Last spring, Lori had espoused the benefits of preparing several weeks' worth of meals in one weekend. She described the peaceful time in the late afternoon when she pulled out a casserole and popped it into the oven. Then she nestled on the couch reading stories to her children.

The idyllic image was so alluring that I ignored Kevin's raised eyebrows and decided to become Julia Child for a weekend. I chopped, fried, and assembled enough meals for two weeks and even remembered to label most of the Ziploc bags. Then I gave up in fatigue. Still, I felt smug today as I pulled homemade spaghetti sauce from the freezer. I turned on the burner under a kettle of water and unearthed a box of spaghetti noodles.

I settled Dylan at the table to copy his spelling words and

let Kelsey help set the table while I cleaned up all our spilled flour.

Dylan chewed his pencil and sighed. "When's supper?"

"When Dad gets home." My washrag flicked some flour into the sink.

"When is he getting home?"

"He said 5:30."

"Mom, it's 5:37."

Why had I ever taught him to tell time? We went through this same litany every night. Kevin might have wanted someone to fetch him a pipe and slippers when he came in the door, but he usually was hurried to the kitchen table instead.

I squeezed the frozen sauce into a microwave dish.

Lumps of potato escaped the ice-coated bag and plopped into the container. The spaghetti sauce was actually a bag of potato and hamburger hot dish in a tomato-soup base. Not exactly the thing to serve over noodles. Sigh. So much for efficiency.

Kevin's car pulled into the driveway, but I didn't hear the slam of the car door. I looked out the kitchen window. When Kevin finally stepped from his dented Datsun wagon, he moved as if pressing through a dense fog.

I ran to open the door for him.

His briefcase hung from his hand. He stood still, as if he couldn't remember what to do with it. I eased it from his fingers and set it aside, then hugged him.

His head sagged against my shoulder. "Are we still following the policy of me telling you everything?"

I ran a hand over the back of his head. "Whatever you want to tell me."

"I'm downsized." He stepped back and slipped into jokester mode, patting his stomach. "Do I look downsized to you?" He tried to laugh, but the sound was hollow and full of hurt. "The boxes are in the car. They had me clean out my desk today."

I buried my face against his chest. "Shh. It's all right. We'll be okay."

"How? How will we be okay?"

I rose up on tiptoe to whisper in his ear. "I don't know how. But we will."

He gave me one more squeeze, then turned to greet the kids, pouncing on them with playful love as if he had never been wounded.

A brave man.

Kevin even managed to tease me about the odd supper of potato hot dish with spaghetti noodles.

Homework, chores, bath time, and reading *Harold and the Purple Crayon* filled our evening. Finally, with the dishwasher humming, we settled onto the couch, side by side, like teenagers who couldn't bear any distance between us.

"I called City Life." Kevin took one of my hands in both of his, twisting my wedding ring from side to side. "They've already filled the Grand Marais position."

"Hey, you prayed about it. That job wasn't meant to be."

"But you were right. I should have taken it. We could both have a fresh start."

I shook my head. "No. My Plan B was all about running away. That's not what God wanted."

Kevin released my hand and tilted his head back against the couch, staring at the ceiling. "They're so strapped, I won't get any severance. And unemployment will only be a fraction of what my salary was."

"We'll manage. We always do." My worry for him transformed into blame for myself. "It's my fault. If I'd been supportive, you wouldn't have turned down the City Life job. If I'd realized what was going on at the church, I could have found work somewhere else . . . work that would have brought in a little income. And if you didn't have the kids and me to worry about, your life wouldn't have all this pressure. I've brought so much chaos into your life."

He raised his head and blinked at me, as if studying a particularly complex actuary table. He clearly couldn't fathom my logic. So he did the best possible thing instead. He ignored my torrent of self-recriminating words, pulled me close, and kissed my nose. "You matter to me. My life would be boring without you."

I burrowed my anointed nose into his shoulder. "Peaceful, you mean." I turned my head. With my ear pressed over his heart, I heard the deep rumble in his chest as he laughed.

"Boring. Besides, none of this is your fault. Lots of businesses are downsizing. I'll find something new."

I smelled the hint of fabric softener on his shirt and felt his arms around me like a blanket from a warm dryer. As I began to relax completely, the slimy viper returned. Doubt. Suspicion.

I eased back. "Kevin, is Renee attractive?" Other than her name, I knew nothing about the office manager he had worked with all these years.

He gave me a bewildered look. "I guess so."

A sudden vision of a sultry blonde in a red dress tormented me. "Really?"

"Sure. She looks pretty good for someone in her fifties."

My icy apprehension melted and relief loosened my tight

muscles. "Oh, that's good," I said vaguely.

Kevin gave me a puzzled double take but then shrugged. "I'll buy a paper tomorrow and start the job hunt. Make a few calls on Monday."

"You'll find something fast. Companies will be fighting over you."

He smiled, and some of the defeat riding his shoulders eased back. "Yep. Stick with me, lil' lady."

I stared deep into his eyes. I couldn't read everything behind them. No one could. But I knew he was laying all his cards on the table. Still, dread weighted my mind. The chips were down, and our hand was looking very weak.

# SEVENTEEN

"I'll e-mail you the document today,"
I whispered. "Just be sure it runs on Sunday. This
deserves heavy coverage." I slapped my cell phone shut and
returned it to the hiding place behind the headboard. Posing as a
woman in her eighties with early-stage Alzheimer's had been my most
challenging undercover journalism project yet. The spirit gum under my
latex wrinkles itched, and my muscles ached from hunching over. But it
was worth it. This story would rock our city. Maybe it would trigger
reform. Not to mention furthering my career.

I had toured many facilities as I began research for this report. When
I found Elder Home, I knew it deserved deeper investigation.

My instincts were on target once again. During one week in disguise, I uncovered Medicaid fraud, overmedicating of patients, neglect,
and even direct abuse. When I peeled back the surface of this place, the
details scurried around like roaches.

A cart rattled in the hallway, and I tugged the sheets up to my chin.
The burly orderly who shoved the door open growled a good-morning
around the cigarette dangling from his lips. Ashes fell onto the uncovered
bowls of Dickensian gruel on his cart.

I decided to skip breakfast.

The woman in the bed near mine moaned. When she saw the
orderly, she lifted one frail hand. "The pain is worse today. Please,
would you tell the doctor?"

He shrugged. "Yeah. Whatever. I think he's supposed to check in
on Thursday."

*I propped up onto my elbows. "But she's in pain now." I concen-trated on keeping my voice thin and hoarse—the elderly timbre that was becoming harder to maintain.*

*"Quit yer griping and eat." He stomped from the room.*

*I resisted the urge to fling my bowl at his back. My revenge would be much sweeter than that. The article in Sunday's paper would name names, quote from documents, and reveal the need for a legal investiga-tion. Satisfaction welled up in my chest. My words could make a tre-mendous difference. A force to be reckoned with.*

*"Use the power wisely, young Skywalker," I murmured.*

The phone rang, and the noise jerked my head up from my blank page. I was supposed to be writing my paper on educa-tional trends, not an exposé. The kitchen table was scattered with note cards, pages of rough drafts, and stacks of books and educational journals. The ringer trilled again. I rubbed my temples, grateful for the interruption.

"Hello?" My voice croaked a bit.

"Is this Becky?"

I cleared my throat. "Yes . . ."

"Oh, I'm so glad I caught you. This is Victoria Spring."

I smiled at the vibrancy in her tone. "It's great to hear from you. The ladies at church are still talking about what a great speaker you were."

"That's nice to hear. Listen, I'm in a bit of a bind. My folks arranged a surprise trip for all their kids and grandkids, but I was scheduled to speak at the Women in Church Work conference. The other speakers in my network are booked up, but I thought of you."

I gnawed the corner of my lip. "I can't think of anyone to recommend. Last year's retreat speaker is out of the country right now—"

Her laugh trilled through the receiver. "No, no. I meant you. I was so impressed with the women's program at your church and the way you organized the retreat. You'd have a lot to share."

I gulped. "What were you going to speak about?"

"Discerning your call in church work. Using your gifts. Stuff like that."

*Should I tell her I'm no longer a leader of a women's ministry? Nonsense. I'd had years of experience. That's what mattered.*

My breath quickened and I couldn't form words.

"There's an honorarium, of course." Victoria mistook my pause for reluctance. "And it will be worthwhile. They're expecting five hundred women in professional church work."

"Sure. I'd love to," I squeaked. "What's the date?"

"Well, that's the problem. It's the first Saturday in December. My parents sprang this trip on us at the last minute, and I don't want to hurt their feelings. They really don't understand my work. You know how it is."

I stared at my calendar. One week after Thanksgiving. Five hundred people. Professionals.

*I can do all things through Christ who gives me strength.*

"Sure. No problem."

We wrapped up details, and I hung up the phone and whooped. I wished Kevin and the kids were home. He had taken them all along to drop off Dylan at a birthday party. Kelsey needed new shoes, so they planned to stop at the thrift store to see if there was anything in her size. When he left, Kevin had kissed the top of my head. "Maybe now you'll have some quiet to work on your paper."

My research books had been gathering dust in my recent preparing-for-Judy's-visit frenzy. So when Kevin and the kids left, I had pushed aside my cookbooks and Thanksgiving to-do lists and settled at the table to play college student. My enthusiasm had lasted until my mind wandered into the daydream about journalism.

Now, after Victoria's phone call, I'd never be able to concentrate on the paper. Who cared about a college degree? God had just given me the opportunity to impact hundreds of church leaders, who in turn would impact thousands of parishioners.

The feeling of power made me giddy.

I stacked my books and shoved them to the side. Grabbing a yellow legal pad, I jotted notes for my talk.

*Bible verses. That would be good.*

I jumped up and ran to the bedroom to grab my Bible from the nightstand, then raced back to the kitchen table. More brainstorming. More scribbling. More excitement.

At one point, I was tempted to comment on churches that didn't fully appreciate the efforts of their volunteer staff. The jab would be so satisfying, and no one would know I was speaking about my own church.

*No, too petty. This isn't about revenge. Keep your motives pure.*

An hour later, Kevin, Kelsey, and Micah raced through the door. They hurried to slam the cold air outside. Kevin stopped on the throw rug by the door and stared at me.

He had always been good at reading my moods. Pretty easy today, since I was vibrating with excitement.

I waved my Bible in the air. "You'll never guess what happened!" I gulped a big breath of air. "I've been asked to speak at a big Christian conference. Isn't that amazing?"

His grin was enthusiastic and genuine, and his feet started moving in my direction immediately. Some men would have a hard time celebrating their wife's success when they had just been laid off, but Kevin grabbed me in a bear hug and then released me so he could flash his wide smile again. "I'm so proud of you! When is it?"

"A week after Thanksgiving weekend."

His brows shot up.

I squared my shoulders. "I can do it."

Kelsey skipped to the table and picked up a pen, ready to embellish my notes.

I pulled her away. "No, honey. Don't touch Mommy's work. Hey, let's celebrate. Let's go out for bagels." We deserved a small Saturday splurge.

Kevin hesitated but then smiled. "Leave your coat on, Kelsey. We're going out."

My expansive mood felt terrific after the weeks of discouragement. Everything was going to be fine. I could see the headlines now. *Kevin Finds New Job. Becky Collects Invitations to Speak—Impacts Millions. Miller Children Thrive. Judy Awed at Thanksgiving Dinner.*

Wait until my Thursday night Bible study group heard about this. And I'd finally have something of interest to put on my *Women of Vision* questionnaire.

All weekend I alternated between a happy glow and panic about my talk. I filled page after page with notes, then struggled to organize the thoughts. I prayed, I wrestled, I strained to give it my all. By Sunday night I decided I was neglecting my family and set it all aside.

Monday morning, in a burst of inspired thoughtfulness, I left Micah, Kelsey, and Dylan squirreled up next to Kevin in bed. I bundled up and jogged down to the corner to buy a newspaper. When I got home, my ears burned with cold and my nose was running. But the brisk air had infused me with energy.

While the coffee brewed, I grabbed a yellow highlighter and began to mark every want ad that looked like a possibility for Kevin. I turned the last page and circled another listing with a flourish.

Kevin appeared in the kitchen carrying Micah, with Kelsey piggybacking on him—her arms clasped to his neck.

I rescued him from the kids and plopped a box of Cheerios

onto the table. Kelsey pulled out spoons. I was so touched by her helpfulness that I didn't point out they were huge soup spoons.

"What are you up to?" Kevin rubbed his shoulder and yawned.

I returned to my chair and waved the newsprint. "Finding you a job."

His eyebrows came down for a minute, but then he forced a smile. "Working on Plan C already?" An edge of sarcasm shaded his tone.

His lack of appreciation stung. "Don't you want my help?"

Kevin planted both hands on the paper and leaned forward, his eyes gentle but firm. "No. I don't."

I sat back, indignant. "Fine."

He turned to pull a coffee cup off the shelf, then filled it and handed it to me. "Hon, let me handle this, okay? You've got enough to deal with."

But dealing with things was what I did best. Plan B, Plan C, Plan XYZ. Forging ahead held the fear at bay. I sipped the coffee, letting warm steam condense on my face. "Okay. I won't nag. But let me know if you want my help, okay?"

His nod was noncommittal.

Yeah, right. Like that would ever happen. Asking for help was not in Kevin's genetic code. I rubbed my forehead. Let him play it his way. He was right. I had enough to keep me busy for now.

Kevin spent the day visiting every friend he had in the industry. Later that afternoon, he pulled up right behind Dylan's school bus. His face was grim. He pulled off his suit jacket and loosened his tie while the kids made like homing pigeons to the table for an after-school snack.

I raised my eyebrows. "Well?"

He flopped into a kitchen chair. "Everyone seems to be

restructuring or cutting back. Even some of the independent agents are pulling out of the business." He forced a big smile. "Hey, kids, Daddy gets to spend more time with you this week."

Dylan and Kelsey pulled their attention away from their graham crackers and cheered.

Sometimes Kevin carried his positive attitude too far. But I decided to play along. "Look at the pinecones Kelsey found today. We're going to have the best Thanksgiving decorations ever."

Kelsey beamed. "I get to sleep with you."

"Not until Aunt Judy comes. Then you'll give her your room."

Her face wrinkled. "It's *my* room."

"Yes, but you get to share." I spoke faster, a sideshow barker determined to make a sale. "And it's only for a few days. And you get to use the sleeping bag."

Her eyelids shot upward toward her short, spiky bangs. "Dylan doesn't."

Now Dylan's dark mop of hair jutted over a thundercloud face. "No fair. She can have my room. I want the sleeping bag."

Kevin ruffled Dylan's hair. "No way, buddy. You and Micah are too cool for that. You guys get to keep sleeping in your big boy beds. Hey, wanna play some football before supper?"

Kevin and Dylan blinked identical beseeching eyes in my direction.

I laughed. "All right. But bundle up. It looks like it might snow."

Kevin bounded down the hall to change, with Dylan galloping behind.

I'd feel less anxiety if Kevin were poring over help-wanted ads and showing a little honest fear, but I was determined not to push him. He'd spent the day networking. He deserved to relax tonight. I canceled my plans to ask for his help with hanging garlands. I'd iron napkins instead.

After supper and a timely devotion about perseverance, I threw plates into the dishwasher and ran downstairs to start a load of laundry and tackle the ironing. My old tablecloth had more wrinkles than an octogenarian. Years in the back of a cupboard had that effect. I had trouble unfolding the ironing board—rusty from disuse.

In spite of deciding to focus solely on Thanksgiving plans, as my iron swept back and forth my mind drifted to the upcoming talk. What should I wear? My blazer with a dark skirt would probably work. Should I try curling my hair? Better not. Last time I tried, my waves stuck out in random directions like the long-haired guinea pig at Kelsey's preschool. My happy fog returned as I envisioned the articulate and faith-filled message that I would deliver. If there was a hint of "I'll show them" when I thought of my church's rejection of me, who could blame me?

Tuesday was Kelsey's last day of preschool before Thanksgiving. I rushed through last-minute shopping with Micah and nabbed a rather pathetic turkey from the bottom of the grocery's near-empty freezer. Apparently the organized women in town had finished their shopping long ago.

When I picked up Kelsey, she proudly presented me with a turkey drawn with the outline of her hand and covered with glued on sunflower seeds. More edible art. I promised her the masterpiece would go straight onto the refrigerator.

After Kelsey and I unloaded the groceries, Dylan arrived home from school with an essay on what he was thankful for. Another adornment for the fridge door.

I was proud of his handwriting, even if the list made me shudder. Super Mario Brothers, Hot Wheels, football, pizza, recess, and friends. Conspicuously absent were parents and siblings. I asked him about the omission.

"Mom." Dylan stretched the vowel with exasperation. "Everyone knows I'm thankful for you guys. It doesn't need saying."

*Oh, but it does need saying. It needs saying often.*

I hugged him and admired his bounding glee as he broke from my arms and charged through the kitchen. He was a chip off the getting-older block. He and Kevin would laugh in the face of calamity, as long as they had a ball to bounce or toss or hit and some turf to tear up. Life was one jolly adventure after another.

I went in search of Kevin. He was hiding out in the basement, sitting on a broken armchair he kept meaning to repair, cell phone pressed to his ear and pages of notes drifting from his lap to the floor. He grinned up at me and clicked the phone shut. "Another answering machine. Amazing how many offices are already closed for Thanksgiving. Guess I'll have to wait until next Monday to do any serious hunting."

"But—" I clamped my mouth shut. *No nagging. No solving. No badgering. He wants to handle this. He wants my faith in him. Focus on your own challenges.*

I sank into his lap, causing the chair to list dangerously to one side. He took advantage and tilted me back for a long kiss, effectively chasing away my worry about his job.

But as soon as we stood up, my mind went back to whirling like my washing machine on spin cycle. We had almost no savings. How fast would he find a job? Would he waste too much time trying to find an exact match, when he might need to try a peripheral career?

I scurried around the basement picking up toys in time to my racing thoughts, tossing them into their storage basket.

Judy planned to arrive tomorrow. Would she try to be supportive, or would she drip disdain?

I trudged up the stairs and looked at the living room and kitchen, seeing the rooms with her eyes. My budget attempts at cozy decorating looked tacky to me now. And the meal. She ate in gourmet restaurants all the time. Would she scorn my marshmallow-coated yams?

I pulled open my kitchen cupboards, wishing for a set of beautiful china instead of battered Corelle.

The cupboard door closed with a bang, and my gaze traveled to the clutter on the kitchen desk. After Thanksgiving I would have just over a week to come up with deep spiritual insights and some zippy one-liners, too. The speaking engagement was a vortex pulling all my thoughts in its direction. I had to be stellar. I had to make my words sing.

Words have power. I was excited to hold that power in my hand. The sense of raging ambition caused an uncomfortable itch in my soul, but I decided not to worry about it. An opportunity this great had to be God's call, didn't it?

*Lord, thanks for giving me a chance to make a difference. Help me craft every single word of the perfect speech. But first help me get through Thanksgiving.*

# EIGHTEEN

*I pulled my guitar* closer and settled it
in my lap. The D string had a habit of slipping
flat, so I tuned once more. My fingers moved into place
on the second and third frets. Chords resonated through the room,
and my children—all twelve of them—began to sing. A stairstep of talent, sweet voices rose around me as we clustered in our living room. The
older girls glided into a pure descant while the four boys carried a tenor
line. Even the three-year-old chirped a solo verse with precocious intensity.

When we finished, the television journalist stepped through the children to sit beside me on the couch. "Everyone wants to know. How do
you do it? You homeschool, don't you? How do you manage that along
with your recording career?"

I ignored the cameraman, who kept shifting to get a better angle. "I
love them. That's all a family needs. Love. And organization, too. I
have a monthly menu plan, and chore charts, and a meticulous schedule
for our curriculum each day."

"Well, that may explain your amazing home life. But how do you
account for the extraordinary sound of your music? The intricate harmonies?"

I smiled. "That's the word. Harmony. Family is all about harmony. Our love helps us blend, so why shouldn't our voices blend, as
well?"

"How do you manage the constant travel with such a large brood?"

"Oh, my sister always comes on the road with us. She loves the kids like her own, handles all our PR, and smooths out the details."

The interviewer turned to one of my sons sitting by my feet. "And what do you think about being part of a family that's a role model for our whole country?"

My son grinned. "I love it. And I love my mom." He jumped up to throw his arms around my neck.

The journalist laughed and looked into the camera. "There you have it. Harmony and a good dose of love. That's the anthem of this family." As she wrapped up the show, the doorbell rang.

I shook potato peels into the sink and dried my hands on a dish towel, running to answer the door. Judy was early. I wanted to have the spuds in a kettle of water in the fridge, ready to be boiled and mashed tomorrow. At least my pies were finished. Pumpkin, of course, but also cherry because Kevin loved it.

I threw the door open, and Judy burst in like a force of nature. "Hey, sis! I caught an earlier flight. I couldn't wait to see you all. What's for lunch? Where are the kiddoes?" Her hand hooked a large bag over her shoulder like Santa. "I brought them a few things."

I laughed in spite of the entertaining-my-successful-sister stress. "Peanut butter and jelly. Dylan's at school. Micah's napping—or he was, and Kelsey's moving some essentials out of her room. Why don't you come in?"

She dumped the bag onto the living room floor, gave me a brisk hug, and wheeled her efficient black carryon toward the hall. "I'm staying in Kelsey's room?"

I chased after her. "Yeah, but like I said, she's not moved out yet."

She ignored me and pulled her bag into Kelsey's room. "Hey, sweetie! Oooh, I love what you did with your Barbies. Cool hair."

"Aunt Juju!" Kelsey's obsession with candy had warped her understanding of my sister's name, and Judy got a kick out of it, so we never corrected her.

Micah howled and began banging his crib. He didn't want to miss the fun, so I popped into the boys' room to lift him out and carried him into Kelsey's room. She was already introducing Judy to all her stuffed animals—many of which were gifts from Judy.

My sister pivoted on her leather stiletto-heel boots, and her perfect blond bob swung with her. "Oooh. And there's the precious baby." She grabbed him from my arms and nuzzled him. "You have grown up since summer." His grin showed off his white Niblet-corn teeth. "Look at the sweetie peetie."

I shook my head. Hearing Judy indulge in high-pitched baby talk seemed as incongruous as Pastor Roger dancing a jig in front of the church. Micah squirmed, and she handed him back to me.

I set him down so he could show off his skill of pulling himself to a wobbly stand using Dylan's bedspread. She didn't notice. She flashed around like a firefly. I'd forgotten. She spoke fast, moved fast. Every visit she zipped across our lives like Dylan on his skateboard.

She didn't offer to help me cook or clean, and I didn't expect her to. While she was settling into Kelsey's room, Dylan bounded off the school bus and flung his backpack to the floor. Judy squealed and ran to meet him.

He gave her a huge hug. I wondered how much of his

enthusiasm was because she kept him supplied with video games.

She marched to the living room and collapsed on the couch. Dylan and Kelsey leapt onto her in a giggling pileup. She smiled at me, a bit smug. "Sis, how about if I take the kids to a movie and get them out of your hair?" Her gaze raked my rumpled sweatshirt. She reached up to pluck a potato peel off my sleeve. "You know, we could just go out for dinner tomorrow."

I was horrified. "On Thanksgiving? No way. Besides, you said you were hungry for some home cooking."

She shrugged. "Well if you're gonna fuss, let me take the two oldest off your hands for a few hours." She squeezed both kids. "What movie do you want to see?"

Time for me to regain a measure of control. "Only something rated G."

Judy rolled her eyes. She tickled Dylan. "Your mom is such a fuddy-duddy."

I planted my fists on my waist.

She sprang up. "All right, all right. G it is. Come on kids. Let's head to the Mega Mall. We can stop at Lego Land."

They grabbed coats and raced out the door—a conspiracy of giddy pleasure.

Micah crawled out to join me.

"Guess it's just you and me, bud." Judy's visits always triggered an undercurrent of irritation.

He gave me a fat-cheeked grin, and my frustration melted away. I turned on the stereo and headed back to the kitchen. Kevin was down at the unemployment office filling out forms. The house seemed almost peaceful. "Come on, Micah. Let's make this the best Thanksgiving ever."

The next morning, inevitable conflicts began marring my dream Thanksgiving like scuffs on linoleum. I got up early to slide the turkey into the oven. Even though it was a scrawny bird, it would take several hours to cook and could roast while we were at church.

An hour later, I stood in the bathroom, trying to make my hair wave back and frame my face. Instead it poked up in odd directions.

Dylan charged into Judy's room. "Time for church. Wake up, sleepyhead."

Judy's sleepy answer carried through the doorway. "I'm not going. I don't really like church. Remember? But you go have a good time."

Dylan turned on his lecture voice. "But church is God's house. You have to come talk to Him."

"If I wanted to, I could talk to Him fine right here. It's not important to go to a fancy building. You know, pal, lots of people believe different things than you do. That's okay. You need to respect that."

Dylan trudged out into the hall and hovered in the bathroom doorway. He glistened. With his dark hair slicked down, wearing a crisp white shirt and dress pants, he presented quite the contrast from his jeans and sweat shirts. "Mom, how come Aunt Judy doesn't like God the way we do?"

"Honey, some people just don't know Him yet. We can tell her how much we love Him, but we can't make her go to church."

Judy groaned from Kelsey's bed. "Dylan, if your mom is going to preach, shut the door, would you?"

Kelsey squirmed during church, and I handed her crayons and coloring books. To be truthful, I squirmed a bit myself. It still hurt to be among people who looked down on me.

Rejected me. Even worse was the pity I saw in the eyes of friends. With effort, I drew my mind back to the hymns. I sang loud and clear, as if the words of praise could drive the pain from my heart. In some measure, they did. I had so much to be grateful for. God's love for me and Christ's sacrifice on my behalf overrode my petty worries.

With my heart lightened, we returned home. I buzzed around the kitchen getting the dinner prepared and hummed the hymn the trumpets had played at church. Kevin disappeared into the boys' room with Micah. If Kev could coax him down for a nap now, our dinner in a few hours would be much more cheerful.

Judy sat in the living room, playing dress-up with the kids. The chest in the corner by the lamp doubled as an end table and a storage spot for hats, capes, and other costumes. Above the giggles, Judy's voice carried to the kitchen. "Let's all be witches with magical powers and cast a spell on your toys to make them come to life."

I stopped stirring the green beans and stuck my head around the corner. "Judy, we don't play witches in our house." I enforced my words with my firm-mom face to the kids.

Judy squared off with me. "You have rules for everything, don't you? Lighten up."

More sour notes in the day. Why couldn't she just follow along in my key?

She must have noticed the hurt flicker across my face, because she turned back to Dylan and Kelsey. "Okay, who do you want to pretend to be?"

"The Good S'maritan," Dylan shouted.

"I wanna be the donkey," Kelsey yelled.

Judy ran a hand through her slick, perfect hair, bewildered. I ducked back into the kitchen to let the kids explain. She wasn't about to listen to anything I had to say about the Bible. Maybe the kids would plant a few seeds.

By 2:00, the turkey was ready, its aroma merging with the scent of my cranberry stuffing and sweet yams. I lit the candles on the table and called everyone together. Micah looked sleep-dazed but happy. Dylan's hair had forsaken its part and was back to a Beatle look. Kelsey's blond curls were rumpled, and her long flowered dress had clumps of Play-Doh stuck to it. Kevin had shed his suit jacket and rolled up his shirt sleeves. There was something about Kevin in rolled-up sleeves that made me want to forget the dinner and lure him to the bedroom. Judy wore trendy black pants with a coral silk blouse, and a rare relaxed smile.

My family. Warmth welled up in me, and I was glad for every bit of preparation I'd put into the meal.

Kevin leaned forward to take Micah's hand and mine. "Let's share a few things we're thankful to God for."

We went around the table after a brief fight between Kelsey and Dylan about who should go first. When it was Judy's turn, she shrugged. "I'm glad that if we want something bad enough we can make it happen. I'm thankful that my positive thinking got me a terrific job."

I stared at my plate and tried not to frown as she continued to thank herself instead of God. Then my conscience gave an annoying tug. Was I really so different? I had fought for a job at the church, and when that didn't work, I'd made plans for a speaking career. Had I stopped to ask God what His plans were? Or had I been too busy with Plans D, E, and F?

Kevin gave Judy a warm, nonjudgmental smile, and then studied the table, sparkling with candlelight, gold-painted pinecones, and serving dishes. "Let's pray."

I caught Judy rolling her eyes, and I quickly looked down,

frustrated again that nothing seemed to get through to her.

Kevin led us in a short, heartfelt prayer. When he finished, I passed a basket of rolls to Dylan and noticed Judy blinking away a bit of moisture in her eyes. I didn't want to embarrass her, so I quickly handed Kevin the carving knife and teased him about last year's mangled bird.

The mood around the table eased into laughter and appreciation of great food. No one mentioned my lumpy gravy or the slightly overcooked yams. Instead, Judy praised the table decorations and the home-cooked meal. "I eat out all the time. It gets to be a real bore."

She didn't mean it as a dig. But I thought about how we could barely afford a monthly trip to Burger King and began comparing my life to hers—again.

*Lord, forgive me for my envy. I have everything that matters right here. Even Judy has told me that.*

After dinner, Judy strolled into the kitchen. She helped me stow the leftovers, she loaded the dishwasher, and she dried the pots and pans as I washed them.

"This has been nice," she sighed. "But I couldn't handle three kids 24/7. How do you do it?"

Another opportunity to share my faith. Zeal chased away my turkey-induced lethargy. "It's because of my faith in God. He promises to give us strength for whatever work He calls us to."

When she frowned, I knew I was pushing the limits again, so I changed the subject. "Hey, guess what? I was asked to speak at a big women's conference next weekend."

"Sis, that's great!" She dropped the dishtowel to the counter and gave me a big hug. For a woman who had appeared on the *Today* show, her enthusiasm for my little success was very generous.

"I know it's not a big deal. But I'm hoping it will lead to more opportunities. I like the idea of sharing my faith with larger groups. Having an impact."

She turned away. "Just don't cram it down their throats."

I stopped scrubbing the roaster. "I'm sorry. I don't mean to annoy you when I talk about God stuff. It's just such a big part of my life."

After a long silence, she made a growling sound in her throat. "Remember Dad's and Mom's funerals? I hated all that prattle from the preacher. 'They've gone to a better place. We shouldn't grieve.' Well, I grieved." Her jaw clenched. "And what kind of encouragement is it to be told we'll be floating around on clouds playing harps? Why couldn't he be honest? When you're dead, you're dead."

Ready to jump in and argue, I bit my lip instead. "There's nothing wrong with grieving." My words were quiet—as conciliatory as I knew how to make them. "I didn't have the best relationship with them, but I miss them, too. I wish they could see their grandchildren grow up." Tears threatened, and I pinched the bridge of my nose.

"Yeah." She softened for a moment. "But why are you filling the kids' heads with all these fairy tales about God? It's only setting them up to be disillusioned."

I bristled. "Judy, it's not a fairy tale. God loves you. He made you. He wants to have a relationship with you."

She set the kettle down with a thump. "Well, I don't have time for that, Miss Holy Roller." She stomped from the kitchen and down the hall. Kelsey's door closed with unnecessary vigor.

I slumped into the kitchen chair. For a few hours, I'd believed the fantasy of a perfect, always-loving family. The kids didn't squabble, Kevin pushed aside his job worries, I focused on gratitude instead of my elusive goals, and even Judy seemed to enjoy herself. But it was a short-lived illusion.

My inadequacies rolled back into my thoughts, and I could no longer remember the tune of the Thanksgiving hymn.

# NINETEEN

**The tour group** *wandered along the grassy path, voicing gratifying oohs and ahhs. I kept a close eye on them so none of them would tread on the mulch protecting my prized plants.*

*We paused to admire a raised bed with artistic color combinations. Masses of cobalt lobelias tumbled down the wooden box. Lowly marigolds provided a layer in front of pure yellow day lilies. A few blue irises that I had coaxed into late blooming completed the striking display.*

*We continued to my pride and joy. The rose beds. Peach, yellow, white, and crimson blooms bobbed in the slight breeze. As I lectured on hybrids and the new varieties, I allowed the group to step closer and sample the aroma of the roses bred for their scent.*

*Then I led them to the international champion rose that had been named after me. My legacy to the generations of gardeners to come. More photos snapped. The peach blooms with a hint of coral along the bottom of each petal also boasted a rich, almost spicy scent.*

*One woman in a broad-brimmed hat and filmy dress looked as if she'd stepped from the pages of* The Great Gatsby. *"Have you always been a gardener?"*

*I smiled. "From childhood. I've always been fascinated with making things grow."*

*One of the men looked up from his notebook where he frantically sketched the layout of my herb garden in the distance. "As a master gardener, do you have any favorite suggestions to share with us?"*

*"You simply must match each plant to the correct location." I slipped*

into lecture mode. "Blueberries need acidic soil, but that would wither many other plants. Lilies of the valley are poisonous, so you don't want them planted in your yard if you have small children. Ferns love shade, but roses need full sun.

"Of course you want to prepare the soil, fertilize, prune, weed, and eradicate pests. But the true secret to successful gardens is simple. Place each plant in the situation where it is meant to be."

I pulled my stare away from the garden photo on our kitchen calendar, hunched over the table, tapped my pencil a few times, and scribbled more notes. "Match each staff person and volunteer with the place they are meant to be." I infused my voice with authority. Giving a lecture was kind of fun. At least it was when I was alone in my kitchen after the kids had gone to bed. Time for a tougher test run.

I stacked my note cards and jogged from the kitchen to the living room. "Okay, I'm ready to practice."

Kevin was sprawled lengthwise along the couch. He closed his copy of *What Color is Your Parachute?* and gave me his attention. "Go for it."

I launched into my speech. After pacing the room and expounding on several key theories, I looked up. "Does that make sense?"

"Sounds good to me." He grinned. "You're so cute when you're concentrating."

I made a huffing sound and tried to give him a stern professorial glare. "Let's continue, shall we?" I cleared my throat. "You may choose to use a spiritual-gifts inventory or simply interview each member if your church is small enough. Another tool is a talent survey. Put it in the church bulletin or newsletter. Invite each person to select areas where they feel gifted and called. It's all about matchmaking."

I threw down my note cards. "Oh, Kev. I'm going to make a fool of myself. They already know all of this. I'll probably trip walking up to the podium and be too scared to squeeze out a single word. They'll probably run me out of the conference on a rail when they figure out what a fraud I am."

Kevin launched from the couch and pulled me close. "My adorable noodle-brain. You worry too much." He rubbed his cheek against mine. "Relax. They'll love you. You care about this stuff so much—that's what matters."

I snuggled deeper into his chest. "I just want to inspire them. Help their ministries grow."

"You will." His voice was gravelly and warm.

Time to stop rehearsing my speech and spend some quality time with my husband. We pulled apart just enough to turn out the light and walk down the hall. I was grateful that Micah was sleeping through the night again. And that our bedroom door had a lock.


After a week off, our Bible study group was ready to resume on the following Thursday. Thanksgiving hadn't gone as well as I'd hoped. I was sad at the rush of relief I felt when Judy went back home. In many ways, my Thursday night gals were my true sisters.

Because we were meeting at Sally's, I took care not to arrive first. I wasn't ready for much time alone with her. I wanted to support her, but my heart wasn't quite in the right place yet. She had stopped reporting the scoop about the inner workings of church decisions, for which I was grateful. The less said, the better.

My friends all knew about the speaking engagement coming up on Saturday. I'd sent them giddy e-mails the night I'd been invited. I toned down my happiness when I e-mailed Doreen. I knew how hurtful it could be when your friends were perky in the face of your inner pain. We'd invited Doreen to spend Thanksgiving with us, and so had Lori. But she took her kids and drove across several states to be with her parents.

As we sat gingerly on Sally's French Provincial furniture, I wondered how she kept her white carpeting so pristine. Sally's girl, Chelsea, was as meticulous and prim as her mother, and I supposed having one ten-year-old daughter was very different than chasing around three young kids.

Doreen looked drawn, as if life as she knew it had ended. And it had. "I keep asking myself if I caused this. Then I feel so much rage I don't know what to do. I try praying, but I just can't forgive him."

Lori sidled closer to her on the couch. "Give yourself time. You don't have to act like some super-Christian. God understands that you're hurting."

Doreen nodded and waved a hand, fighting back tears. "Come on, I don't want to be the group's project for the night. Let everyone else share their prayer requests."

Sally turned a page in her planner. "All right. But we care about you. You aren't a project."

Heather fingered the fringe on her macrame belt. "We need each other. That's what friends are for."

Lori nodded, then cleared her throat and took the uncomfortable attention off of Doreen. She smoothed her denim dress. "Abby was called the N-word at the park this week. I don't know how to handle it." Pain shone in her dark eyes. "Our church is so diverse, and all of us are such close friends that I sometimes forget there are still people who won't accept our skin color."

We all bristled with outrage and offered to track down the offender and visit his parents—armed to the teeth.

She managed a small smile. "It's not just that. Noah got pulled over last week, driving home from work. He wasn't doing anything wrong. The police stopped him and ran his license. They figured he was a crook because he was driving through a nice neighborhood."

We all gaped at her in silence. I'd rarely thought about her race or the unique challenges she faced. I suddenly felt ashamed for how oblivious I'd been.

She gave us a lopsided grin. "It gives me practice in forgiving. Like when a salesgirl keeps a close eye on me when I'm shopping. Anyway, pray that I can explain this to Abby—and respond in a Christlike way."

We nodded, and the eyes turned to me. I tried not to bounce up and down with excitement. "Please pray about my talk this Saturday. I'm thrilled but scared. Oh, and I feel like I'm coming down with something. My throat's been sore all day."

Heather leaned forward with a worried expression. "Maybe God's trying to tell you not to go."

"Not at all." Lori shook her head. "I'm sure it's Satan harassing her, because he doesn't want her to make an impact for God's kingdom. We need to pray against this attack."

Doreen leaned back and sighed. "When I was working, I'd get sick when I was under too much stress. You should think of ways to relax."

"Or it's just germs." Sally unexpectedly came to my rescue. "We live in a fallen world, and people get sick. Don't your kids have colds?"

I nodded. "All three of them. Well, whatever the cause is, would you pray that it gets better?"

We settled into prayer time, and I felt the strength of joined faith and the soothing comfort of God's presence with us. The evening flew past.

Saturday morning I woke up at 4:00 and tossed and turned until 5:00. I finally gave up on sleep and headed to the shower. After I put on my blazer and dress pants, I panicked and decided to switch to a skirt. I'd heard that some conservative Christians preferred women to wear skirts. But when I checked myself in the mirror, the skirt looked too short. I tried some different slacks that were wide and flowing. They looked ridiculous with the blazer. I tossed the blazer and found a flouncy blouse, which made me look like a Scarlett O'Hara parasol. Back to the blazer and dress pants, with a wispy scarf around my neck to add a feminine touch.

My throat was sore and my head ached. We'd been passing this cold around our family all week.

*No, Lord. You wouldn't do that to me. This is hard enough.*

The pain increased as I downed my morning coffee and greeted Kevin and the kids as they stumbled their way into the kitchen in shifts. Worse, when I practiced the opening of my speech, my voice came out hoarse and cracked.

"What am I going to do?" I grabbed Kevin's biceps in a panic.

He pried my fingernails from his arms and drew me close. "Just hum while you drive there. And bring a water bottle." He stroked my hair. "Happens all the time to me when I'm giving a presentation. Humming helps keep your vocal cords loose."

Great. I could see myself walking into the conference humming and guzzling.

After pacing the kitchen like a nervous bride, I decided to leave early. Kevin pulled me to the couch and held my hand, offering up a quiet prayer for me. I don't think I'd ever loved him more. Then I belted my coat like armor and marched to the van.

I didn't realize there was a computer show at the convention center that morning. Traffic was fierce. As I crawled along the freeway toward downtown, I alternated between hyperventilating with fear of being late and humming to soothe my throat.

I had to park several blocks from the church where the conference was being held and barely made it in time. My shoes were coated with slush by the time I ventured into the lobby. The program director hurried up to me with a smile. "Thank you so much for filling in at the last minute. I'll be introducing you. Could you tell me a few things about yourself?"

I froze.

She tried again. "You know. Your college, your background in church work, any publications?"

I stammered. "I just organized the women's program at our church. From the ground up. Victoria thought that would give a new slant for all these professionals. You know? The role of volunteers? Discerning their gifts? Bloom where you're planted? That kind of thing."

She flinched, and her smile tightened. "All right. That's fine. Oh, and we're running a bit behind schedule, so could you shorten your talk from thirty minutes to twenty?"

No problem. I'd only timed my talk a dozen times in the last two days, creating the perfect thirty-minute presentation. I shuffled my note cards, desperate to find a few points to toss away.

She led me toward a side door that would send me out to face the rows of hundreds of women. After the current speaker finished to whooping laughter and thunderous applause, a piano signaled a praise and worship song. The song whisked along, and I wished it had more verses.

Cold dread contrasted the burning pain in my throat.

The program director sauntered out and gave me a brief introduction. Her open arm beckoned me, but my feet stuck to the floor as if I were treading my kitchen linoleum after the kids spilled lemonade. I made my way out, trying not to look at the faces in front of me.

I leaned toward the microphone. "Hello—" Feedback shrieked, and I pulled back in alarm. A few chuckles sounded from the pews. I winced and tried again.

"Women's ministry is all about matchmaking." I gave a broad smile and launched into my talk. I looked at the women spread out before me. They were no longer frightening jurists waiting to pass judgment on me. They were women like me, longing to serve God. They were friends I could serve and inspire.

My words progressed from a stumble to a confident flow. I had them. I felt them in the palm of my hand. In spite of the occasional cracks in my voice, and even when I rushed to cover all the important thoughts, I saw people lean forward, nod, smile. The twenty minutes passed in a blur.

I acknowledged the applause and strode with confidence back to the wings.

I'd done it. I'd found a skill and vocation even better than working for my church. No, that wasn't quite right. This was all part of the same gift. I loved to make things grow. I'd nurtured the women's ministry into a strong program. Seeded, watered, and watched it bloom. Now I was encouraging others and sharing all my tips for their own work. Over the coming year, many churches would benefit from the ideas I'd shared today.

A warm glow of satisfaction wrapped around me. Or it could have been a growing fever. My throat hurt so badly, I probably had strep.

The program director thanked me with a genuine smile of approval. She promised the honorarium would be mailed to me next week and invited me to stay for the rest of the conference. I would have loved to listen to the other speakers, but my head throbbed and I felt dizzy. I also was feeling the effects of guzzling so much water.

As I hurried back to the lobby to find the bathroom, I resisted the urge to do a Snoopy dance.

*Thank you, Lord. That was so great! Please give me more opportunities like this.*

I pushed open the rest room door with the confidence of an important person with things to say. The buzz of fulfillment tingled in my cold-stuffed ears. Everything was finally coming together. I still didn't know how we'd survive if Kevin didn't find work soon. My honorarium for today's speech wouldn't go far. But certainly this was a sign that things were turning around.

As I entered a stall, I heard several other women walk into the bathroom and cluster by the sink. I grinned. Maybe they'd discuss the great speech they'd just heard.

## TWENTY

*I climbed the* rope ladder to our carefully designed tree house. Palm fronds formed an
adequate roof, although they needed frequent replacement.
Hurricanes and squalls—the same sort of storm that had
destroyed our ship—hit the island far too often.

Months ago, we had struggled up on the sandy shore, half drowned.
My husband had flint in his pocket and, after drying out his tinder, was
able to light a fire against the oppressive darkness. We knelt on the beach
and thanked God that our three boys had survived and that we were all
together.

The next day's exploration revealed the shattering truth. We were
on a deserted island.

In those early days we would have died without provisions that
washed ashore from the broken frame of the ship. Each item was precious. Rope, knives, salted pork, even kegs of whiskey that would form
the basis for our medical supplies. A few rifles and some fishing nets
gave us hope of feeding ourselves until a passing ship found us.

Ingenuity kept us alive. My husband and sons thrived on the challenge of building a home with unusual luxuries such as a dumbwaiter
to lift water buckets from ground level up to the first platform. I wove
palm fronds to create baskets, hats, and floor mats. We learned a dozen
uses for the hairy-husked fruits that my husband said were called coco-
nuts.

*Unfortunately, we found little else that was edible. Our early optimism faded in the face of hunger. Today I stared at the meager collection in my hands—a basket with a few clams. The boys' cheeks were sunken, and they no longer wasted energy on pranks or roughhousing.*

*My husband climbed down from his lookout post higher in the tree. "No sign of ships today. But there's always tomorrow."*

*Tears sprang into my eyes. "How many tomorrows will we have? Look at our sons. We are all starving."*

*He frowned, but then his expression softened. "God will provide." His voice carried over the splashing of tropical rain against palm fronds. "We must not give up hope."*

"I hope I make it through the rest of this conference." A woman's voice carried over the sound of washing hands.

I was in the nearby stall, tucking in my blouse. I reached for my purse.

An automatic hand dryer hummed into action. "Yeah. It's been a long day. And that last speaker didn't help."

I froze. My purse remained on the hook as I strained to hear the two women.

"Where did they find her? Doesn't she realize how impractical those suggestions are?" A bitter edge tinged the voice.

"I wish they didn't bring in folks who don't have a clue about what we face."

The women left, completely unaware they had shipwrecked my spirit in a few precise sentences. I hid for several minutes to make sure no one saw my exit. I slunk from the church, then ran all the way to my car. All I could think about was getting away.

I drove home in a tired daze. Conflicting impressions battled in my heart. I'd done a great job. The audience's reaction had been enthusiastic. The program director seemed genuinely happy.

Yet the words of those two women repeated over and over in my head. My initial joy dropped like a falling coconut. By the time I got home, I could barely trudge into the house. I muttered a vague answer to Kevin's eager questions about the conference.

"Looks like you've got a fever, honey." Kevin's concerned face swam into focus. "Go crawl into bed. I'll bring you some tea."

The sore throat and fever were the least of my problems, but my pillow enticed me. I pulled up the quilt and fell asleep.

After my nap, I wandered into the living room to fill Kevin in on how the talk had gone. And also the conversation I'd overheard.

"Oh, sweetie." He edged closer to me on the couch and reached his arm around me, tugging until I relaxed my head against his shoulder. "They were just a couple of sourpusses. Probably so burnt out on their jobs they didn't want to consider new ideas."

He always knew the right thing to say.

I swallowed hard and winced from the pain. "But I was so happy. It felt so good to use my gifts."

He felt my forehead with the back of his hand, then smoothed back my bangs. "That hasn't changed. You did use your gifts. You use your gifts every day. Don't let a few grumps steal that from you. Come on, you need some aspirin."

I didn't have the energy to protest. He steered me back into bed, and I lay awake pondering my lack of joy now that my dream had come true. Would other speaking engagements end with this strange mix of satisfaction diluted with fatigue, doubt, and confusion?

Later that week, an enthusiastic note arrived along with my

honorarium check. The organizer of the event raved about my talk and even asked me to speak again at next year's conference. I was cheered for an hour or so, but then the words of the women in the restroom returned to squash my confidence.

In the coming days, my worry was pushed aside by activity. My cold improved, but Kevin caught one, which didn't help his energy for job hunting. The kids were wrapped up in pre-Christmas mania. Even Kelsey had practices for the Sunday school pageant. Micah had his appointment with the audiologist, who recommended surgery to insert tubes.

One night after Micah fell asleep, Kevin and I huddled at the kitchen table. I'd brewed the last of our coffee and had started a new grocery list. Kevin punched numbers into the calculator and sighed at the pile of bills at his elbow.

I handed him a cup of coffee. "Enjoy it. It's the last of the coffee, and it looks like we may not be able to afford more."

My joke fell flat. He rubbed his head. His dark hair was growing longer. The sight made me sad. His military cut represented his confidence and control. Tonight he looked as defeated as his unkempt hair. Miserable eyes met mine as I sat across from him.

"You know we can't pay for next semester's college class, don't you?" Remorse creased his brow.

"Who cares?" I grinned and waved a hand dismissively. "I need a break anyway. I have to finish last semester's paper. And who knows? I might get busy with speaking engagements."

Dylan bounded into the kitchen. "Can I have a snack?"

"Sure," I answered, distracted. "Carrots, celery, apples."

"Mom, I meant a real snack."

Kevin gave our son "the Look." Normally the epitome of

easygoing, Kev still could intimidate when his dark eyebrows zagged down and his eyes threw sparks.

Dylan's eyes widened. "Never mind." He disappeared down the basement stairs.

I stood and walked around behind Kevin's chair. I massaged his shoulders, trying to knead out his pain. "Is it really that bad?"

"Worse. I can pay the mortgage and electricity this month. But our insurance is gone. Unemployment might cover grocery money. But we have to sell one of the cars."

"But—" *How would I do errands? Drive Kelsey to preschool?* I swallowed. "No problem. I'll arrange car pools for Kelsey. Well, not exactly car pools, since I won't be taking a turn. Rides. I'll arrange rides." Babbling covered my anxiety.

Kevin groaned and shoved the calculator away. "I'm sorry."

"What for?"

"It's my job to provide for our family."

I took a steadying breath. "Wrong. That's God's job. Let's pray about this."

Before we could join hands, Kelsey wandered into the kitchen, already in her pajamas. "What's this called?" She planted her palm against her upper torso. She was still working on learning body parts.

I smiled. "Your chest."

She shook her head. "No, there's another name. 'Member?"

We had looked at a picture book from the library that afternoon. She was fascinated by drawings of the inner workings of the human body.

"Oh, you mean your lungs."

She bobbed her curls up and down. She pulled out her other hand from behind her back. One of her punk-haired Barbies jutted out of her fist, stark-naked. "Mommy, why does Barbie have such big lungs?"

Kevin choked on his coffee and started laughing—the rich deep laughter I used to hear every day. I pulled my daughter toward me for a big hug. "Honey, when girls grow up to be women, their . . . er . . . chests are bigger."

She stared at my sweater. "Yours isn't."

Kevin hooted and doubled over. He laughed so hard I thought he'd pass out. I tried to glare at him. Now that Micah wasn't nursing much, I was wearing more of my prepregnancy clothes. Apparently the shapeliness brought on by breastfeeding had disappeared.

Watching Kevin dissolve into hysterics filled my narrow torso with so much relief, I couldn't hold on to my frown. I swept Kelsey into my arms. "Come on, sweetie. Time to brush your teeth and tuck you in."

After reading *Green Eggs and Ham* and *Go, Dog. Go!* I returned to the kitchen. Kevin was staring into space. I called his name twice before he blinked and noticed me.

I took his face in my hands. "It's going to be okay."

He leaned against one of my palms, then grabbed my hands and pulled me onto his lap. "You're right. Let's pray." With my head against his shoulder, holding on to each other like drowning victims, we began to pray—our thanks to God for being trustworthy, our honest fears, our questions, our pleas for a job for Kevin, and our wobbly words of trust and surrender.

We continued to pray as December moved along. I'd always been good at pinching pennies, but now I had to squeeze them and wring them out.

Selling the van brought in some money and lowered our car

insurance. Kevin swallowed his pride and admitted to broader circles of friends that he needed a job. He called it networking, but I knew he believed it was begging. I saw the strain growing in him as each day passed.

We used our extra family time to create homemade Christmas gifts, go sledding when the first serious snowfall hit, and invent other ways to cheer ourselves. We attended Dylan's holiday program at school wearing bright—even if not always authentic—smiles.

Judy called. Even though she had left in a huff after Thanksgiving, she planned to join us at Christmas. I dreaded Judy's reaction to our scaled-down Christmas—and another chance to feel embarrassed by my life in comparison to hers. But I resolved to focus on making her feel welcome and to back off on my judgmental attitudes. With the building anxiety in our home, she might even provide a welcome distraction.

My fear grew at the same pace as our pile of bills. Kevin swung between honest discouragement and a more frightening self-containment and withdrawal. My attempts at cheerleading sometimes slipped into nagging. "Have you checked the bulletin board at the unemployment office again? Did you go through today's paper? What about the Internet? Did you submit your résumé to companies that way?" No wonder he seemed more irritable every day. I hadn't realized how much strain his job loss could put on our marriage. No matter how much I reassured him, he admitted he felt like less of a man. No matter how confident his swagger as he headed out for another interview, I worried we'd lose the house and end up in a cardboard box on skid row. We both put our best faces on for each other, but the effort was pushing us apart.

As always, my Bible-study group provided a strong support. Sally reported that the church had decided she wasn't right for the job and had offered the job to Julie Henderson—the energetic recent college grad from Chicago. Sally was content to continue as church secretary. I lost my stiffness with her.

Doreen was struggling through a mediation process. Jim had refused to reconsider the divorce, so Doreen faced the grueling process of dividing possessions. Worse, they were dividing time with their children.

"I know I could push harder," Doreen said one night, her ramrod spine a bit droopy these days. "He's the one who wronged our family. But I don't want to shut him out of the kids' lives. I don't want to try to wring every ounce of child support out of him, either. It just feeds my anger. Mediation feels like a more Christian approach to this than hiring lawyers to fight it out."

My jaw sagged as I listened. This from the woman who had wanted me to sue the church for not hiring me.

Lori leaned forward. "Good for you. Sounds like God is giving you grace for this awful time."

Doreen fingered a strand of her smooth auburn bob. "But I still get mad."

"Of course you do." Lori's words were warm with acceptance. "Like I did when those kids at the park called Abby names. Or like Becky did when the church overlooked her. But we can't hang on to bitterness."

All our heads nodded. "We need to keep praying for each other," Heather said, brushing crooked bangs away from her eyes.

Sally pursed her lips. "Heather, no offense, but where do you get your hair done? It looks like you cut it yourself. I could give you the name of my hair stylist."

Heather's laughter chirruped like a songbird floating above the world of mere human concerns. "I *do* cut it myself. I don't want to waste money at a salon."

"But . . ." Doreen crossed her legs and flexed her ankle. "Ron's a doctor. You can afford a haircut for pete's sake." Finally someone had raised the question we'd all wondered about. Heather's home was furnished simply, with a style barely beyond college-dorm days. She shopped at thrift stores, but I'd never asked her why.

She hadn't been embarrassed by Sally's criticism of her hair, but now she looked down at her peasant skirt, her face turning pink. "Oh, when Ron paid off his med-school loans, we decided to support a clinic in the Dominican Republic." She shrugged.

I sank back in my chair. My flighty, care-for-the-earth-live-simply-eat-lentils friend had put her money where her mouth was all these years. And we never knew.

"Wow." Lori summed it up for all of us. Then she tilted her head, stretching her swan neck. "So will you let us know if we can help the clinic?"

With childlike excitement, Heather looked around at our faces. "You'd want to do that?"

"Well, duh," Sally said. "Hey, we could have a bake sale at church. Oh, and do they need clothes for the clinic? We could do a clothing drive. And I could donate some makeup."

Doreen rolled her eyes in my direction, and I fought back a grin. Then we all plunged in with suggestions and ideas as Heather watched us in amazement.

Eventually Lori called us back to prayer time. "How's Kevin's job search going?"

My light mood dimmed. "Nothing yet. He's worked like crazy, but no one is hiring. He was going to apply for a night janitor position, but it paid less than his unemployment checks, so until they run out, he wants to keep hunting for something a little closer to his field."

"Hmm." Sally looked up from drawing stars next to my name in her planner prayer list. "Sometimes when God doesn't answer our prayers, it's because He's trying to teach us something. Maybe He'll give Kevin a job once you figure it out."

The comment stung, but it took me a while to figure out why.

*So because you and your husband have secure jobs, God doesn't need to teach you anything? Kevin and I are the remedial children?*

I chewed at my lip, fighting back the words. Heather cocked her head, frowning.

Doreen drew her brows together in worry. "If this is a sign Becky needs a lesson, what does it say about me? My life is a huge mess. Does that mean it's God's judgment on me?"

Lori shook her head. "Of course not. He loves you. Sure you may come out of this with deeper faith, or new understanding, because He doesn't let suffering go to waste." She gave a level look at Sally. "But that doesn't mean God is zapping you with trials because you're worse than the rest of us. We're all failures apart from His grace." Lori's voice trailed off, and she stared at the wall across from her. A flicker of pain crossed her usually tranquil face, and I waited for her to say more, but she sat quietly, apparently lost in thought.

Sally tapped her pen. "Okay, then. So Becky, are you getting excited about the *Women of Vision* article? Have you figured out what you're going to tell them about living the victorious Christian life? This is a super chance to let non-Christians see what they're missing."

Would it disrupt Bible study too much if I ran screaming from the room?

I took a deep breath. "How about if you all pray that something in my life goes right in time for them to write about it, okay?"

Heather patted my foot from her place on the floor. "You don't need to impress anyone."

Her words soothed my prickly feelings a bit, but my brain kept chomping on my inadequacies all evening and had trouble paying attention to the discussion.

As I pulled on my coat to leave, Lori pulled me aside and handed me an envelope. "Just a little something to help you out."

Inside was a generous gift card for the local grocery store.

"I can't take this."

She hugged me. "Of course you can. Noah and I want to help. Please let us. You'd do the same for us."

Gratitude and humiliation churned inside me. We couldn't afford stubborn pride right now. I nodded and hurried out to the car. Even with warm support from friends, at times Kevin and I felt like castaways. In a culture that defines a person by their job title, we often felt deserted. I was starving for normalcy.

When I got home and dragged into the kitchen door, Kevin was sprawled at the table, feet up on a chair, reading the maize-colored church newsletter. "I know just what we need," he announced before I even said hello.

His enthusiasm made me wary. "What?"

"This Saturday, our church is distributing food baskets to the poor, and they need volunteers to drive the baskets out to people's homes." He flapped the pages in my direction. "It'll be great. Cheer us up. The kids can help, too."

"Okay." I stepped in behind him and wrapped my arms around his neck, dropping a kiss onto the top of his head. "Good idea."

After all, what could be better to give us a sense of perspective and lift our spirits?

# TWENTY·ONE

**It was dark.** The kind of dark that sticks to your skin like slime. I'd hunched in the alley for hours, watching two silhouettes pace behind the tattered shade on the third-floor apartment across the street.

Stiletto heels made my feet hum with pain. The shoes weren't a practical choice, but with a tight skirt and deep red lipstick, they provided a convincing disguise if someone passed by.

Rain drummed onto the street. Anyone with sense was snug at home tonight. But I'd never had any sense. Otherwise, I'd have known better than to open my own detective agency.

The awning above me dripped, and water tickled my neck. Why had I taken this case?

I smelled trouble the instant he strolled into my old third-floor office. I also smelled Old Spice. I'm a sucker for a guy in Old Spice.

He spun some tale about stolen documents. His story was about as thin as the corner deli's pastrami.

I tried to say no, but instead I rocked back my battered chair and balanced it on two legs. Overdue on rent, no other clients battering down my door—there was no choice.

"Fifty dollars up front." I drilled him with a glare. "And don't play games with me. I need all the info you have."

He gave a lazy grin and handed me a file. "It's all in here."

The case had been a nightmare. Mr. Old Spice had thrown me so many curves he should have pitched for the White Sox.

*So now I was staking out a gangster that even the Feds stayed clear of.*

*Suddenly an old Packard squealed around the corner and pulled to a splashing stop right in front of my hiding place. A thug jumped out and muscled me into the backseat before I could pull out my Colt.*

*The goon behind the wheel gunned the engine and headed toward the pier. "You been pokin' around where you're not wanted, girlie." Cursing myself for getting into this mess, I stared out the rain-streaked window, planning my escape. I hated my high heels, but cement over-shoes would be even worse.*

"Hon, are you getting out?" Kevin's voice held a mix of exasperation and humor as he held the car door open for me. Kelsey and Dylan were running laps around the car, and Micah wiggled in Kevin's arms.

"Sorry. I was daydreaming." The nippy air woke me up fast as we crossed the church parking lot.

Volunteers scurried around the church basement, adding bright bows to big laundry baskets stuffed with food. We lined up to get the name and address for our delivery.

Greg, the elder who had cheerfully killed my dreams at the board meeting, checked off names on a clipboard. "Ah, the Millers. Good to see you. Well, you've got an easy delivery. Just grab one of the baskets and load it up." He handed me a card with an address.

I glanced at it. "Whoops. There's been a mistake. We need the name of the family who's getting the food donation. This card has our name."

Greg beamed at us. "That's right. Pastor told the committee about Kevin being out of work. You need this as much as any family on our list."

I looked at Kevin. It didn't take a detective to see how he was taking this kind—but humiliating—gesture.

Kevin transferred Micah into my arms and gave Greg a tight smile. "You sure about this?"

"Yep." Greg's expression slipped out of cheerful corporate organizer to something sympathetic. "Please take it. We all care about you. You can deliver two baskets next year, if that would make you feel better."

Kevin stared at the basket as if it were armed with explosives. Accepting it would be a confession of need. He took a slow breath and nodded. "Thanks. We'll do that." He hefted the basket and carried it to the car in silence, with the rest of us trailing behind.

When we settled everyone into the car, I tried to gauge Kevin's mood. "That was sure nice of them."

He refused to look at me and started the car. The engine sputtered before turning over, and I bit my lip. We couldn't afford a car repair.

*No, Lord. Not one more problem. We just couldn't handle it today.*

Maybe it was just the cold weather. I shivered. Winter would get a lot colder than this.

Kevin's gloved hands flexed around the steering wheel.

I rested a hand on his arm. "They wanted to do it."

He clenched his jaw. "I know they want to help. But now our family is the local charity case."

"They don't look at it that way."

He stared out the windshield and didn't answer.

"Okay, think of it this way. I worked as many hours as most part-time jobs. For three years. For free. Pretend it's a salary bonus. An employer's gift basket."

The corner of his lips twitched. Some of the tension eased out of his shoulders, and he eased the strangle grip he had on the steering wheel.

When we got home, excitement erased our shame for the moment. We unloaded and exclaimed over each item. Dylan and

Kelsey skipped around the kitchen table and cracked each other up singing "Old MacDonald" and inserting names of food items. Old MacDonald was a lucky guy. He had a turkey, a bag of russet potatoes, canned vegetables, and luxuries like a piecrust and apple pie filling. The basket also held staples like rice and beans to take us into the new year. We'd been scraping by for weeks, and this wealth cheered me up. Pretty soon I was humming Christmas carols as I put away all the food.

In the middle of celebrating our bounty, the doorbell rang. The mailman had a package for us from Florida. Kevin's mom hadn't been up for a visit in years, but she never forgot to send gifts for Christmas. They were the same each year—handmade scarves for each of us. Grandma Miller exemplified frugality, so she used leftover bits of yarn for her creations. I unfolded the tissue paper and handed out the presents. Kelsey whooped over her orange and purple scarf, and Dylan grabbed a black, green, and mauve number with long tassels. Micah chewed on his baby-sized gift while Kevin and I each wrapped our multi-colored scarves around our necks. Never mind that Kevin and I each had ten of them already—one for each Christmas since we'd married. Never mind that the colors were garish. Getting a present was always fun.

Kevin cranked up the stereo and shoved Kelsey's play table to the side. He grabbed my hand and we danced around the living room under garlands of red and green construction paper loops. Micah held on to the couch and bounced on his chubby legs. When I collapsed to the floor out of breath, I called Micah, but he didn't respond. His hearing hadn't improved. We'd have to come up with the money for his surgery somehow.

I shoved aside that worry. When Micah turned and saw my open arms, he tried to take a step toward me. As soon as he let go of the couch, he plopped onto his bottom.

Kevin sank down next to me. "He'll be walking soon."

Micah crawled over to Kevin and was treated to airplane rides over Kevin's head. Eventually, Kevin stood up and flew Micah around the room.

Watching Kevin's eyes sparkle and the energy return to his spirit was a better gift than all the cans of food and scratchy scarves.

Dylan and Kelsey jumped up and down yelling, "My turn." The phone rang, and I ran to the kitchen to grab it.

"Hi, Becky. It's Victoria. I'm so glad I caught you in."

I smiled. As if my social life were so busy she'd have a hard time tracking me down. "What can I do for you?"

"First, I have to tell you, the Women in Church Work conference folks were thrilled with you. Absolutely thrilled."

"Thanks. Good to hear." I savored her words. It seemed I couldn't get enough reassurance that I had done a good job.

"That's kind of why I'm calling. Now hear me out before you answer, okay?"

I hooked a kitchen chair leg with my foot and slid it close. "Okay. Go ahead."

"Every December I speak at a special women's retreat in Chicago over Christmas—a group of widows and other single women without families."

I sank into the chair. "Sounds like a great ministry."

"It is. Loneliness is a big problem for lots of people this time of year." She paused. "Anyway, since the surprise trip with my folks a couple weeks ago, my mom has been sick, and it looks like she'll be in the hospital during the retreat. I don't feel comfortable leaving her."

"Sure," I murmured with sympathy.

"So I'm calling to ask if you'll take over. You'd give a devotion on Christmas Eve, and then two talks on Christmas afternoon. It's a beautiful retreat center. Nice folks. You'll enjoy them. And you can expand the issues you spoke about at the last conference. Just change the focus to discerning and using your gifts. And did I mention there was a big honorarium? They're very generous. Oh, and of course they'll fly you out."

I finally interrupted because I thought she wouldn't stop talking until I said something. "Wow. Sounds wonderful. But I have a family, and I can't leave at Christmas."

"I knew you'd say that. But Becky, you've got to think about your dreams. You want to develop a speaking career. This would open a lot of doors for you."

She was doing some fast talking, and she had a great sales pitch. "Listen, this center holds some major retreats during the year. If they like you, they'll invite you back for some of the big national events they host. If you miss this, you won't have another chance like it.

"And then there's the need. You're good at this. I think God wants you to reach out to those women. I know you'd be a blessing to them."

I couldn't fly off to Chicago over Christmas. It was impossible.

But Victoria kept talking, explaining more about this unique retreat center and how their events had launched her own career. A bubble of excitement grew in my chest. She was right. This was the kind of opportunity I had prayed for. And the honorarium was huge. We needed the income. And I was scared that if I missed this opportunity, offers would dry up. When opportunity knocks, you don't roll over and pull up the covers.

Conflicting thoughts seesawed in my brain. Firmly in the center, one notion swung into focus—I couldn't face this decision alone. "I'll need to pray about this."

Victoria took a slow breath. "But I need to know soon. It's less than a week away. Please, Becky." She choked up. "If I don't find someone to replace me, I can't be with my mom if she needs surgery."

I wavered, but the impression was too strong. "I need to talk to Kevin and we need to pray."

"All right. But call me back in one hour, okay?"

I found myself agreeing to at least that much before I hung up the phone. Even though time was short, I couldn't seem to move from the chair. Dazed and excited, I imagined myself flying to Chicago. Imagined the faces of the women I'd be speaking to. Women who needed encouragement. Women who would gain inspiration from my words. Kingdom work. It was exactly what I'd dreamed of. I'd finally make a difference—a big difference.

Kevin wandered into the kitchen. "Who was that?"

"Quick! Pop in a movie for the kids. We have to talk." I glanced at the clock on the stove. "We have fifty-five minutes."

He stared at me for a moment, taking in my panicked exhilaration. "Okay." Bless his heart for not demanding an explanation immediately. He took the kids downstairs and started a video while I set buckets of toys around Micah in the living room. He crowed and was chewing on a plastic cow by the time Kevin joined me on the couch.

"So what's up?" He shuffled his fingers through his ever-longer hair and watched me with concern.

I took a deep breath. "Victoria called and wants me to speak at a big women's retreat. The honorarium is huge—just what we need for next month's bills. She really needs my help because her mom is sick. She said this could open a lot more doors for me."

He grinned. "Honey, that's great."

I turned away and picked at a hangnail. "Yeah, but there are a few problems." I dared a sideways glance at Kevin.

"Let's hear it." His tone made my stomach drop.

"The retreat's in Chicago."

His frown relaxed and he shifted into problem-solving mode.

"It could work. If I still haven't found a job, I could take care of the kids while you're gone—if you leave me a list. Their schedules boggle my brain. When is it?"

Micah crawled toward us. I gathered him up to put him on my lap—a bit of a shield before the next revelation. "Well, they do this retreat for women who are alone." I gave him my earnest look. "You know how folks can get lonely over the holidays?"

He nodded as I spoke and kept nodding after I stopped—for two more seconds. Then he froze. His eyebrows climbed. "What holidays?"

"This Christmas," I squeaked.

Rare anger flashed in his eyes. "You can't be serious."

Micah did his limp-fish impression and slithered out of my arms. I faced Kevin squarely. "Sometimes God asks us to make sacrifices."

His face didn't soften. "So you think God wants you to do this?"

"I don't know." My voice slipped into a wail. "That's why we have to talk. Victoria needs to know in . . ." I grabbed his wrist again and twisted it to see his watch. "Forty minutes."

"I can't believe you're even considering this—"

"But . . ."

"Judy's coming. The kids are wound up."

My excitement fizzled, drowned out by guilt. "Are you saying I can't go?"

"We've never spent a Christmas apart." He reached for my hands, hanging on as if he wanted to squeeze sense into me. "How could she even ask it?"

"It would just be this once. Victoria said if I don't do it, I'd be missing out on lots of other possible speaking engagements."

"In Chicago?"

"Yeah. But it's a short flight, and their other events aren't at such inconvenient times."

Kevin took a deep breath, letting it out through his nose like a snorting bull ready to charge.

I met his eyes. "Please? Could we at least consider it? Pray about it?"

He nodded stiffly. "You're right. Let's switch sides." We'd discovered this technique during our early marriage arguments. When we had heated and opposing views, we'd pretend we were the other person and argue their point of view.

Twenty minutes later, we had more compassion for each other's desires but were still at an impasse.

Kevin took charge. "Time to pray."

In evidence of his integrity, he didn't pray for God to knock some sense into me. He asked God to reveal a direction for us, to give us unity. I prayed the same thing. After the amen, our eyes met.

I broke the silence first. "I'm afraid if I turn it down, I'll be missing a once-in-a-lifetime chance."

Kevin wrapped an arm around me. "Is fear a good motive in making a decision? If God wants this for you, couldn't He bring you another opportunity later?"

"It's really important to me." I leaned against Kev's shoulder, willing him to understand. "I can't ignore God's open door. Those people need me."

Kevin had worked hard to hide the devastating blow his job loss had caused to his self-esteem. But now he looked deep into my eyes and gave me a glimpse of his pain. "*I* need you."

I knew he wouldn't force me to refuse this chance. Especially when I sensed God's leading. But I felt torn in two.

Sure, there were risks in taking this job. But the opportunity had a lot of appeal. I was good at inspiring. I'd be doing something important. We needed the money. I couldn't afford to be choosy about what I took on right now.

My instincts warned me that I might be heading down some dark alleys. But I could handle it. God never said life would be easy. I sprang from the couch and headed for the phone.

## TWENTY TWO

*Mist rose softly* in the valley—a gentle
contrast to the rugged terrain of my highland home.
From the cliff's edge I could scan in a wide arc. Chill waters
tumbled below in the burn, flowing into a nearby loch rich with
fish. An occasional ewe bleated. Peat smoke rose from farmhouse chimneys, dispersing a scent like the undercurrent of fine scotch whiskey.
Lavender heather painted muted hues on the hillsides.

All this I absorbed with longing and tenderness. I refused to look
directly behind me. My father's battlements would glower down with a
stony stare, reminding me of my duty to the clan. A wool blanket in
MacHemple colors wrapped my shoulders, but it couldn't warm the cold
misery in my heart. Today would be the last day I would wear my
family's plaid.

Horse hooves pounded behind me, and still I refused to turn. Feet
thumped to the hard ground. I heard the swish of leather as rapid hands
tied reins to a nearby tree.

"Are ye grievin', lass?" The young voice was rich and smoky like
the hall I had fled an hour before.

I squared my shoulders. "Nay. I know my duty."

Firm hands gripped my arms and spun me to face him. Fierce blue
eyes studied me. "It's more than duty I'm hoping for." Oldest son of
the McMiller chieftain, Kevin was wide of shoulder, with long black hair
as untamed as his laughter. In his dress kilt with claymore hanging from
his side, there was no doubt that this was a man of strength.

He brushed a stray lock of hair from my face, where the wind took *it again and tossed it behind me. "Our clans need this alliance, aye. But often . . . love has come from these sorts of marriages."*

*"Love?" I meant to scoff him, but the word came out as a startled gasp.*

*His grip on my arms relaxed to a nervous caress, as though he were soothing a skittish horse. "The priest arrived. They sent me to find you. Are you ready?"*

*I gave him a firm nod. Duty was a strong master. But maybe McMiller was right. Perhaps one day our lives could be sweetened by more than duty.*

I stared at the telephone for one more minute. What did duty demand? I dialed Victoria, still not sure how to answer her. Kevin stood in the doorway. Tiny creases at his temples reminded me of the stress he'd worked so hard to hide in the past weeks. The slump of his shoulders betrayed his discouragement. But his eyes spoke the loudest. I stared again into the dark caramel eyes, which pleaded to me in silence.

"Victoria? Hi, it's Becky. I'm sorry, but I can't speak at the retreat. My family needs me right now. I'll pray that you can find someone else to fill in for you." I wrapped up the conversation quickly, before she tried again to convince me.

Several expressions flickered across Kevin's face. I read the relief and the gratitude, but also some regret that I had been forced to walk away from this important step toward my dreams. "Thank you." His voice was hoarse.

"Family comes first," I said firmly.

He stepped closer and held my arms, staring hard into my eyes. "Are you sure you won't resent me for this?"

I met his gaze squarely. "Of course not."

I expected to feel relief after sacrificing my desire out of duty to my family. I expected Kevin to rejoice over my decision. Instead, the following days produced rumbles of tension and heaviness in the air that warned of an approaching storm.

Kevin had made his rounds—visited everyone he knew. He

had tweaked his résumé and mailed copies to every likely company, and plenty of unlikely ones, as well. For now, all he could do was make follow-up calls and wait to get some interviews. Meanwhile, he collected want ads for minimum wage jobs—a backup for when the unemployment checks ran out. His Plan B.

That folder of clippings frightened me. Kevin wasn't a Plan B kind of person. His enthusiasm and determination overcame any obstacle. He was slow to commit to a project, but once he did, nothing could stop him. For him to expect failure in his job search was completely out of character.

I doubled my efforts to be encouraging—and even managed not to offer suggestions. But nothing seemed to help Kevin's mood.

He wasn't used to being around the kids all day. He didn't know how to schedule phone calls to nap times or print letters when kids weren't nearby eating jam sandwiches. The daily mishaps familiar to me hit him hard. He didn't talk about his annoyance. He just smoldered like a peat fire.

The children began to tiptoe around him. Kevin no longer roared and chased them around the house unleashing a torrent of giggles. He spent hours on the computer searching for leads, while I tried to keep the kids entertained in the basement so they wouldn't bother him.

One afternoon, after a meager lunch that my husband ate in stony silence, I needed a break. When Kevin flopped on the couch with a library book about career changes, I grabbed my scarf and mittens. "Honey, after I drop Kelsey at preschool, I'm going to stop at Lori's for a while, okay?"

"Fine. Why not?" He slammed the book and tossed it aside.

I bounced Micah on my hip and looked down at Kevin. Discouragement I could understand. But something else brewed under the surface. I forced a smile. "Are you sure? I don't have to go if you need the car."

Cold, hard eyes rose to meet mine. "Why would I need it? Go."

"Mom." Kelsey tugged my coat.

I hovered in uncertainty. "Are you sure? Do you need anything?"

"I'm fine."

The indifferent dismissal hurt. I wanted to say something else, to bridge the cracking fault line between us. Instead, I watched the fissure deepen and backed away.

"All right." I adjusted the hood on Micah's snowsuit. "See you later."

I fled the house, wondering when it had become a place I ran from instead of the refuge I had always run toward.

Lori's home opened its arms to me. Abby lifted Micah from my grasp and carried him off to play. Lori poured me some tea—Constant Comment, with a hint of clove and orange—not the moss and weeds that Heather drank.

I settled in my favorite wing chair, the one Lori had rescued from a yard sale and restored. Lori was great at patching things up. Maybe she could help me with my marriage. She waited for me to open the conversation.

I sipped the tea and wondered where to start. "Kevin's been acting weird."

"Weird? Like thinking-he's-Napoleon weird? Or discouraged-because-job-hunting-is-hard-work weird?"

I managed a small grin. "Okay, I know he's having a hard time. Anyone would be. But it's more than that."

"Have you asked him about it?"

"He just says, 'I'm fine.'" My gruff impression was pretty accurate. "'Can you keep the kids quiet? No, nothing's bothering me. Stop nagging.'"

Lori raised her eyebrows.

I held up my hand. "No, I promise. I haven't been nagging anymore. I know I did that first week, but I backed off."

She nodded. "This has been hard on both of you. Does he have any leads?"

Her sympathy warmed me as much as the tea. I shook my head. "Maybe he's mad at me because I wasn't excited about moving to Grand Marais when he first mentioned it. He turned that job down because of me."

"But it was his choice, too. Didn't he say he believed God wanted him to trust?"

"So maybe he's mad at God."

"Maybe." Lori's face creased in concern. "Do you want to pray about it?"

"That would be great." My prayers lately had stumbled along with the same questions and pleas. Praying with a friend often helped me to focus, to look beyond the tight bubble of my needs and fears.

Lori dove right in. "Thank you, Father, for being sufficient for all our needs. Thank you for loving us. You are wise, and tender, and creative, and can solve every problem."

I nodded, already feeling some of the weight lift from my heart.

"Lord," Lori said, "I hold up my dear friend Becky. She needs your comfort today. She wants your direction. Give her grace to support Kevin in his struggles and wisdom to know how to respond."

We continued to pray, affirming our trust, asking for help, thanking God for being in control. We wound down and let healing silence hover around us.

Abby tiptoed into the room. "Sorry. I wanted to get your bag. Micah needs a new diaper."

I grabbed a tissue and blotted my eyes. "Oh, thank you. I left it by the door."

Lori waited while I blew my nose. "Better?"

I smiled. "Much. I didn't have a plan for this in my playbook, and it's left me feeling pretty shaky."

"God is still in control." Lori stood up and collected our empty mugs. "But I know it's hard. I wish you weren't going through this."

I followed her to the kitchen and admired the kids' art that she had framed and mounted on the wall. Abby's watercolor of a castle on a cliff evoked the sound of bagpipes.

Lori reached for a note pad. "Oh, I almost forgot. There's a great Christian support group for folks in a career change or job hunting. They meet at Faith Church in Woodbury." She scribbled down a phone number. "If Kevin's shutting you out, maybe he could open up to these guys. They're going through the same thing."

Driving home with Kelsey and Micah, my spirits stayed high. The time of prayer had strengthened me, and the slip of paper in my pocket gave me a tangible way to help.

Micah fell asleep in the car, so I carried him inside and eased him out of his snowsuit and into his crib. Kelsey held a finger to her lips as we tiptoed out of the room with exaggerated care.

Kevin wasn't in the living room or kitchen, so we trotted downstairs to find him.

The television blared, and Kevin didn't hear me walk up behind the old couch. He was twisting something around in his hands.

His old baseball trophy? Kevin wasn't usually nostalgic. His team won a tournament when he was twelve—a few months before his dad's fatal car accident. The trophy usually rested on the basement shelves, but I hadn't seen him look at it much in the past ten years of our marriage.

"Hi, we're home," I called over the game show host.

Kelsey ran past me and around the couch to show Kevin the picture she had colored at preschool.

He picked up the remote and the picture blinked out. "How's Lori?" His voice was flat with disinterest. He barely glanced at Kelsey's drawing.

"Good. It was nice to spend some time with her." I nodded at the trophy. "Remembering your glory days?"

My teasing didn't elicit a grin. He stood up and studied the inscription on the base. "Did I ever tell you my dad didn't make it to see me pitch in that tournament?" He held his body stiff and set his unshaven face into hard angles.

Kelsey jumped up and down on the couch behind him. "Daddy, Daddy, can we go to a movie?"

I ignored her capering, focusing on Kevin. "No. I thought his accident came later."

He nodded slowly, as if the pressure in his head hindered its movement. His knuckles turned white with his grip on the golden batter.

Why was he obsessing over a Little League trophy? He had been withdrawing from me more each day, and I didn't know how to reach him. Now fear melded with my confusion. This man was a stranger. How could I help him if I didn't even know him?

Kelsey kept bouncing and whining.

I pulled the note from my pocket. "Lori sent some info about a support group for job hunters—"

"Quit pushing me!"

I'd never heard him shout like that. Maybe on the basketball court. Never at me. My eyes widened and I took a step back, stuffing the note back in my pocket. "I'm sorry."

Instead of becoming remorseful, he grew angrier. "Do you think I'm not trying? Do you think—"

Kelsey tugged on his arm. "I wanna see a movie."

He whirled around—probably to scold her, but she was bouncing forward—and the trophy in his hand clocked her on the forehead. She fell back to the couch. Her stunned silence lasted two long seconds. Then she screamed such a full-throated scream I could see her tonsils.

Kevin backed away instead of reaching to comfort her.

I shoved past him and gathered Kelsey in my arms, murmuring standard soothing mom-speak. Still worried about Kevin, I looked over my shoulder. His face was gray, his eyes glazed. The trophy fell from his shaking hand and hit the floor with a thump.

"Shhh. Kelsey, it's okay." I was trying to reassure Kevin, as well.

"I knew it. I knew." Kevin's choked words were barely audible over Kelsey's crying. He turned and ran for the stairs.

I heard the side door in the kitchen slam. He had raced out so fast he couldn't have stopped to grab his coat. I frowned. We never ran out on each other when we had a disagreement. It was one of our rules for fighting fair.

I lifted Kelsey and headed for the stairs, still soothing her. "You have a little bump. I'll get you a bag of frozen peas for your forehead."

As I smoothed her stubby bangs away from the lump, my wedding ring flickered in the stairwell light. When Kevin and I married, I held my vow as solemn and permanent. We made a pledge to serve God together, and over the years we had formed a family. Our union was about more than just ourselves. Although love held us together most of the time, occasionally we needed to rely on loyalty and duty—on the words of our promise—as well. This was one of those times. I squared my jaw. Kevin could pace the backyard for a while and cool off. As soon as he came back in, we'd talk. I'd figure out how to help. I'd kiss away his owie, like I did for Kelsey.

When we reached the kitchen, I heard our car tear out of the driveway.

# TWENTY·THREE

*I held my breath* in awe. Liquid light
swirled and pulsed inside the round framework.

"If she changes anything—anything at all, it could
have a catastrophic effect." Dr. Burton nudged his glasses back
to the bridge of his nose and glared at my commander. "The world as
we know it may shift into something completely different. We might not
even exist."

Commander Green looked at me with stoic control. "She
knows."

I nodded. "Doc, there's no time for cold feet now. We need to find
the source of the virus."

He snorted. "Time is one thing we have. But you're right. The
machine is flawless." He scratched his head. "Unfortunately, people are
not so flawless."

The commander stiffened. "She knows what to do."

I tightened the belt on my jumpsuit and grabbed the harness of my
pack. Clothes, money, and maps for the time period. Dr. Burton claimed
his research was so accurate I would emerge just outside New York City
in precisely 1891.

The "super strain" that was decimating the United States could be
traced back to a mutation of a polio bug prevalent that year.

The doctor chewed on the end of his stylus. "Bring back more than
one sample."

I was impatient to dive through the portal of throbbing colors—the first human to ever travel back in time. *"Doc, I know. You've told me a thousand times."*

*Perhaps I sounded cavalier, but his constant worry was getting on my nerves. He treated me like a brainless lab assistant.*

*Commander Green snapped me a salute.*

*I faced the Time Tunnel—our affectionate nickname for the project, coined by one of the team who collected discs of old television shows. Before Doc Burton could start fussing again, I threw myself into the vortex. Going into the past was our only way of saving the future. Like streams of light, the very essence of time spiraled around me.*

Occasional headlights flickered past the living room window. From the vortex of my rocking chair, I could feel time flow past as I waited for the sound of the car—for Kevin to tiptoe in and explain why he was acting so weird. I hugged a throw pillow while I fought back tears. Minutes sludged by as I swayed forward and back, afraid and alone. Kevin was the person I usually turned to with my fears. Now he was the cause of them.

*Kevin, what's wrong? I know you're worried about finding a job. Do you still think I wouldn't want to move? I'll move to Timbuktu if it will chase that fear and pain off your face. And the temper. What's that all about? Have I done something wrong?*

Slowly my twisting thoughts untangled into prayer.

*Lord, show me how to love Kevin. Bring him home. Let him be okay. Please. Let him be okay.*

Long after midnight, the lock rattled at the side door. My heart double-thumped with middle-of-the-night fear of burglars until I heard Kevin's familiar sigh as he walked into the house. Tempted to jump up and run to him, I gripped the rocker instead, uncertain. I didn't want him to feel like I was pouncing on him.

He rattled around the kitchen for a minute, running the

faucet, setting a glass down with a soft clink. Then he came toward the living room.

He hovered in the doorway, backlit by the overflow light from the kitchen. "Becky?"

"I'm here." My voice was froggy from tears and exhaustion. "Are you okay?"

He sank onto the couch without turning on a light—a dark form hulking in the shadows. "Yeah. Look, I need to explain."

Relieved that he was home and willing to talk to me, I darted across the room and threw my arms around him. "I was so worried." I kissed him, squeezed him, and petted his cold skin, the way I had when I'd found Dylan after he'd once wandered off at the park.

"Glad to see you, too," he said wryly.

His humor eased the last of my fears. I kissed him again. "You're back."

He knew what I meant. "Yeah. I'm back."

"Let me get the light."

He fumbled for my arm in the darkness and stopped me. "No."

I sank next to him on the couch and leaned my head on his shoulder. Our position stirred memories of our first intimate talk on the bleachers back in college. The darkness all those years ago had helped him feel safe enough to open his heart. Maybe tonight's shadows would help him again.

After a long silence he tightened his arm around my shoulder. "See, my dad lost his job when I was a kid."

I made a sympathetic sound in my throat.

"He tried like crazy to find something. Times were tight. Mom ended up getting a job at the drugstore. It drove him nuts that she was the only one providing for us."

The sadness I felt for him threatened to overwhelm me.

"Oh, sweetie. No wonder this has been so hard on you."

"There's more." He coughed, his shoulders convulsing the way Dylan's did when he cried.

I reached up to grip his hand that rested on my shoulder. He was thawing from his mad race into the winter night, his skin slowly warming. "It's okay. You can tell me. I love you." I wasn't sure if he heard my low words.

"So he started drinking. It wasn't so bad at first. We figured he needed some comfort. Hanging out with his friends at the bar. But then he turned mean. He'd come home drunk and yell at my mom. Started to shove her around. Hit me." His words moved faster.

Cold horror filled me. Then anger rushed in that anyone had dared hurt this man I loved so much. I squeezed my lips together so an outburst from me wouldn't interrupt his story.

"One night he didn't come home. The police came to the door about three in the morning. I heard my mom talking with them. He'd been drinking and took a turn too fast. Hit a tree and—"

He cleared his throat. "I decided right then I'd never be like my dad." He stopped as if that explained everything.

Why hadn't he told me before? Why had he rewritten his past? I squeezed his hand. "But you're not like that."

He rested his head against the top of mine. "But Dad wasn't, either. I remember playing catch in the backyard. He used to come to all my games. He laughed. He would swing my mom around the kitchen. Until he lost his job."

The pieces fell together. "So you were scared you'd change. Like him?"

His silence answered me.

Words of reassurance chased around my brain. I chose them carefully. "Kevin, listen to me. You are the same wonderful man I married. You aren't your dad. You've never—"

"I hit Kelsey."

"That was an accident. She's fine."

"And I was so mad. I yelled at you . . . and . . . it was like . . . All of a sudden, I knew how my dad felt back then." Next to me, his body tensed again.

I wanted to chase away his fears—the monster rattling in the closet. When Kelsey was afraid, we got out a mister of water we called "Monster Repellent" and sprayed it around her room. Kevin's dark fears would require more ammunition.

*Lord, help me know what to say. Help him. He's hurting so much.*

I nestled closer to him, hoping he would feel my trust and love for him. "Shhh. You're frustrated. So you got mad. Who wouldn't? I forgive you."

He shook his head, and we sat in silence. The furnace kicked in with a soft whirr. Ice clattered in the freezer's ice maker. A car swooshed past on the snowy street. In time, Kevin's tight muscles eased. We leaned back against the couch, and I pulled my legs under me to curl up against him with a contented sigh.

Kevin let his breath out with a huff. "Do you know where I went?"

Drowsy, and relieved he was home, I managed a non-committal murmur.

He moved his hand off my shoulder to finger my hair. "I drove to a bar."

I sat up and stared at him. "But you don't drink." With my parents' history of addictions and the chaos we'd seen in some of our friends' lives during college, we had decided to avoid alcohol.

In the gray hint of light from the kitchen, he gave a sheepish wince. "Like I said. I started to understand my dad."

"So you were going to follow in his footsteps?"

"Something like that. I figured it was inevitable anyway."

I shook my head, bewildered. "What happened? You don't sound drunk."

He gave a short laugh. "I sat in the parking lot, feeling like my head was going to explode. And I started telling my dad what he'd done to me . . . how mad . . . how terrified I was to be like him. And somehow, the conversation changed and I was talking to God." He looked away. "You know?" he said softly.

"I know." I wrapped my arms around him. "I'm glad you guys had a chat. I've been worried about you."

He shifted. "Yeah. Sorry." He shoved up from the couch and offered me a hand. "Come on, let's get some sleep."

Kevin had stretched way past his usual limit for serious conversation. I wanted to ask him about his prayer time—what secret intimacies had passed between him and God in the foggy interior of our old car, parked behind a bar. But more probing would leave him feeling overexposed and awkward. Maybe he'd tell me more one day. I took his hand. "I love you."

We leaned against each other for support as we walked down the hall. My mind swirled with the revelations about his past. Family had a way of coming back to haunt us, even when we reinvented our past and ourselves.

I thought of Judy. She and I seemed trapped in the competition begun by my overachieving dad. She chased the elusive dream. I struggled with jealousy and insecurity. No wonder tension mounted every time we were together. Maybe if we ventured back in time—talked about our childhood and memories—we could spray away some of the monsters between us.

Kevin and I nestled together under the quilt, exhausted by the trauma of the evening. I reached out to find his hand under his pillow and wrapped his fingers with mine. "Are you okay now?"

"Well, I still don't have a job." A tinge of humor warmed his voice. "But, yeah, I'm okay."

My eyes closed in relief, and I was almost asleep when I heard him sigh.

"Thanks," he said.

To me? To God? I wasn't sure. But I feel asleep content.


Judy blew into our lives the next day. I was thankful Kevin had returned to his genial enthusiasm for life. He greeted her with a bear hug. "How's my favorite sister-in-law?"

She grinned. "I'm your only sister-in-law."

Their traditional greeting. The familiarity of the exchange comforted me after the stress of the past weeks. I wiped frosting off my hands and ran to hug her. "Want to decorate some gingerbread men?"

The kids' Christmas vacation had started, and we were making good use of the time.

She smirked. "Betcha I can make a cuter one than you."

For once her competitive spark didn't hurt me. "You're on. Loser makes the cocoa."

She tossed her coat toward Kevin, and we ran to the kitchen giggling like Dylan and Kelsey.

An hour later, the kitchen was splattered with dough and smelled spicy and a little burnt—from forgetting to set the timer on one cookie sheet. Judy's prize cookie wore a stylish business suit with silver bead buttons and a lovely blond hairstyle. I gladly conceded her win. Besides, I wasn't sure if she could make cocoa anyway. We settled at the kitchen table with our mugs. The kids, sated with gingerbread and pilfered marshmallows, headed downstairs to play.

Kevin came in and tossed an armful of mail on the table.

"Looks like more Christmas cards. I've gotta run some errands; see you later."

I smirked. "Hmm . . . it couldn't be a little Christmas shopping, could it? It's way too early for you to be thinking about that. Christmas Eve isn't until tomorrow."

He winked at Judy. "Keep her in line, would you? I have to shop at the last minute. Otherwise she messes up the garage with her snooping."

He charged out the door, a man on a mission, and I stared after him with a grin stuck on my face.

Judy shuffled through the mail. "Ooh, this looks good. Mind if I read it?"

I turned back. Another shiny face taunted me from the glossy magazine she held up. I moaned. "Oh, no! They're sending me issues."

"'*Women of Vision*. The monthly magazine for successful women of the Twin Cities.' Good for you, sis. You should read more of this kind of stuff."

"No, no, no. You don't understand. They're going to feature me in April. I was trying to forget."

She slapped the magazine down. "What? Beck, this is great."

"No it's not." I pointed to the cover. "Look at her."

Judy scrutinized the cover woman then did a quick scan of my hairstyle (unflattering), makeup (nonexistent), and fashion sense (regrettable). I saw her trying to think fast. Then she tapped a manicured nail against her brilliant front teeth. "They can fix all that with a little airbrushing."

"Thanks a lot." I pulled a jelly bean from my cookie's tummy and threw it at her. "But that's not the worst. I have to make my life sound inspiring. These women all have hot-shot jobs."

"Hey, don't fuss. It says this lady is a stay-at-home mom."

"Really?" Hope flared. I grabbed the magazine from Judy and flipped pages to find the article. I found another photo of the featured woman and read the caption. "Great. Just great. Says here that she and her husband have adopted ten special-needs children."

I shoved the magazine back to Judy. "This is hopeless. My life is so ordinary next to everyone else."

She snorted into her cocoa. "Oh, come on. Play the religion angle. Sweet Mrs. Church Lady, taking care of everybody."

I rolled my eyes and bit into my cookie with a pout. "It's going to be a pretty short and boring article."

Judy tossed aside any concern for me along with the magazine. She looked at the kids' art on the refrigerator. "I've been thinking about Christmas when we were kids," I said.

Judy breathed in her cocoa and relaxed in her chair.

How had she kept her wool skirt and tailored blouse spotless? My country-snowman sweater was dabbed with every shade of frosting. I took a slow sip of my drink. "Dad was gone for a lot of them."

Judy's brows drew together. "You're right. I'd forgotten that." She ran a finger around the rim of her mug. "He sure loved his work."

"Or loved *to* work. He never slowed down."

Judy grinned as if that were a good thing. "Yeah, and you're a lot like him."

"Me?" I choked on my marshmallow. "You've got us confused. Me: boring housewife. You: corporate giant."

She handed me a paper napkin. "But you push yourself just like he did. You work all the time. Being the best wife and best mom. Creating a cozy home." Her nose wrinkled as she took in my stenciling work along the top of the walls. "That stuff you did at your church. You remind me of him."

Horror widened my eyes.

Judy laughed. "Sis, it's a good thing. Sometimes I think I'm more like Mom."

"No way. She was—"

"Remote. Distant. Lonely."

An unwelcome surge of old hurts shot through me. "She was an addict."

Judy lifted her shoulders. "She popped a few pills and drank. Her way to cope. I work eighteen-hour days for the same reason." A rare glimpse of genuine pain flickered across her face.

Tenderness prompted my hand to reach for hers. "I don't want you to feel lonely, Judifer—to rush through life so you can shut out everything."

She squeezed my hand. "Thanks, sis." She pulled back and sniffed. "But don't you start preaching at me now."

Hours of prayer had prepared me for this moment. I knew when to ease off. I pushed back my chair. "Come see our tree."

She followed me to the living room and bit her lip as she examined our decorations. She assessed the ornaments the kids made. Juice lids, tin foil, yarn, Styrofoam balls, and glitter. "Cute." Her eyes dropped lower. "You've only got a couple presents under here. Did you hide the rest?"

I took a steadying breath, pushing back the shame that wanted to knock me over. "We're keeping things simple this year. You know. Kevin's still job hunting, so things are a little tight."

She brushed aside the embarrassing moment and slipped into snipe mode. "And what's with that wrapping paper?"

I slapped her arm. "Hey, it's pretty." I'd cut up grocery bags and used the brown paper. Stamped with an ivy rubber stamp and dark green ink, tied with raffia, the packages had a rustic elegance.

"Good thing I brought a few gifts."

Once she unpacked, our humble tree would be surrounded by piles of glittering boxes. So much for our simple approach. Oh well. The kids would love it. I just wished I could be the one providing some of the glitz.

Kelsey clumped up the stairs in cowboy boots from the dress-up box. She raced to Aunt Judy for a hug.

Judy knelt awkwardly on her stiletto boots and returned the embrace. "So what's the schedule, sis? When do we open presents?" She tickled Kelsey.

My daughter giggled and raced around the room. "Presents! Presents!"

I caught her and plopped onto the couch, holding her in my lap. "The candlelight service for Christmas Eve is tomorrow at 7:00 P.M." I smiled in anticipation. "When we get home, we let the kids open one present each. Christmas morning they get to open their stockings before we go to church. When we get home we open the rest and have a feast."

Judy pursed her lips. I could see her fight back words. She surrendered to the impulse. "What's with your obsession with church? We never did that when we were growing up. Can't we do it like we did when we were kids?"

Kelsey turned a puzzled face to me.

I bristled, ready to remind Judy what childhood Christmases had really been like. Dad calling from some faraway city to deliver a distracted greeting. Mom slapping two TV dinners on the table for us and retreating to her bedroom. But I remembered the glimpse of honesty that Judy had showed me in the kitchen.

"I hope you'll come with us. I think you'll like it." No

pressure. No tossing guilt grenades at her. Only a quiet invitation.

Judy rolled her eyes and strode from the room to unpack.

Kelsey slithered from my lap and ran behind her to help.

I stared at our tree. Was I really like Dad? Driven to excel? Was Judy as lonely and lost as my mom? Traveling back in time was a tricky maneuver. It had seemed to help Kevin to delve into the past. But memories could distort and blur like an eddy of colored lights. Could Judy and I ever find common ground in our past, so we could have a better friendship in our future?

# TWENTY·FOUR

*Complete precision* helped me as I
reached into a back walkover. Midway through the
movement I paused in a handstand, demonstrating perfect
balance. As I finished the move, I slid into splits. The beam
beneath me felt smooth and familiar. When I leaned forward I could
smell years of chalk and sweat permeating the wood.

Some competitors hate the beam. I love it. My scores had blitzed past
everyone else's at the Olympic trials. Balance beam was the ultimate test.

My right wrist throbbed from jamming my hand on a tough vault
four days earlier. My shins wore bruises from small mishaps on the uneven parallel bars. I shut out the pain. Launching through the air was
as exhilarating as flying. It was flying.

Today at the Olympics, years of training assisted me. I blocked out the
cheers from the crowd as one of the Romanians landed her vault. I ignored
the music from the floor exercise and the pounding of blood in my ears.

I flung my body into a breathtaking series of back handsprings.
Momentum rocketed me from the end of the beam. I twisted and flipped,
spotting the floor. Force jarred through my ankles on the landing. I
coached my knees to absorb the shock as I found my placement. Joy
exploded through me when I straightened without adjusting either foot.
A perfect landing.

I ran off the platform and hugged my coach. We turned to watch the
scores come up on the board. Our team needed every fraction of a point
to pull ahead. My routine had been flawless and phenomenal. I'd introduced new elements of risk and skill no one had seen before.

*Our team gathered among our warm-up gear and water bottles, eyes straining at the board. Had my efforts been enough? I studied the judges' faces, hoping for a clue.*

Judy's face didn't reveal a thing. I studied her expression and quickly looked back down at my hymnal. "O Holy Night." The congregation strained on the high notes, and the violin whined slightly off key. Our church pulled out all the stops at Christmas. A flute for the prelude, the violin on the first hymn, and even a Celtic harp for one song. Enthusiasm outweighed skill, but it was still a moving service.

When the children had begged and pleaded, Judy had agreed to come. But she wasn't looking very happy about it. We sat in a pew near the front—Judy on one side of me and Kevin on the other—because the children had a part in the service. I also hoped it would keep Judy from skedaddling.

She shifted in the pew, craning her neck to study the surroundings as if she were at a sporting event.

*Lord, let something soak in. The reading of Scripture, the songs, the children's brief pageant, the sermon. Anything. Help Judy see you tonight.*

Judging from the bored expression on her face, she wasn't absorbing much.

Pastor asked the preschoolers to come forward. Kelsey squeezed past Judy and skipped to the front. About fifteen little ones turned to stare out at the congregation. One boy picked his nose. A girl pulled her skirt up, showing off her white tights. Kelsey waved at us, eliciting giggles from a few parents.

The piano banged out their introduction and the children launched into "Away in a Manger" with choreographed arm gestures reminiscent of synchronized swimmers.

Next the older children enacted the Nativity, waved forward by Sally, who directed from the side. Dylan proudly carried a spray-painted shoebox embellished with glitter to the manger. His tinfoil crown slipped over one eye, but he still maintained a somber dignity as he knelt and presented his gift.

No one dared suggest to Sally that the wise men didn't arrive the same night as the shepherds. She had directed this pageant for years, with the fervor of a Romanian gymnastics coach.

Smiles and sighs around the church proved that her approach was effective, if not always historically accurate.

Judy pulled out a nail file during the sermon. I kicked her and gave her the small shake of the head usually reserved for when Dylan folded paper airplanes out of the bulletin. She rolled her eyes and rummaged for something else to entertain herself. She pulled her PDA from the purse and raised a questioning brow again.

I gave a vehement shake of my head. What did she think she was going to do? Play Tetris? Or make notes for herself about the stock option report for the next committee meeting?

She scowled and sank back against the pew. My prayers took a sharp left turn.

*Lord, let us get through this service and back home without Judy doing something completely embarrassing.*

"Silent Night" provided a stirring end to the service—until Kelsey pierced the stillness of the last fading chord by shouting, "I'm hungry. When's supper?"

Beet red, I edged my brood toward the side aisle, hoping to escape without more mishaps.

"Becky," Heather called from several rows back.

The women from my Bible study raced to the front of the church like salmon swimming upstream against the current of parishioners leaving.

My stomach did a flip-flop. They'd all heard about Judy and prayed for her. Would they drop some clunkers? "Judy! So nice to meet Becky's heathen sister." Or "We've heard all about you and the bad influence you have on your niece and nephew."

Instead, they surrounded us with unabashed warmth, eager to welcome Judy. Doreen showed particular enthusiasm. Her parents had flown in to town for the holidays, and they watched her children near the back of the church. She introduced herself to my sister.

As I watched Doreen and Judy chat, remarkable similarities emerged. Both had sleek flawless hair—Doreen's auburn and Judy's blond. Both wore elegant black dresses and tasteful silver jewelry. I wore a rolled-paper-bead necklace Dylan made at school. At least his teacher wasn't obsessed with food art. I could be wearing Fruit Loops.

Lori pulled Kevin aside. I overheard her ask about his job search. He answered cheerfully and entered an earnest conversation.

I was boggled. Why was he so comfortable talking about the tough subject with her? I turned back to rescue Judy.

"So our profits are up," Judy said. "But middle management is a mess."

Doreen gestured with excitement, her red nails flicking like sparklers. "I know exactly what you mean. I climbed the corporate ladder in the fashion industry, and we had the same problems."

Judy's face lit with pleasure. Their discussion ramped up to the high bar as they babbled an insider language I couldn't follow.

Heather handed me a block wrapped in tulle. "Merry Christmas. I made you a special lemon and lavender soap. Lemon stimulates and lavender soothes."

So would it make me restless and sleepy at the same time?

She joined hands with her girls and they snaked their way across the front of the church. I thought for a moment I saw Heather skip, and rubbed my eyes.

The rest of the congregation cleared out, but our group kept talking. "I need to get Micah from the nursery," I said in Kevin's general direction.

Kevin nodded in acknowledgment then turned to help Sally take apart the manger scene. Judy ignored me. She and Doreen had moved on to the topic of men. Kindred spirits on this issue, they filleted the whole gender up one side and down the other. I hoped Kevin wasn't listening.

By the time we got home, I was wound as tight as Dylan's pull-back-and-zoom race cars. I braced myself for Judy's attack. For the hurtful scoffing.

She settled into my favorite chair and crossed her long legs. "I like your friends. They aren't what I expected."

I hung up my coat and came to sit near her, confused. "Really?"

"Yeah. I figured they'd all be glum and disapproving."

"Oh. Like me."

She laughed. "Something like that. But you aren't glum. Just a little . . . puritanical. Or else I thought they'd be shiny Barbie Christians with big plastic smiles."

I found that ironic, coming from the queen Barbie doll supplier. "Did you like the church service?"

Judy checked to see that Dylan and Kelsey were busy rattling packages under the tree and not listening. "Boooring. I don't get what you see in it. But I was really surprised. That one hippie lady . . ."

"Heather?"

"Yeah. I didn't think Christians could be . . . well . . . so different."

I smiled. "She's different all right."

"And Doreen. How cool was that? We have so much in common."

"I've noticed the resemblance before," I said dryly.

"Of course, I told her to sue the creep for every penny he's got. She said it's more important to forgive him." Judy shrugged. "Other than that she's as smart as they come."

Did Judy think all Christians were idiots? "Of course she's smart. And Heather's creative, and Lori is involved in a bunch of political causes, and Sally—well, Sally is Sally. They've all supported us in tons of different ways this past month."

Judy set aside her faux sophistication and met my eyes. "I'm happy for you. It's got to be great having friends like that. I don't really have friends; I have networks." She examined a long fingernail, and her superiority slipped back on like a silk robe. "Of course, you have to make some sacrifices if you want to be on top."

A feral excitement built inside me. I was ready to vault forward. To capture my sister for the kingdom. I could tell her that Jesus would be her true friend. I could tell her about the wonderful fellowship possible among flawed but loving Christians. I could tell her all her sacrifices were winning her a prize that wouldn't satisfy.

Dylan exploded out from under the tree with a huge box. He charged over to me and launched into my lap. Even in second grade, he was still cuddly sometimes. He rattled the box. "I pick this one."

I was grateful he still let me hold him, but now that his baby fat had melted off, he had a bony backside.

He squirmed. "Can I open it now?"

"No. Me first!" Kelsey jumped up and bumped the tree.

Kevin grabbed it before it could fall over. "First we share our gifts with Jesus."

Judy gave a long-suffering sigh. "Didn't church count?" she muttered.

Kelsey dropped her box and spun in a circle. "Me first."

I squeezed Dylan to keep him from arguing. "Okay, honey. Go ahead."

She sobered and drew herself up with the intensity of a diva. "Daddy, you have to sing the song."

They'd obviously rehearsed, because he didn't have to ask "What song?" He began singing "Angels We Have Heard on High."

Kelsey stopped him. "Wait. I wasn't ready." She repositioned herself, and he started again, his rich tenor voice filling the room. Kelsey moved to the music, performing an interpretive dance that would have made Martha Graham weep—from joy or horror, I wasn't sure which.

As angels sweetly sang over the plain, she flapped her arms and ran on tiptoe back and forth across the living room. During the *gloria*s she turned lopsided somersaults. I wasn't sure how her gymnastic moves depicted the celebration of an angel choir, but I decided it was appropriate. God turned the world upside down on Christmas.

Even Judy added to our enthusiastic applause. Dylan wriggled off my lap and stood stiffly in front of the tree. His white church shirt hitched out of his pants on one side. The knees of his dark trousers sported dust from crawling under pews with Doreen's son Josh. Yet he carried a somber dignity as he stuffed his hands into his pockets and cleared his throat. He'd been working for several weeks on the gift he wanted to share with baby Jesus. He recited the angel's proclamation to the shepherds. When he reached the sentence about hosts of angels singing "Glory to God in the highest," Kelsey dashed forward to start somersaults again.

Dylan glared at her. "Mom, tell her to stop. It's my turn."

Kevin pulled Kelsey back and shushed her wails. Dylan started over.

I glanced sideways at Judy and saw her shoulders shaking. But she kept an admirably straight face.

When it was Kevin's turn, he pulled out a wooden toy—a "Jacob's ladder" with a small character that "walked" down the ladder, and when it was turned upside down, walked back to the beginning. "I made this for Jesus."

"How are you going to get that to Jesus?" Dylan asked.

Kelsey shoved him. "Silly. The angels do it."

Kevin sat down on the floor and gathered the kids closer.

"I'm giving it to Peter Henrick. He's really sick."

The kids nodded. The Sunday school had made cards for Peter one week.

Dylan frowned. "But you're supposed to give the present to Jesus."

Kevin moved the toy out of reach of grasping fingers. "I am. Jesus said that whatever we do for other people, we are doing for Him."

Impatient to open their one Christmas Eve choice, they dropped the subject and turned to me.

"My special gift to Jesus this year is the Christmas retreat I didn't go to."

"*Mom*," Dylan moaned. "That's not a present."

Kevin got up and came to sit by me on the coach. He wrapped an arm around me and gave me the smile that could still make me melt. "You're wrong. It was a very big present."

Christmas passed in a happy haze. I released any stray regrets for missing a great job opportunity. If I'd gone to Chicago, I couldn't have introduced Judy to my friends. They had done more to open her eyes about what it meant to be a Christian than I had been able to accomplish in ten years.

I needed God to help me find the center of the beam—not ignoring or hiding the faith that was my reason for being, but not hitting Judy over the head with it, either. For once, I had seemed to find the balance.

Christmas might not have scored a perfect ten, but it came close.

The next day, when Judy prepared to head to the airport, she gave me a brisk hug. "Do a good job on that magazine interview. I can't wait to read it."

"Yeah, no problem." She zipped out the door, and I closed it behind her. Then I softly banged my forehead against the wood again and again.

## TWENTY FIVE

**"Your Honor, please** direct the defendant to answer the question." The prosecutor stomped past the jury box and glared at me. When he leaned closer, his breath smelled of onions. "Did you refuse to give full information to the police?"

I swallowed hard, struggling to find words. "Yes. I mean, no. It's not exactly—"

"Mrs. Miller," the judge cut in, "do you need to hear the question again?" He slowed his words as if I were a remedial student. Someone in the back of the courtroom giggled at his mocking tone.

I stiffened my spine. "No, I understand the question. It's just not a simple answer. I need to explain. . . ."

"Your Honor," the prosecutor protested, "I fear this woman's stubbornness will keep us here for days." He winked toward the jury. "And some of us have lives to get back to."

I felt my face burn. "Yes. All right? Yes. But—"

The prosecutor looked at me as if I were gum on his shoe. "So you admit your report was incomplete."

I glanced at the jury, searching for compassion in their eyes. Twelve faces conveyed varying degrees of disgust. An elderly woman shook her head and turned away with a sigh. One man in a business suit frowned at me then looked down to scribble some notes.

I dropped my chin. "I'm sorry. It's just I didn't—"

"Louder, Mrs. Miller," the judge admonished.

I cleared my throat and turned toward my defense attorney, but she *was filing her nails and grinning at something her assistant was whispering in her ear. Tension and panic sparred in my stomach. No one understood.*

"You see, my son has been sick, and my husband . . . Well, never mind. I was waiting to find out about a new career direction, and then—"

Stephanie Maxwell's impatient voice on the phone cut in again. "I understand. But I need to get the general slant of the story, and your questionnaire didn't give me much to work with."

Why was I even bothering to solicit sympathy? The *Women of Vision* journalist sounded young, energetic, and organized. She'd been badgering me with questions, trying to fill in gaps from the forms I'd mailed back to her. All I wanted to do was drop the phone and run away. Besides, it was Sunday afternoon. Didn't she know she wasn't supposed to be working?

"At any rate"—she obviously had no intention of losing control of the conversation—"with each featured woman, I shadow them so I can really enter their world. It's time for me to come out and spend a few hours with you."

"What?" Surprise raised my voice two octaves.

Dylan heard my shriek and barreled into the kitchen. "Did you see a bug?" He galloped around me, tugging my arm. "Where is it, Mom?"

I waved him off with one hand, my other knuckles turning white around the phone. "But I'm not in the issue until April."

"Mrs. Miller"—Stephanie pushed her words out, as if her teeth were clenched—"the feature articles need to be finished well in advance of release date. How is tomorrow?"

I could imagine the notes she had jotted in my file. "Uncooperative. Evasive." And I was supposed to be making a good impression. Time to play along.

Trying for casual, I gave a trilling laugh. It came out

somewhat maniacal. "That would be lovely. I'll look forward to meeting you."

I hung up the phone and dropped my head onto the kitchen desk. My forehead hit the computer keyboard, sending a string of *y*'s across the screen. Why, indeed. Why had I agreed to have the inadequacies of my life examined by an outsider and reported in a public forum? This was a nightmare.

"Mom, where's the bug?" Dylan poked me, holding up a big jar full of various decaying insects. "I need it for my collection."

I lashed the family with my panic for the rest of the day. A blitz of cleaning did little to soothe me, but I did make the bathroom shine. *Ms. "Women of Vision" Maxwell just better need to use it, after all this work.* I even pulled out some decorative hand towels stored under the sink. I was desperate enough to try anything to bring some style to our household. Kevin talked me out of rearranging all the furniture, but I did dig out pillar candles to set around the living room. Micah got ahold of one and chewed it, but the tooth marks only showed if you looked closely.

An afternoon of frenzied cleaning left everyone cranky, and my adrenaline finally burned off, leaving me with tired despair. Kevin and I tucked all the kids in, letting them listen to quiet worship tapes as they fell asleep. I hoped the peaceful music would counteract all the shrill commands and scolds I'd filled the air with all day.

"What am I going to wear tomorrow?" I stared into my closet.

Kevin collapsed onto the bed with a groan. "Anything. You always look good."

"And what should I make for supper? I don't think macaroni and cheese will impress her."

He sprang up, grabbed my waist, and pulled me away from my closet and away from my obsessions. "Honey, it'll be fine."

We tumbled onto the bed together. "Just be yourself."

I crawled across him to my side of the bed and burrowed under the covers. "Yeah, right. That's what all the successful women of the Twin Cities want to read about."

"Oh, I don't know. I bet they get tired of reading about nuclear physicists and mountain climbers." Kevin slid under the quilt and wrapped warm arms around me. "You'll be a refreshing change of pace."

I was too tired to think of a good verbal reply, but my very cold foot found his calf and elicited a satisfying yelp.

Monday morning, Dylan's bus carried him down snowy streets right before Stephanie Maxwell's car pulled into our driveway. Kevin jogged out to meet her and asked her to move the car so he could pull out.

Once our wagon was idling by the curb, her Miata slipped gracefully up the drive. Instead of coming back to the house, Kevin waved at me from his car door. "Have a good day. See you at supper. Love ya." Then he jumped into the car and skidded away, far too eager for his day of job hunting. When I'd asked if he would be around at all during Stephanie's visit, he had rattled off a long list of places he needed to follow up with now that the holidays were over. I couldn't prove it, but my guess was half of those companies didn't exist. He just didn't want to be anywhere near the line of fire.

I pasted on my best Susie Homemaker smile and welcomed Stephanie into our house. Her rich brown bob almost matched her leather jacket. She was a sleek and intimidating twenty-something.

I had dressed to the nines that morning, too. But now my best sweater was in the laundry hamper. Micah had vomited all over it right after breakfast. Not decorous, little-baby spit up, either. Unintentionally, I was following Kevin's advice and being myself, in my comfy old sweat shirt and jeans.

I ushered our guest into the hall with Micah wedged on my hip. He rested against my shoulder, sucking his middle finger. We'd tried to steer him toward his thumb, but he found more comfort in the middle finger. The problem came when he pulled it out.

Kelsey trotted into the kitchen, clutching a fistful of toy horses. "Wanna play?" She offered Stephanie a palomino with an unevenly cropped mane and no tail. Not exactly Emily Post manners, but at least she was sharing.

Stephanie handed me her coat and looked down at Kelsey. "Maybe later. I need to talk to your mommy."

Before I could officially welcome the woman, the phone rang. "I'll let the machine get it," I tossed over my shoulder as I struggled to hang up her coat with one hand.

"No, go ahead. I want to watch your typical day play out. We can talk later."

Dodging Kelsey, I raced across the kitchen to the phone.

"Hello?" I nabbed the phone right before the machine kicked in. Micah wriggled down my leg and crawled to the narrow cupboard where I stored cookie sheets. I kept one eye on him and one on Stephanie, who had perched on a kitchen chair and opened a notebook. The scratching of her pen terrified me.

"Hi, Becky." Doreen's voice trembled. "Are you busy?"

"Not at all. What's wrong?"

"Nothing new. It's just one of those days. It's all crashing in."

Micah provided sound effects by caber-tossing a cookie sheet onto the linoleum. I angled away from the noise and turned my back on Stephanie.

"Tell me." I put every ounce of "I care about you" into those words. Then I listened hard as Doreen processed some of the hurt and anger threatening to overwhelm her.

When she wound down, she asked with a catch in her throat, "Could you pray for me?"

"Let me pray now, so I don't forget." I lowered my voice, feeling awkward with a stranger at my table. "Lord, thank you for Doreen and the wonderful person you've created her to be. Remind her that she's precious. Give her strength today—strength to forgive again and again. Give her some little blessings to sustain her."

I would have said more, but a strange sound caught my attention from the middle of the kitchen. "Oops. Amen. Doreen, I've gotta go. Micah just threw up."

I dropped the phone, grabbed the paper towels, and raced to Micah.

When I glanced back at Stephanie, she had stopped writing and her nose was wrinkled. She pointed to the mess on the floor and Micah's overalls. "Mrs. Miller, why is his vomit purple?"

Things never really improved from there.

I assured Stephanie that it was medicine, not a strange diet that made Micah so colorful. Then I disappeared to clean him up and get him into a fresh outfit. I started a load of laundry, praying our washer wouldn't throw a tantrum.

After a heart-wrenching crying jag, Micah settled down for his morning nap and Kelsey disappeared to watch *Sesame Street*. I poured coffee for my guest and tried to muster some warm feelings for her. After all, this was my chance to share a glimpse into the life of a Christian mom for a readership like my sister, Judy, who might assume we were all frumpy, grumpy, and lumpy.

But as Stephanie badgered me, I wished for a defense attorney to jump up and object to the line of questioning.

"What's your typical day's schedule?"

I'm sure she thought it was an easy question. "Um. Well . . . that's the thing. There is no typical day. I get everyone up and dressed and Dylan leaves for school. On Tuesdays and Thursdays

Kelsey has preschool in the afternoon, and Micah and I run errands. Except now when Kevin needs the car for interviews." I continued rattling off the weekly and biweekly events at church and school. "And then there's my Thursday night Bible study."

Stephanie's eyes began to glaze. "So when do you work? On the application your friend said you're a leader at your church. Why don't you tell me about that?"

I squirmed, wondering how to explain. I stammered a few things about the programs I'd developed. "But now they're hiring a full-time staff person to take over that role, so I'm not over there as often for meetings and things."

She gave a matter-of-fact nod, as if there was nothing humiliating about the church's decision, and I stopped chewing on my thumbnail and relaxed a bit.

"And what are your goals and dreams now?"

My answer blurted out from the place of deep longing inside me, before I could stop myself. "I want to do Big Things for God."

Her pen stopped moving, and she raised an eyebrow. "And what would that look like?"

I was saved by the doorbell. Charity and Grace were tromping through the neighborhood helping Heather sell granola to raise money for the clinic. Heather waved from the sled she was pulling along the sidewalk, then stopped to make a snow angel in our front yard while I bought a large sack of "Peanut-Butter Soynut Surprise" from the girls, not wanting to know what the surprise might be.

After they left, Micah squawked from his crib. He felt warm again and was tugging his ear, so I sank into my rocking chair to give him a comfort nursing. Kelsey scattered Tinkertoys at our feet and sang to herself. Stephanie settled on the couch with her notebook to continue her interrogation.

Our conversation was interrupted by more phone calls, but I did my best to describe my life to the reporter.

When she asked about my daily goals, I thought of the accomplished women in her magazine and sighed. "I used to have a list to follow, but my life doesn't work that way. Things come up. I have to change directions."

"But if you haven't delineated your specific goals, how do you measure your success?"

I felt the jury of modern-day culture glaring at me in disgust. Shamed, I stared at the floor. "I guess I'm not a success. I'm just really ordinary."

Somewhere I heard a gavel crash.

# TWENTY·SIX

*My pager vibrated* against my hip.
"I'll be back to check on you later, okay?" I
smoothed bangs from the clammy forehead of a ten-year-old
girl and scribbled a note in her chart.

The girl managed a weak grin. Her parents watched my every move
with worried eyes. I offered a few words of reassurance and then hurried
down the hall, checking my pager on the fly. Red numbers flamed from
the small device.

I skipped the poky elevators and slammed the stairwell door open.
My jog down five flights took me to the ER in record time. The trauma
center screeched with lightning-fast action.

One of the nurses called to me. "They're just bringing him in.
Three years old. Traffic accident. No car seat."

I trotted to the end of the hall. The paramedics pushed a gurney in
from the ambulance bay with firm strides. In smooth concert, they transferred the tiny boy onto the exam table. One of the men untangled an
IV line and hooked the bag onto the waiting stand. The other turned to
me with his clipboard. No wasted motion. No wasted words.

"Pulse ninety. BP ninety over forty. Looks shocky. Head trauma
and lacerations. Complained of stomach pain before he lost consciousness." He tore off his assessment sheet and handed it to me.

My brain raced, organizing priorities. "Parents?"

The paramedic jerked his head toward the waiting room. "The mom
was with him. Shook up, but no major injuries. We steered her out there
for now."

*I nodded my thanks to the rescue team, and they disappeared as smoothly as they had arrived. I spared a quick glance at one of the nurses. "Get consent."*

*She ran to grab the forms from the station and headed out to the mom. We needed a parent signature if we went ahead with emergency surgery.*

"I think this is an emergency."

Kevin pinched the bridge of his nose, resting his elbows on the kitchen table. "Honey, I'm worried about it, too. But we can't afford the surgery right now. I might have a new job in another week or two."

"Or you might not." I stroked his arm to soften my words. "You heard the doctor. Micah can't keep going through this. And the audiologist said we should do it as soon as possible."

My chaotic visit with Stephanie Maxwell had been cut short by another flare-up of Micah's earaches. She made her escape, and over the wails of my miserable baby, she promised to call me to finish our interview another day.

Kevin and I had spent another night pacing the floor and a long afternoon at the clinic. Now we both slumped at our table, searching for a solution.

Micah whimpered from his infant seat. We had carried the removable chair in from the car. Micah seemed to rest more comfortably propped up rather than lying down.

I left Kevin to puzzle over the piles of insurance paper work and ran to get the baby Tylenol.

Micah was too miserable to fight me. Kevin was just as miserable but still had a lot of fight left in him. "I've managed to keep paying our major medical, but the deductible is too high. We'd be covering most of the operation ourselves. And we can't. We just can't."

I poured Kevin a cup of tea. He took a sip and winced.

Guess my frugal inspiration to reuse the tea bags several times wasn't such a good idea.

I sat down and pulled Micah's baby carrier closer to the table, rocking it with my foot so he would doze off. "Kev, I have an idea."

He pushed his chair back, folded his arms, and narrowed his eyes.

Not an encouraging start. "Okay, don't say anything until I finish." I waited for his slow, single nod. "SuperAmerica is hiring for the night shift. I figured I could work there for a while, just to help out. You could watch the kids while I'm at work, and its close enough for me to walk in case you need the car."

He was frowning, so I hurried on. "I know that when your dad lost his job and your mom starting working it drove your dad crazy, but this isn't the same thing. I'm not saying I'll take over providing for the family forever. I just have to help."

"You want to work a night shift after taking care of kids all day?" His tone gave nothing away. Micah's eyes drooped closed.

I stopped rocking the baby seat. "Oh, I'd get some sleep after Dylan leaves for school. At least on the days that Kelsey has pre-school. If Micah naps. But we'd have a little income for Micah's surgery."

"You've got it all figured out."

Had I pushed the wrong buttons? Was he going to explode again?

Kevin leaned forward and took my hands. "You don't need to be the savior." His voice was gentle but compelling. No wonder he used to sell so much insurance.

"But I—"

He shook his head. "Remember when I said it was my responsibility to provide for us? You said I was wrong. That God provides for all of us."

"Well, yeah, God provides—but I could help out in the meantime."

Kevin stared at me until I heard my own words.

I rubbed my temples. "I'm doing it again, aren't I? Plans D, E, and F."

He laughed. "I'd call this one an F. You want to work nights at the place that gets robbed about once a week, take care of the kids during the day so I can job hunt, and—what—perform a few brain surgeries while you're at it?"

My grin held a whole flock's worth of sheepishness. "Point taken. But this is an emergency."

Micah yawned his baby yawn—jaw canting sideways and a tiny squeak at the end.

I reached down to feel his forehead with the back of my hand. Heather claimed she could tell a child's temperature within a fraction with this technique. "Micah's going to be learning lots of words in the next year or so. He's got to be able to hear."

Kevin studied Micah with the grave and tender weight of a father's responsibility. "I know. And if I don't find something soon, *I* can take the job at SuperAmerica. Okay?"

I nodded. "It's a deal. Besides, you'd look cute in their uniform."

He grinned. "Yeah, and I bet I could have all the free coffee I wanted."

"You don't like my tea?"

We stacked up the bills and papers, carried Micah's infant seat to our bedroom, turned out the light, and prayed that God would help us trust Him.

As we advanced into January, Kevin focused even more energy on his job hunting. He was hoping potential employers had returned from vacation days in a good mood.

I couldn't decide which trauma to focus on first. Kevin's morale, Micah's ears, my sister's need for Christ, or the mess I'd made of my interview with *Women of Vision*.

Victoria called to report on the Chicago retreat, adding to my angst. "You really blew it. The woman I found to take my place has been invited back to speak several times during the year—and all for generous fees. If you're serious about wanting to do more speaking, you need to set some priorities."

Her words stung. I hated to think I'd lost my chance to do something of value. Especially after seeing my job at church go up in smoke—virtuous, religious, holy smoke, maybe, but the board of elders had reduced my dreams to cinders all the same.

Their rejection continued to smart. Sally told me that after Julie Henderson turned down the position, the board had decided to offer the job to Teresa Vogt, the woman from Faith Church in Woodbury. Quite an irony, since that's where the job search support group met.

After talking with Lori on Christmas Eve, Kevin had decided to visit the group. The Wednesday night of his first meeting, he came home so fired up I wanted to kiss Lori. But I settled for Kevin.

I only managed a quick peck on his cheek. He was hard to catch as he bounced around the kitchen. "You wouldn't believe how many great guys I met. They aren't losers at all. Like one guy said, in today's economy, divisions get cut, downsizing happens, and we need to be flexible and patient. And keep looking. And praying."

Watching him prowl the kitchen with some of his old zest gave me a distraction from refining my worry list. He talked for ten straight minutes about what he had learned, waving his arms.

I perched on the kitchen counter. "Hon, did they have coffee at this meeting?"

He pivoted to look at me, arms frozen in midair. "Yeah. Why?"

"No reason."

He dove back into his recap and his new plans for the coming week.

I pulled my legs up to sit cross-legged and watch him with a contented smile. I probably looked like a serene statue of Buddha, but without the round tummy. Well, maybe a bit of the round tummy. After all, I'd had three kids.

Kevin might have gone on for hours, but the phone interrupted him.

I reached to grab it. If Kevin got on the phone, some poor telemarketer would hear a full report on job trends in the current market and networking techniques.

"Hi, Becky. It's Lori. So did Kevin go to the meeting?"

"I'll say." I shifted the receiver to my shoulder. "Sweetie, could you check on Dylan? He's been sneaking a flashlight under the covers to read again lately."

Kevin headed down the hall, and I lowered my voice. "He loved it. He can't stop talking about it. Thanks so much." Now that Kevin's ebullience left the room, my worries began pulsing like the blips on intensive care monitors. "But the bills are still piling up, and Micah's got another ear infection, and—"

"About that," Lori cut in. "The Wednesday morning mom's group has been praying for Micah."

"That's sweet of them." I hadn't ventured back in the past weeks. The committee heads were managing Moms' Time Out without me. I figured I was doing well to even show my face at church on Sundays. Besides, I was afraid that if I spent time around this group of young moms I might say something to point out the injustice of the board's decision or undermine the new staff person who would be taking over soon. The temptation to play on their loyalty was too great, so I stayed away.

"Yes, but they wanted to do more than pray," Lori said. "So they took up a love offering for Micah, and one of the women got her husband's company to match it. I've got the check for you."

"But we can't accept that."

"Why not?" Lori spoke with steel in her voice. "Aren't we part of a body? Aren't we supposed to help each other?"

"Yes, but—"

"All right, then. God cares about you and all you've been going through. We're excited that we can be a part of showing you a little of His love."

"Yes, but—"

"So I'll bring the check to Doreen's tomorrow night."

I could see I wasn't going to get anywhere arguing with Lori. I felt the same uncomfortable squirm behind my sternum as I had when the church gave us the Christmas basket of food. Deep gratitude wrapped around me like a bandage, but it was threaded with dark colors of helplessness and shame.

"Is Doreen up to having us over?"

"She said she's looking forward to it." Lori sighed. "I'm bringing Abby to watch Doreen's kids, since Jim won't be there."

"Is there anything we can do for her?"

Lori made a humming sound. "Pray for her. Let her know we care."

I scratched my head. "But I want to help."

"You mean like we all wanted to help Micah?" Affectionate humor softened Lori's teasing comment.

"Point taken. But seriously, I want to do something."

"Charge in and rescue her?"

"Ha, ha. Just because I'm a little—"

"Driven?"

"Focused. I don't like sitting back when I see a need."

Lori's peal of laughter echoed through the phone. "You can

say that again. I'm still shocked you turned down the Christmas retreat. But proud of you, too."

"Yeah, well," I grumbled. "Victoria says I've blown my best chance to get more speaking engagements."

"If God wanted you traveling and speaking, don't you think He could open those doors?"

"Sure, but we're supposed to be knocking on doors, too. Right? He wanted me to develop a women's ministry, and look what happened to that."

"I know that hurt you." Lori's tone turned tender. "But the story isn't over yet. God doesn't fall in line with our playbooks. He doesn't always make sense to us. That doesn't mean we're supposed to take over and do everything ourselves."

Okay, maybe Lori was right. Maybe I was a teensy bit driven.

After I hung up, I tiptoed to the boys' room. Kevin was still there, sitting on the side of Dylan's bed. Dylan sprawled with seven-year-old abandon. Dark lashes—a smaller version of Kevin's—rested against his cheeks. The play of shadows on Dylan's jawline hinted at how he would look one day as a gangly teen. Kevin would teach him how to shave. He'd borrow the car and bound out of the house to take a sweet young girl on a picnic. A poignant longing hit me. Time was sweeping by too quickly. For all my love of rushing headlong and conquering every obstacle, I suddenly wanted to sit still and soak in the moment.

Kevin stared across the room past the rails of the crib, like a prisoner looking for rescue. Micah slept with his knees under him and his bottom hunched up. His fat cheek scrunched against the mattress, and his mouth pursed open as if he were whistling.

I reached for Kevin's hand. "The Moms' Time Out group put together a gift for Micah's operation." Neither of our boys stirred as I whispered. "Lori insists we take it."

Kevin's head dropped. Then he nodded. "I'd rather have God

provide for our family through my job. But I'm not God. If He wants to help us this way, it wouldn't be right to refuse." He faced me with a blaze of determination. "But I've lined up two interviews for tomorrow."

"That's great. And I'll talk to Micah's doctor and set up the surgery for him. They said it will only take a few hours, and we can bring him home right away. Of course that doesn't keep it from costing an arm and a leg."

"Well, doctors have to pay back their student loans somehow." Kevin grinned. "Maybe I should go into medicine."

We tiptoed out of the boys' room and checked on Kelsey. Curled on her side, clutching a hot-pink stuffed octopus, she sighed in her sleep.

The kids drove me crazy most of the day. But after they fell asleep, an appeal as strong as pheromones grabbed at my heart. Awe that God entrusted them to our care blended with a yearning to protect them every second of their lives.

I smiled at my erratic emotions. Impatience and love. Restlessness and contentment. Fear and trust. My soul strained between old nature and new.

*Lord, I'm tired of all these trials. And I'm tired of striving. I'm supposed to find my purpose and use my gifts to serve you, but nothing is working. Please open a door for me.*

The next evening, I left the household in Kevin's care. His interviews that day had ignited his hope, and he looked forward to some playtime with our kids. Driving toward Doreen's, I wondered what I could do to offer her support during her divorce. Little e-mail prayers and occasional cards didn't seem like enough. Maybe I could—

The truck shot out from the left cross street like a surreal chase scene from a bad movie. Shock stopped my breath, my pulse, my brain cells. Some limbic reflex made me hit the brake long before I understood what was happening.

"No!" The scream tore from my throat. A strobe of images flashed. The fierce grill of the truck bore down. A giant fist slammed me. Glass shattered. Brakes squealed. Steel crumpled. I felt a moment of surprise that this was how it would end. This suddenness that crushed all life from me.

"She's had some head trauma." The voice was tired and sympathetic. Scattered noises of an emergency room confused me. I was in a car, wasn't I?

"We'll need to wait and see what happens after the swelling goes down."

*Don't be silly. I'm fine.*

I opened my mouth to say the words. I even willed my body to sit up and smile.

Nothing happened.

## TWENTY SEVEN

*My cape gave me* stability as I flew
through the air. Skyscrapers spiraled below me. I
felt protective of the throngs hurrying along the streets, the
taxis and buses scurrying about their business. When I did my job
right, most of their lives were never interrupted by crisis. They never
knew I had shot from the sky to rescue them. Quick as a hawk, I dove
and stopped the semi with faulty brakes, or toppled the mugger in the
alley, or shored up a bridge wobbling in a gale.

Other times, it was impossible to hide my presence. Last week I had
rescued a dozen people trapped in a burning building, flying them down
to the street one by one. I heard the gasps. "Supermom! It's her."

I disappeared as mysteriously as I had arrived. Better to remain
shrouded in myth. Not everyone was a fan.

My archnemesis had made his presence known in the past months.
Stolen uranium, an influx of criminals into town, kidnapping of top
scientists—all signs that Corporal Chaos was planning another attempt
at world domination.

My search through Metropolis had proven futile. I had yet to find
Chaos's lair. Coasting over the warehouse district near the waterfront, I
felt a unique distortion of energy. A sure signature of my foe.

Zeroing in on the sensation, I zoomed toward one of the buildings.
Suddenly an airborne ship exploded from a hidden entry and hurtled
toward me. Chaos's face sneered from inside the plasteen windscreen of
his ship. He fired supersonic corporeal realignment rays in my direction.
One of the beams grazed my shoulder. The force sent me into a violent

spin, and I tumbled toward the earth.

*I had miscalculated. As the ground seemed to rise up to meet me, I realized I wasn't going to make it.*

"Will she be okay? Can I stay with her?" Kevin's throat sounded raw and cracked with emotion.

I reached my hand out to comfort him, but my hand wasn't there. Panic raced through me. I was disembodied. A horrible image of a brain trapped in a sphere flashed through my mind— some recollection of an old sci-fi movie.

"You should go home and rest." A calm, deep voice sounded somewhere above me. "We won't know much until tomorrow, and we've got her medicated. She won't be able to respond."

"No, I need to be here." Kevin's words were firm.

*Yes, yes. Don't leave me. I'm trapped in a jar. Keep talking.*

Other sounds sorted themselves out. A distant intercom from a nurses' station. A blip from a monitor. A hiss.

"I'm here, Becky." Kevin's familiar voice hovered near. "Hang on. You're going to get through this. Oh, Jesus, help her."

A slow tide of reassurance pulled its way across my consciousness. The car accident. I was in a hospital. I couldn't move yet, but I wasn't in a jar.

*I'm here. I'm all right.*

I felt a flare of frustration that my eyes wouldn't open and my voice wouldn't obey my prodding. Then the feeling faded into lethargy, and I floated somewhere warm and detached.

Velvety dreams swam in and out of my awareness. I flew above treetops, savoring the varied shades of green below. I swam in deep water, searching for treasure. Children's faces looked up at me from hospital beds, comfort and gratitude shining from their faces. Throngs in auditoriums listened to me sing. I slew dragons and dodged arrows astride a marvelous stallion.

Then a voice called me toward a street lined with elms. I sat on an ordinary lawn, yellowed from summer heat. From behind me, firm arms wrapped around me. A young girl, no more than Kelsey's age, skipped along the sidewalk nearby. Ordinary brown hair bounced behind her, and her features were plain. Yet with her carefree joy, she radiated beauty.

Suddenly, she stumbled. An uneven stub of concrete caught her foot. Her hands flew forward as she pitched headlong. She gasped and began to cry with the pain. When she rolled and sat up, blood branded her dirt-scraped knees.

I wanted to run to her, but the arms held me. A voice whispered, "Watch."

From somewhere behind us heavy footsteps pounded. As a man raced past, I had no doubt that this was her father. I held my breath, waiting for his chiding words. "Why are you so clumsy? Stop your fussing. Big girls don't cry."

Instead he swooped her into his arms. "Oh, sweetheart, I'm so sorry. Are you all right?" With a tender hand he brushed the tears from her cheeks, still cradling her against his chest. "Let's go inside."

"I got an owie." The girl's wail had already calmed to a whimper.

"Yes, you did. But you're so brave. We'll put ice on it and it won't sting so much." The father kissed the girl's forehead and carried her into the house.

My heart raced with a greater thrill than I'd felt when flying over the fields and forests. I longed to be loved that way.

*You are, sweetheart. You are loved. Stop trying to be a savior, and let me carry you.*

The words held the same tender concern as those from the little girl's father. I relaxed back into the strong arms and sighed. "But there's so much to do."

A deep-throated chuckle sounded in my ear.

*There will always be much to do, my busy one. But you can skip along your path. You don't need to trudge under a heavy weight. And when you stumble, let me hold you and heal your wounds.*

Soporific sunlight flickered through elm leaves. Crickets whirred and a squirrel scolded from above us.

Tension melted from my muscles while chaotic striving dissolved from my thoughts. My eyes grew heavy. When I opened them again, I swam in a lake coated with the worries of my life. Diapers and dishes. Grocery lists and bake sales. E-mails to answer and term papers to write. Books about how to be better at everything. They floated all around me, then scattered in wide ripples until they dispersed. Some strong person had set his ship in my waters, and the surface was broken.

Then I was in the sailboat with him. As we glided through still waters, more ripples ribboned in our wake, chasing away the poisons that had once smothered the waves around me. I watched my goal of Big Things for God disappear behind me.

"Just that one?" I asked in a flare of panic. "Can't we bring that one along? We could tow it along behind us."

*Shhh. Trust me. There is purer water ahead.*

"Water." My voice rasped. Thirst clawed at me.

An arm reached awkwardly behind my shoulders and propped me up. A plastic straw brushed my lips.

I sucked in the stale-tasting liquid, then opened my eyes.

Kevin's grin stretched his whiskered cheeks. His dark caramel eyes were red-rimmed but warm with relief and a hint of tears. "You're back."

I refused to say, "Where am I?" Even in my half awake state I knew that was too cliché.

When I struggled to scoot up, pain grabbed my leg, and I abandoned my attempt to move. "What happened?"

"A truck hit you. How do you feel?"

I winced a small grin. "Like I was hit by a truck." My words sounded slurred.

Kevin laughed more than the feeble joke deserved. He

wrapped his arms around me. I tried to reciprocate, but a tangle of IV tubes in my left arm limited my reach. Even hobbled by technology, I held on to him as my mind struggled to catch up. The car accident. Pain. Confusion. A happy dream I should remember, whose wispy truths were already escaping me. I grappled to put the pieces together and squeezed Kevin's warm and solid arm.

*I'm alive. I'll be okay. So hard to concentrate. To remember. But I'll be okay.*

I eased my head back against the pillow. "Where are the kids?"

"Heather's watching them. She had them all finger painting—even Micah." Kevin settled on the edge of the bed.

Forming words took huge effort. My brain still felt incompletely present . . . not quite connected to this unfamiliar room. But I circled back to the image of Micah set loose with paint. "I hope she has plenty of Spray 'n Wash on hand."

My eyelids felt heavy and I felt a soft pull back toward my dream. A place that was so peaceful, I didn't have to make sense of anything. I was tempted to float away, but some responsible gene in my DNA clamored to figure everything out first—to take inventory and make sure it was safe for me to drift off. I forced my eyes open again. A white board hung on the wall across from the bed. Large green letters insisted *Today is January 14.*

I rubbed my forehead with my right hand. "I was out for two days?"

Kevin nodded. "Don't do something like that again, all right?" His mock scolding aimed for playful, but he couldn't hide the evidence of two days of anxiety. The muscles around his eyes looked rigid, frozen in a squint of worry. He watched me hard. I used to watch Dylan that way when he was a baby—secretly afraid he'd stop breathing.

My fingers found the bandage on my head. More inventory. "Hey, where's my hair?"

"They shaved away a little patch by the wound."

I harrumphed. "Oh well. Maybe it'll grow back blond." The thought tempted me to giggle. Was the pain medication making me silly? I frowned, fighting off the mental fog. I tried to focus on my husband. Tried to find the right emotional tone. Reassure him. Care for him. "You look tired."

Kevin rubbed the top of his head, riffling his dark hair. He still needed a haircut. "I'm fine. I was worried about you."

Poor man. He'd lost his dad to a car accident. What had it done to him when he heard about my crash? More memory pieces coalesced. His voice. His prayers.

He still watched me intently.

I reached up to touch my face, making sure all the important parts were intact. Even gentle pressure hurt. I must have been banged up pretty bad. But my nose, eyes, ears, and lips all remained where they belonged. "So, when can I get out of here?"

Kevin looked at his watch. "I don't know. The doctor should be by in about an hour. The nurse told me he stops by at eight." He had switched from staring at me to avoiding my gaze and fiddling with his watchband.

Anxiety bloomed slowly in my stomach when he continued to look away. I wanted to ask what else he needed to tell me, but I decided I wasn't ready to know. "Hey, I'm hungry. Do they have any cheeseburgers in this place?"

Kevin looked up and grinned, his ease returning. "I think you'd better start small. The nurse said the morphine might make you queasy."

"How about a Popsicle?"

Mr. Fix-the-Problem lit up, eager to help and happy for a diversion. He lurched off his perch on the side of the bed, then winced and hopped around in a silly flamenco dance. "My foot's asleep." When he was able to walk without limping, he headed for the door. "I'll go up to the birthing rooms. They had Popsicles in the freezer when you had Micah. Root-beer flavored?"

I nodded.

He zipped out of the room.

His bouncy stride reassured me that everything would be okay. The thought of Kevin invading the maternity wing to steal a Popsicle made me smile.

Then my mood sobered. I pushed aside the cotton blanket and took an assessment. My lower left leg was in a cast. But even worse was the metal contraption pinned to my hip and upper leg. Now that I could see it, I felt desperately trapped—caged by some medieval torture device. I tried to shift, but even small movement made my hip throb like a sore tooth.

As suddenly as a book closing, my energy shut down. My mind slipped into a doze in the space between breaths. The image of the truck bearing down on me flashed through my thoughts. I shuddered, quickly opening my eyes. I didn't want to relive the accident. Yet even the brief flare of memory resurrected the shock of impact, the sound of breaking glass and twisting metal, the acidic smell of powder from the air bag.

A moan issued from the other side of a curtain.

Startled, I realized I wasn't alone in the room. I wasn't in a sociable mood, so I didn't call out to introduce myself. Rustling noises and the whir of the bed sounded from my roommate. Then the television clicked on. The screen was angled toward my neighbor, so I could barely see it. She shuffled through channels and finally centered on an early morning cartoon. A caped crusader battled villains at high volume.

*Kevin, get me out of here! I want to go home.*

A nurse slipped in on rubber-soled shoes. She fiddled with the IVs and showed me the button to push to adjust my pain medication. She explained the external fixator that was keeping my hip immobile and warned me against disturbing anything. I didn't pay much attention. I was too tired to focus, and her determined cheerfulness made me depressed.

The room faded for a while. When I opened my eyes, Kevin had returned and triumphantly waved a Popsicle. Niggles of nausea came and went with my headache and morphine, but the icy treat felt wonderful along my dry throat. Promptly at 8:00, a man in a rumpled white coat with minty breath arrived to poke and prod and ask numerous questions in rapid succession. As he examined my head wound, I could smell the antiseptic on his hands.

"So, when can I go home?"

He straightened. "Let's not rush things. Of course you'll need to come in for physical therapy once the cast is off. Has your husband talked to you about your injuries?"

Kevin edged away from the bed to watch the television as an animated hero flew to the aid of a runaway train.

"No. I just woke up. We haven't had a lot of time to talk."

The doctor cleared his throat.

Cold dread hit me like a blast from my freezer. I wished the doctor would sit down so I wouldn't feel quite as helpless looking up at him.

"As you probably noticed, the injury to your left side was extensive. We were able to set the lower leg without too much trouble. It should heal up just fine. I want you to avoid soft drinks, take extra calcium . . ."

I nodded the grateful, subservient nod I always used with doctors. "That's not so bad. A broken leg and a few bumps and bruises."

He paused a fraction too long. "And serious damage to the knee. Actually the worst damage is your pelvis. It sustained a crack." He traced a diagram in the air. "We put in some pins, but you need to understand that many people with a hip fracture don't ever return to full function."

Full function? What did that mean? "Exactly how crippled will I be?"

The doctor winced. "We have no way of knowing at this point." He patted my arm. "You're lucky you survived. Just concentrate on getting well."

He moved quickly around the curtain to examine my roommate. Kevin turned away from the TV and walked toward me.

"Honey, I'm so sorry." He tugged at the collar of his wrinkled shirt. "Don't worry. Doctors don't know everything."

Tears leaked from my eyes even when I willed them to stop. "Yeah. I'm not really crying, you know. It's just the pain-killers."

How bad was this going to be?

How was I going to take care of my busy family? And chase the kids in the yard? How was I going to lead the bake sales, and take on speaking engagements, and encourage Kevin while he found a job?

I gasped. "Kevin, how are we going to pay for this?"

He bent down to kiss my cheek. "Don't worry. Car insurance covers this kind of thing."

"But—"

He sank onto the edge of the bed. "Shh. It's all going to be fine." The sag of the mattress reactivated my pain, but I wasn't about to tell him. I was too desperate to have him close.

My eyelids sank of their own accord. Sleep tugged me into a haze. "I love you." The words were a clumsy murmur. I hoped Kevin heard me.

I dozed in and out, too stunned and medicated to link my thoughts into a coherent train. Sometime in the middle of the night I suddenly came awake.

Strange noises unsettled me. The sheets felt scratchy. I wanted to curl onto my side but couldn't move. And now that I would welcome the fuzzy oblivion that had annoyed me earlier, my mind lit up with high-definition clarity.

*Lord, why this? Why now?* Wasn't life hard enough? So many things to take care of. So many things I needed to fix. I'd already felt like I was failing. And now this.

All year I'd been sliding further away from the picture of how my life of Christian purpose was supposed to look. The victorious life. The life of worth. The life of a hero.

And now, like Supermom blindsided by one evil villain too many, I plummeted down with a crash.

Instead of serving the world, I had become a burden. I couldn't imagine anything worse.

# TWENTY·EIGHT

**Eerie rust-striped** peaks of harsh rock
hid deep canyons and uneven terrain. This place
was named the Badlands for good reason. I checked my water
supply and coated my skin with one last layer of sunscreen. Even
this early in the day, the South Dakota sun could be brutal.

I hitched up my pack and jammed a baseball hat over my blond curls. I'd rather be loping along a dirt path, but intense hiking over the jagged slate and scree was a valuable part of my training for the Boston Marathon. I had my title to defend. My winning time last year had broken all records.

Joy fed my energy as I clambered over the rocks. Orange metal rods served as guideposts and steered tourists from danger. As I left those behind, I ventured into the true Badlands. Alone except for an occasional circling hawk, I pushed my pace, reveling in hard breathing, sweat, and welcome isolation.

The alien moonscape fooled the eyes. Sudden drop-offs could appear without warning. But I knew the terrain. Bands of hardened volcanic ash separated deposits of red clay, reminding me of a weirdly shaped layer cake. Not so different from my life. A blend of influences. Conflicting layers. Harsh beauty.

I skirted the edge of the butte and searched for a place where I could pick my way down the canyon and over to the next rise.

A lizard burst from behind a rock and startled me. I lurched back. My foot rocked. My ankle bent with an audible crack. The sound raised *a well of nausea before the pain did. I fell to my side, tears of frustration burning in my eyes.*

*I was miles from help, curled in misery under a scorching sun. I tried to force myself up. Pain speared up my leg. There was no way I could put any weight on the foot.*

I squeezed my eyes shut. "I can't do it." I hated hearing the words come from my throat. I was a go-getter, a positive thinker, a person who always had a Plan B. But the pain defeated me.

The physical therapist gave no pity. "Try again."

I lurched another awkward step, holding most of my weight on the parallel bars. I ground my teeth and tried for another shuffle.

The therapist, a young athletic woman with a long blond braid, softened her drill sergeant demeanor. "You're doing better than yesterday." She helped me into the wheelchair waiting at the end of the bars.

I nodded and tried to look enthused. I wasn't about to let her see my misery. After weeks of itching, I was relieved to be out of the cast that had helped my lower leg heal. However, as the doctor had predicted, my hip joint gave me more trouble. The fracture appeared to have left me crippled. Disabled. Physically challenged. Whatever the politically correct term was at the moment. No one seemed to be sure how much it would improve.

As I wheeled from the rehab center to the sidewalk, Kevin and the kids pulled up in our new wagon. At least insurance had covered a replacement car. I forced a bright smile. Kevin settled me in the front seat and folded down the chair to stow it in the back. He'd become efficient at that maneuver in the weeks since I'd come home from the hospital. After he got in the driver's side, he flashed his own false smile. "How'd it go today?"

"Lots better. I'll be running around in no time." If I had to be useless, at least I would fake a valiant spirit. "Hey, kids. How was your morning?"

Kevin pulled out into traffic while Dylan and Kelsey began jabbering at the same time. Even Micah joined in with some happy vocalizations.

Some of my discouragement faded. "Whoa. Slow down. One at a time."

Dylan, by force of first-born status, took over. "Dad let us cook lunch. We saved you the gorilla cheese sandwich."

"Grilled cheese," Kevin explained.

I tried to shake the visual of a hairy primate between two slices of bread. "Wow, you guys are getting really great at handling everything."

"I washed dishes," Kelsey shouted.

I raised my eyebrows at Kevin.

He shook his head. "Don't worry. We were eating on paper plates."

A genuine laugh bubbled up from my heart. A sound I hadn't heard in a while. "Kevin, I'm so sorry about this. You're getting stuck with so much extra work."

He shot me a look full of steel. "Stop saying that. I don't mind. Besides, I figure God knew you'd need me, so that's why I don't have a job yet."

I shook my head. "Now you're sounding like me. Trying to get it all figured out. Wouldn't it have been easier to let you keep your job and just hold my car back by five minutes that night?" A pang of disillusionment jarred my heart—disillusionment that had been too common in the weeks since the accident. Sometimes I felt my soul had become as crippled as my leg. "I've quit trying to make sense of it." I knew the words sounded bleak, but it was too late to pull them back.

Kevin glanced at me and started to say something. He

changed his mind and glared out the windshield. After a long pause, he sighed. "Lori's coming over this afternoon."

I nodded but couldn't muster any enthusiasm. I struggled to adjust my leg into a comfortable position, then rested my head against the window. Stores, cars, people walking dogs—all swept past. Crocuses peeked through the last remnants of snow. An old man raked the detritus of winter from his lawn. The world was going on. Going on without me. I didn't have the strength to merge into the rapid traffic of life. I didn't have the heart to join in anymore.

During the early days in the hospital, my focus had been consumed in learning how to take care of myself and monitoring each sign of improvement. Kevin's mom flew up from Florida for a week to help out, and the kids got to spend time with the grandma who sent them kaleidoscopic scarves each Christmas. Taking advantage of her presence, Kevin took Micah in for his surgery. Our baby did great, even without me there to hold his pudgy hand. His hearing was improved, and he'd had one cold already with no ear infection showing up.

Life had moved forward at church, as well. I learned the next candidate the church had interviewed for the Women's Ministry job, Teresa Vogt, had declined the position. That gave me a moment of dark pleasure. I hoped Greg and his board would have a hard time finding someone. I recognized the thought as spiteful and prayed for forgiveness . . . but I couldn't help smirking.

My sense of vindication had only lasted briefly. The next day Kevin had brought in a fistful of phone messages. One was from Stephanie Maxwell at *Women of Vision* magazine.

Resignation weighted me down as heavily as my cast. "Kev, could you call and apologize for me? I'm sure she'll find someone better to profile."

He stroked my arm. "Are you sure? You were so excited

about it last fall. Your Bible study gals were convinced you were supposed to represent all Christian moms. I could explain what's happened and she could come interview you here."

I turned my head away. "No. I don't want anyone writing about me."

The decision wasn't so difficult. Just one more pain to endure—like the slowly healing bruises, the bone-deep ache in my hip, the throbbing in my knee, and the dark weariness in my mind. I was grateful Kevin didn't argue.

After Grandma Miller flew back home, my Thursday Bible-study ladies cheered Kevin and the kids with frequent visits to the house, bringing a hot dish, or a dessert, or some other treat.

Even Judy had stopped by the hospital twice when she was on layovers. Kevin told me later that she switched to a complex route of non-direct flights just to spend a few hours with me on her trips from coast to coast.

Weeks of flowers, cards, attention, and the distraction of healing kept me fairly optimistic. I pushed aside my big questions for God, and my worries about purpose, and did all I could to get better.

But now that I had been home for several weeks, my mood sagged. Getting through each day was daunting. My physical therapy sessions were a marathon of suffering. Questions I had held off on began to irritate me like squeaky hinges. What if, in spite of my hard work, my leg never returned to normal? And why hadn't God protected me?

That afternoon, Lori brought an apple pie. Abby and Jeffy ran off to play with Dylan and Kelsey while Micah crawled around at our feet.

Lori handed me a plate of pie. "So how was therapy today?"

"Fine." I shrugged. "It hurts, but people have had to deal with worse stuff."

Lori's eyes projected the kind of deep, warm concern that I imagined a mom would show—not my mom, but the eternally empathetic dream mom my friends had growing up. "That doesn't mean your pain isn't valid."

I was thrilled she didn't tell me to look on the bright side. To trust God. Use this disaster for good. Think about others instead of myself. The platitudes that only seemed to wound me.

Come to think of it, few of my friends had said those things. The slogans were voices from my own subconscious—telling me I was a failure for not being happy and noble. Warning me to stifle my doubts instead of examining them.

Micah headed toward the basement stairs, and Lori jumped up to steer him back toward us. "You don't have to be strong. I'd be a mess if this had happened to me." She sat beside me on the couch and rested one hand lightly on my stiff leg. "You can be mad. You can be spitting tacks if you want. I would be."

I pressed my lips inward. Emotion welled up inside me. Her permission to vent was a gift, but it frightened me. I tried so hard to be strong for Kevin and the kids. When I couldn't hold it in any longer and spewed bitter frustrations to him, I always felt guilty afterwards. He had his own battles right now.

I leaned into Lori with a half hug. "Thank you." The word squeaked past my congested throat. "I want to be a good example in suffering, learn the lessons God can teach me here, blah, blah, blah. But the truth is, this stinks."

"It sure does."

Lori's agreement lifted my pain a few inches, enough for me to voice some more of my dark thoughts. "I had this picture of what my life should look like, and it was all falling into place.

Then I lost the job at church. But I figured God had something better for me. I had to put aside my college classes when Kevin lost his job, but I trusted there was some good reason. I thought I'd start speaking. Now that's fizzled out."

She opened her mouth, but I cut her off. "I know. It's enough to take care of my family. But I can't even do that. When Kevin lost his job, I wanted to be the strong one. But I've been more scared than he is. I'm not managing to be much of a cheer-leader for him, and I'm not contributing to the family income. So I tell myself at least I can be a great mom. But my time is used up taking care of myself. Doing my therapy. Eating, wash-ing, sleeping. Everything takes so much effort. It's all I can man-age. This isn't how it's supposed to be."

A wrinkle of pain flicked across Lori's forehead. A hint that she understood disillusionment more than I realized. The thought intrigued me, since in my eyes, she had achieved the victorious Christian life in all its nuances. She didn't give me a chance to delve. "How is it supposed to be?" she asked gently.

I sank back against the couch and tilted my head up to stare at the ceiling. "Parting the Red Sea, slaying giants, healing the lame, preaching before Caesar . . ."

Her laughter drowned me out. "No one will ever accuse you of thinking small."

I felt myself blush. "Well"—I gestured to the room—"nor-mal was bad enough. Now I'm subnormal. Weak. God's taking me in the wrong direction."

Again, Lori met my eyes. "He's not done yet."

I let the words sink in deep and wrap around the aching places. Her visit was one of the little recesses of grace in between the reality of what life had become.

Soon the physical therapist had me hobbling in a walker. I felt humiliated, trailing behind old ladies in their eighties.

They'd outrun me easily. As more days of therapy passed, I began to face the truth. I might be limited permanently. When I would muster determination to face that possibility with some level of acceptance, pain from nerve damage flared up, lacerating my good intentions and driving me back to despair.

One afternoon, the ache in my leg blossomed into fierce daggers, so I retreated to bed. I swallowed a few pills, angry at needing them but too miserable to endure any longer.

An hour later, as I floated in a woozy, somewhat less painful mode, Heather dropped by to visit. She brought her guitar and sat on the end of the bed singing songs. Grace and Charity tiptoed in a half hour later and played some hymns on their Celtic harp and recorder.

Their earnest concentration made me smile.

When they glided away to play with the kids, Heather watched them with affection. She plucked a few soft chords on the guitar and turned back to me with a smile. "Music is very healing, you know."

"I'm as healed as I'm going to get." I tried to hide the sour tang in my voice. My leg resembled my old Skipper doll from when I was seven. Our family dog attacked her and pulled her leg off. Although I wedged the plastic ball of her leg into her hip socket, it never moved right again. There the resemblance ended. Skipper's leg was smooth, tan, and flawless. Mine was scarred, white, and useless. I couldn't bear to let anyone see it. Earlier that week I had gone through my dresser and thrown out every pair of shorts I owned.

Heather gave me a worried frown. "Your spirit can still fly, no matter what your body's limitation."

I forced a smile and a nod, not ready to explain I lived on a slightly more physical plane than she did.

She and the girls left, leaving echoes of ethereal music to hum around my bedroom. But no matter how firmly I told my spirit to soar, said spirit reminded me that my hip hurt.


A few days later, Sally arrived, Bible in hand. She had Post-it notes flagging every key verse she thought I needed to hear.

Even though I braced myself, her efforts to cheer me stung.

She dove into an enthusiastic reading about God never giving us more than we can handle and how we should rejoice in suffering. I wanted to quote back at her "Weep with those who weep," but I held my tongue.

The verses she read were familiar to me. I knew the truth of the words. I believed them. But when Sally banged me over the head with them from her place of relative peace and comfort, it felt like sand rubbed against an open blister.

After a while, I smiled politely and pleaded fatigue.

"Oh, come on," she said. "How can you be tired? You get to sit around most of the day. I should be so lucky."

Sally's vacant smile reminded me of the red-painted lips of a sneering puppet mask in Kabuki theater. I stared at her blue eyelids and faux-rosy cheeks and reminded myself her words were careless, not intentionally cruel.

As soon as she left, bitterness squeezed my throat until I thought I would choke—choke on her clichés, her determination that I should find the silver lining.

One day, maybe. But right now I was in pain. Physical pain barely controlled by drugs that made me foggy. Emotional pain as I grieved the loss of health—and the picture of how I thought my life would be.

When I watched television and saw parents run down a beach with their children, I wept. Never mind that we had no ocean beaches in Minnesota. The point was that even if we did,

I could never run along the seashore with the kids.

I tormented myself by clicking the remote through sports events. Tennis, gymnastics, a triathlon. Oooh, that was the worst. The athletes swam, biked, and then ran a full marathon. Every movement of their legs showed off lean, perfect muscles under a sheen of sweat.

Perhaps I could have clawed myself out of the physical and emotional pain. But the spiritual pain was even more devastating. As Sally was quick to remind me, God has all power, so He could have prevented this.

All I'd longed for since meeting Him in high school was to show my gratitude by pouring out my life in serving Him. Was it St. Therese who said to God, "If this is how you treat your friends, no wonder you have so few of them"?

I'd had challenges before. My soul had hurt and writhed, but I'd always recovered. I'd work up enthusiasm for the next new project and charge into it with energy that pushed past my disappointment.

This time I couldn't pull myself up.

I didn't even have the satisfaction of someone to blame. The driver of the truck wasn't drinking or speeding. It was a quirky accident. A patch of ice. Even top quality tires can skid. Just one of those things.

Except this was my life, not a movie of the week.

Even when some of their comments unintentionally hurt, my friends did lighten my heart a bit. But other acquaintances hadn't been so gentle.

The first time Kevin had wheeled me into church after I came home from the hospital, folks had flocked around me like crows to carrion.

First came the Pity Pats. One elderly woman rested a hand on my head and said, "You poor dear." Her soft tone was overlaid with condescension and the subtext, "I'm so glad it's you and not me."

Next came the Comparing Cathys. One of the young women from the Wednesday Moms' Time Out ran over to me and crouched in front of the chair. "Becky, I was thinking of you all week. I know exactly how you must feel. I had a broken toe once, and it was excruciating."

And of course there were a string of Lecturing Lindas.

"You should really drive down to the Mayo Clinic. They have the best doctors."

"Good nutrition is vital right now. Are you taking vitamins? I sell a great brand. I could come over this week and tell you about them."

"My uncle had the same thing happen to him, and he just prayed it away. Got up and walked every day claiming his healing and threw away his walker."

Never in my life had I been so glad to hear the prelude for the opening hymn. The crows finally flapped away, leaving me in small pecked pieces.

Eventually the novelty wore off and church wasn't as much of an ordeal. Life settled into a new "normal." I limped, cried, and asked God a dozen times a day why He didn't want my service.


Surprisingly, Doreen brought me the most hope. She came to visit on one of the bad days. I was in bed with pillows under my knee and a box of Kleenex at my elbow in case another crying jag hit me.

Doreen sat on the edge of the bed and tugged down the hem of the slim navy blue skirt she wore. The matching jacket framed a crisp white blouse and power scarf.

I glanced down at my rumpled sweat suit. "Whoa, someone's dressed up."

She pushed back a smooth lock of her straight auburn hair and smiled. "I just came from a job interview."

I pouted. "I thought this was all for my benefit."

"Yeah, right." Doreen still had shadows under her eyes, but when she smiled, her cheeks hid the bags and her spine stretched up with more confidence.

"So you'll have to work full-time?" Frustration shot up inside me. "Jim isn't going to give you enough support?"

Doreen laid a manicured hand on my arm. "It's all right. I'd always planned to go back to work someday. It will just be an adjustment for us all. How are you?"

I scooted to sit up a bit higher. "I've been better."

Doreen glanced at my nightstand and my open Bible. "Wow. I'm impressed. After Jim left, I couldn't stand to read mine for quite a while."

She understood. The feeling wrapped me in hope and I smiled. "I started in the New Testament, but the miracles of healing . . . it's like they're mocking me."

"That's too funny. When I finally opened mine, I read all the chapters about marriage. Why do we torture ourselves like that?"

"Hey, it's in the Bible, so it's true and important." The words tasted dry, but I felt compelled to say them. Some remnant of Becky the Super Christian still lurked inside me.

"Yeah, but I think God wrote some parts just for times like this." She leaned across me and grabbed my Bible. "Spend some time in the Psalms."

I nodded. "I think you're right. I've never understood the lines about miry pits and aching bones better than I do today."

Doreen kicked off her pumps, tossed aside fear of creases, and adjusted to sit by my side. She leaned her head against my shoulder. "I always wanted to be the strong one, too. Be the top at work, the best wife and mom, and have it all together. I don't like being weak." Her voice grew soft. "We're all wounded, Becky. Just in different places."

I reached for a tissue, and a moment later she grabbed one, too.

We sniffled together without talking for a few minutes. I blew my nose. "Why . . . why would God let this happen? Doesn't He want to use me? He keeps taking things away and making it harder for me to do anything of worth for Him."

Doreen lifted her head off my shoulder and moved back to face me. "You're precious to Him." I could see why she had always shone in the corporate world. She was firm, convincing, and implacable. "He'd love you if you could never lift a finger again. Hang on to that, okay?"

I let her words sink in and nodded.

She launched off the bed. "Gotta run. My babysitter gets mean if I'm late."

"I thought your mom was in town helping out."

"She is." Doreen gave me a wicked grin. "She's my sitter."

As Doreen minced out of the room in her narrow dress-for-success skirt, I smiled and picked up the Bible.

I wasn't going to be running any races soon, but life was a marathon, not a sprint. And pain was part of the adventure. My fingers flipped through the pages, and names stood out in chapter headings. Abraham, Moses, Joseph, Job. I began to notice how many of God's dear servants suffered—not always because of sin or stupid choices—but because the world is fallen and we have an enemy.

"But it hurts, Lord," I whispered. "Some days I'm not sure I can make it another step. The sun's beating down, I've lost all the guide markers, the rocks are sharp."

*I know.*

And I realized He did. I reached for another Kleenex, but the box was empty. I twisted and braced myself on the edge of the bed, reaching for my walker. I maneuvered awkwardly down the hall.

Kevin paced near the kitchen desk, papers piled around the computer screen, his cheek pressed against the phone. "You're kidding. Really? Yes, that is interesting."

Was he getting a job offer? *Oh, Lord, make it happen.*

Kevin turned with a huge grin and waved the phone in my direction. "It's for you."

# TWENTY·NINE

**Computer keys clicked** an enticing
rhythm under my fingertips. Like an umbilical cord,
my small movements pumped pulsing life from my thoughts
into a screen where words became story. This baby was almost
ready to be born. But labor had stalled out.

I hunched into my tweed jacket with the leather-patched elbows—my
one concession to the writer cliché—and stared out the window at squirrels
in the backyard. Time for a little free writing to clear the cobwebs.

"A squirrel ran . . ."

Not a specific enough verb. Hmm. "A squirrel raced." No. "The
squirrel scrambled up an oak tree and paused, tail arching like . . ."

What was the right comparison?

"Tail arching like an apostrophe." Too prosaic.

"Tail arching like a breaching whale." Naw.

"Tail arched in a tense quiver of fur." Maybe. Good tone if the scene
is going to lead into suspense. What if a perfect fall day is not so perfect?
I could almost hear the scary-music soundtrack.

"Dead leaves crackled under foot, their small corpses popping with
each step I took."

Too macabre? Let's see where it goes. How about a little more sensory description?

"The squirrel scrambled up an oak tree and paused, tail arched in a
tense quiver of fur. Dead leaves crackled under my feet, their corpses
snapping with each step I took. A rich odor of maple syrup coated the
air as the sugar bush boiled . . ."

*Nope, that would be spring, not fall. The sap ran in the spring.*

"Wet bark sent a musty smell of decay into the air." *But if it had just rained, the leaves wouldn't be crackling. Grr.*

"Smoke from a distant bonfire imbued the air. . . ." *Too pretty.*

"Teased my nostrils . . ." *Too anatomical.*

"Tickled my nose . . ." *Too cliché.*

"Smoke from a distant bonfire stirred memories of the accident. Anxiety swirled in my gut like a pile of wind-tossed leaves. No. It couldn't happen again."

*Ooooh. Yeah. This was beginning to set a mood. I could almost smell the smoke.*

A tendril of smoke wafted from the toaster, and I limped across the kitchen, pushing my walker, to pop the release button. Kevin must have been making a snack and the lever had stuck again.

I wrinkled my nose. Even weeks later, the smell jarred me back to the electrical-burn scent of air-bag powder.

Kevin was bouncing on his heels. "Yes, here she is now. . . ." He shoved the receiver toward me. "It's Pastor Roger."

I hobbled my way to one of the kitchen table chairs, and Kevin stretched the phone cord to reach me. My forehead was moist with sweat from the short walk to the kitchen.

Pastor had visited me once at the hospital and again after I got home. His bluff, authoritative voice had been strangely comforting. He read a generic devotion, but the confidence of his delivery pierced through some of my fog and stirred a deep urge to keep fighting the good fight. When he prayed for me, lingering resentment for denying me my dream job had melted away.

So I smiled as I took the phone. Kevin gave me a thumbs-up, and I figured he was proud of my jaunt down the hallway.

"Hi, Pastor Roger. How are you?"

"Great. Great." The hearty voice boomed over the wire. "And you?"

I adjusted the receiver an inch away from my ear. "Getting stronger." It was the expected answer, and I was too much of a "good girl" to veer from the script.

"Well, that's terrific." He cleared his throat in a rare moment of awkwardness. "You see, the board has been talking—by the way, we all admire how hard you're working to regain your strength. It's always great to see you in church. You're setting a wonderful example."

I wrinkled my forehead, feeling puzzled. "Um, thanks." I could have added something about God being my fortress and strength, but that would be laying it on a bit too thick.

"Yes, well." Another harrumph. "I'm actually calling for another reason."

Kevin watched me while shifting from one foot to another, as if he were guarding a soccer goal.

His antsy moves were driving me nuts, and I wished I had a soccer ball handy to kick at him.

I turned away to concentrate on my conversation. "What can I do for you?"

"Perhaps you've heard that Julie Henderson took a different call to a church in Chicago?"

No need to show how closely I'd followed the job search. "Mmm," I said noncommittally.

"And we felt Sally just didn't have the skills for the variety of roles involved."

"Yes, she told me that a while back."

Pastor paused again. "And Teresa Vogt from Faith Community Church has turned down the offer. She feels God is calling her to continue in her work there." He sighed.

Instead of feeling smug at the problems they faced, I felt pity. "I'm sorry it didn't work out. Kevin has gotten to know some of the staff when he goes to the career support meetings over at Faith. They have some great programs over there. Teresa would have done a great job. So, what's the board doing next?"

"Well, that's just it. Becky, we'd like to have you come in and talk about taking back the reins of the program."

My heart double-thumped and I took a quick breath. "As a volunteer?" I asked cautiously.

"No, as a full-time staff member. We're rethinking the need for a degree from a denominational college. And I know you've been working to complete your education degree anyway, so that should be sufficient."

Vindication roared through me like a head rush, and I was glad I was sitting down.

The perfect happy ending. I couldn't have written a more satisfying closing scene for my life story of the past months.

Kevin capered around the linoleum.

I fought back a giggle and put on a professional demeanor. "Well, that's very interesting." I was proud of how calm I sounded. "Let me pray about it and talk to Kevin, and I'll get back to you."

But my heart shrieked, "Yes, yes, yes!"

After we closed out the conversation, Kevin took the phone from my shaking hand and set it in the cradle. Then he swooped me up and carried me to the living room, spinning in circles while we both whooped. When he stumbled over one of Dylan's Hot Wheels, he slowed down and fell onto the couch with me in his lap.

"So what do you think?" He ruffled my shaggy layers of hair.

I waited for my excitement to bloom into a burst of ideas and plans. For my mind to race ahead prioritizing upcoming events. The Grandmas' Tea, the Holy Week prayer night, the craft sale for the women's shelter, new parenting classes.

Instead, my energy seemed to roll to a slow halt, colliding against a solid wall. The thrill burned away, leaving a strange heaviness. I looked up at Kevin. "I'm not sure."

And I really wasn't sure anymore. The realization stunned me. This was exactly what I'd wanted all along. I'd built up a good program, and now I could take it further. I could develop the biggest women's ministry in the city.

But as I visualized my dream, the image felt flat and lifeless.

Kevin looked as stunned as I felt. "How can you not be sure? Isn't it what you wanted?"

"Of course. It's just . . ."

Kevin's bony thigh was sharp against my bottom, and I maneuvered off his lap to sit beside him. "So much has happened in the past few months, and . . . somehow it doesn't feel as important now. I mean, it was my big way to do something for God. But sometimes my plan felt like a lot of pressure. And everything kept going wrong. And now . . ." I nibbled the edge of a fingernail. "I'm not sure this is where God wants me."

Kevin studied me in silence then reached for my hand and turned my wedding ring around my finger. "Is it because of the accident? Are you afraid you don't have the energy anymore? You know we'd all help."

In the past weeks of recovery, my feelings had bounced around like a racquetball. Now I had to take a slow breath and focus to sort out what motives were speaking to me.

Fear certainly pinged around in my head. I grabbed that ball out of the air to examine it. "Yeah, this year I've decided I'm a lot more weak, imperfect, and *limited* than I realized. And now I can't even maneuver very well physically. I get tired easily. So . . . sure, taking on a new challenge right now scares me. I'm not up to being first on the scene and last to leave—the big Energizer Bunny for the church programs anymore. I'm not sure I ever should have been. It was just that drive inside me."

"And it's gone now?"

"Yes. No." I pulled my hand away and brushed my bangs off my forehead. I tossed the fear ball aside and grabbed a different orb as it bounced around my mental court. "I still want to do something big." I pulled my good leg up and hugged the knee. "Part of me still wants to be Billy Graham, or Mother Teresa, or a Fearless Faith Singer, or a full-time speaker like Victoria. Someone special."

Kevin rubbed his cheek against mine. "You are special."

"Or a strong, organized, spiritual woman like Lori. Or creative like Heather." This was a complicated motive to study. "But I know I have to let God lead me to my own place . . . not try to be like them."

Kevin jumped up to pace the living room. He kicked Dylan's cars to the side of the room. "But I thought that leading the moms' stuff *was* your special place." Frustration tinged his words.

I didn't blame him. My lack of wholehearted enthusiasm for this offer frustrated me, as well. "It was. I mean, it was something God inspired in me, and gave me energy and creativity to do. I had plans to do a lot more, too. And, yeah, I did feel like I was in the place He wanted me." I turned and used my hands to help lift my leg onto the couch, stretching out and staring at the ceiling. "But God can change where He wants us, right?"

Kevin had been expounding that theme a lot in the weeks since he had started attending the job support group at Faith Community in Woodbury. He grinned. "Got me there." Then he rubbed his head and paced some more. "But this is nuts. If I got an offer now, after all these months of hunting and doing odd jobs, I'd grab it."

I waited until he turned and looked at me. "Even if you didn't think it was God's will for you?"

He threw his hands up. "I don't know. How would I know? It's not that simple. And what if this is your big chance?"

Another ball of fear ricocheted around my thoughts. "I know. That scares me. If I don't say yes to this I might always regret it."

Kevin finally came back to the couch and lifted my shoulders so he could sit down and let me rest against his chest. "I just don't want you to say no for the wrong reasons."

He was right. What was holding me back? Fear I wasn't capable? Lingering resentment about how they treated me as their last resort? Or was it God's Spirit warning me to slow down?

What was urging me to take the job? A genuine calling? Or my drive to prove myself? Vindication? A fear of missing out?

The emotions and motives rocketed around my brain, and their bounces brought on a headache. "At this point, I don't know if I can say yes, or no, for the right reasons. It's all a muddle."

Kevin stroked my forehead. "Okay, we'll pray. Oh, and I forgot to tell you, I have a second interview lined up for tomorrow."

I lifted a hand to high-five him. "All right. Is this the hotel management place?"

"No, no. They went another direction."

"The carpet sales place?"

Kevin shuddered. "No. I would be thankful for the part-time work, and I think I could move into full-time there eventually, but I hope it doesn't come to that. No, this is the new start-up insurance company. It would be a lower position initially, but the potential to move up would be huge."

Kevin's whole body vibrated with eager energy at the thought of a challenge he could sink his teeth into, in the field he loved. Maybe in the next few days we'd both be starting great new jobs.

When we went to bed that night, I tossed from side to side, shifting awkwardly each time to reposition my bad leg. Finally some remnant of the nearly forgotten dream from the hospital resurrected. I saw the small girl on the sidewalk, crying over her skinned knee, and the father so quick to soothe and comfort her. It didn't answer my questions, but the image helped my exhausted mind relax. God was holding me. He'd show me what to do next.

The next morning I woke up with the clear sense that I needed to turn down the women's ministry position. All my mixed up feelings had calmed, and the one sure direction I felt was a gentle word from God to close this chapter. Fears immediately gibbered at me. "You're missing your big chance. You're letting Kevin down. The church needs you. What will people think? You'll never increase your influence, widen your boundaries, or discover your purpose."

Kevin came out of the shower glistening and whistling. He happy-danced around the bedroom, hitching up his suit pants and pulling out several ties to choose from. Now that he'd survived being unemployed without turning into his father, his optimism had returned in full force. He perched on the edge of the bed. "Will you be okay getting Kelsey to preschool today? I'm taking the bus downtown so you'll have the car."

I smiled. "Sure. No problem. Did you hear Dylan stirring yet?"

He shook his head. "I'll wake him up. Can't believe Micah isn't up yet. He's been sleeping so much better now that he doesn't have all those earaches." He sprang up and wrapped a tie around his neck, tucking it under the collar.

I bit my lip. "Kev?"

"Hmm?"

I could tell he was mentally rehearsing answers to interview questions, but he pulled his focus back to me. I really hoped he wouldn't think I was being a coward. "Hon, I'm calling Pastor Roger today. I don't think this is the right job for me."

Kevin's hands slowed as he knotted his tie. He didn't look at me. "You're sure? You don't want to think about it some more?"

"I know it seems crazy, but I'm sure. I'm not always good at figuring out God's plan. I can't this time, either. But I feel really strongly that He's asking me to walk away from this."

Dark eyes met mine with complete trust. "All right, then. That's taken care of." He leaned down for a quick kiss. "Now pray for God to send some guidance my way, too. Okay?" He winked and zoomed out the door.

I heard him rattle around the boys' room, and Dylan chortled. Micah began babbling, too. He didn't want to sleep in when his brother had to get up for school. I pushed myself out of bed. Time to dive back into the adventures of momhood.

I coaxed breakfast into the kids, Dylan onto the school bus, and Kelsey into clothes without stains. I combed her hair, changed Micah's diaper, and attempted to vacuum while leaning on my walker. Micah toddled along at my heels. He was getting around with more confidence than I was these days.

I got Kelsey to help me make the beds. Every little task took more effort these days, but I managed. And I felt a surge of accomplishment at how much I was able to handle.

After driving Kelsey to preschool, I came straight home. Micah went into his high chair with a hill of Cheerios and a stack of Lorna Doones. I grabbed the phone and said one more prayer. "Are you sure about this, Lord?"

The conviction remained.

Sally answered the phone at church. She must have had some inkling about the offer because she twittered when she heard my voice. I asked for Pastor Roger, and when his voice rumbled through the phone connection I took a steadying breath.

"I wanted to get back to you right away. I've prayed about your idea of having me take over the women's ministry as a staff position. I'm sorry, but I don't think it's something God wants me to take on right now. Thank you for asking me, and I'll keep praying you find the right person."

Yes, it was a rehearsed speech, but it helped me stay firm, even when Pastor blustered and coaxed for a while.

I put the phone down, feeling numb and a bit empty. The job had represented so much to me. It was hard to believe that God had asked me to turn it down.

Some happy ending. I was miles back from where I'd started. I still had the deep desire to serve God, but even less of a clue as to how. I had touched the alluring edge of several great possibilities, only to set them aside. Was I nuts?

And with all that had happened this year, I had even fewer resources to draw from than I had six months ago. Then I'd been a harried, hurried, slightly driven mom, with some marginal successes. Now I was handicapped and tired, without any goals to give me focus other than getting through each day.

Yet a weird peace settled over me.

"Okay, Lord. I'm yours. Use me. Put me on a shelf. It's all the same to me because I know you love me."

Today the words didn't snag in my throat. Warm arms of love supported my spirit.

If I were writing the story of my life, I would have preferred a bold crescendo of triumph for this chapter. But if God didn't need every page in my book to crackle with adventure, I could accept that. What might it look like, to live for God without so much striving?

Micah swept his arm across his tray, scattering Cheerios to the four winds.

I shook my head and laughed. From the sublime to the ridiculous. My life seemed to constantly make that jump. I swept up the cereal and felt a stir of longing move back into my soul.

I lifted Micah out of the highchair and held his warm body against me until he squirmed. When I set him down, he toddled quickly to the kitchen cupboard and began pulling out all my Tupperware. I opened the front door and gathered in the mail.

*Okay, Lord, I know I was supposed to turn down the job at church. I know you love me even if I don't accomplish anything beyond the walls of my home—or even here. But there is still a fire in me to serve you. To help other moms. It's so strong . . . and it hasn't gone away. You're going to have to take that longing out of my heart or I just might go crazy.*

As if to shine a cruel spotlight on my longings, the March issue of *Women of Vision* was in the stack of mail. *I wonder who they'll be replacing me with in next month's issue.* I told myself it didn't matter and tossed the magazine straight into the recycle bin.

# THIRTY

**The engine moaned** as I downshifted into the curve, then roared as I released the clutch and gunned into full speed to blitz by another opponent. Each car I passed in a blur sent a rush of satisfaction through me, which faded as soon as I saw the next bumper ahead of me on the road.

Barricaded with bales of hay and bright flags, the winding streets of the small German town formed a challenging course. Sheep grazed on alpine slopes in the distance, and crumbling castles evoked fairy-tale fancies in those who stopped to look.

But I wasn't here to enjoy the scenery.

Barreling around another turn, I thought of the sponsors who had paid for my upgraded engine. Their names were plastered on my car and my jumpsuit. They expected a win.

My shoulders ached with tension. My body seemed to think it could urge more speed from the car if I gripped the wheel harder.

Ahead of me, a car swung from side to side, trying to block me. "Out of my way." I hissed the threat, even as my foot punched the gas pedal. Raw horsepower surged beneath me, and I darted past my opponent and left him breathing my exhaust.

A few minutes later I spotted the lead car. My determination surged along with my engine.

Suddenly, the car ahead of me shuddered. Within seconds it spun out. In this remote area between hamlets, no barricades cushioned his accident. Squealing brakes accompanied his spin. When the car came to rest against a stand of pines, smoke poured from the hood.

I hit my brakes and skidded to the shoulder. If I'd debated, I might have convinced myself that a rescue crew would be along soon, that this was my one chance to get ahead, that there was probably nothing I could do anyway.

But I didn't take time to listen to the pit crew in my head. I jumped from my car and ran to help.

I heard the engine cut out and a car door slam. I limped across the living room to the front door. I'd been sipping a cup of tea, savoring the quiet, letting my mind drift. Since it was my turn to host our Thursday night meeting, Kevin had taken the kids to the Mega Mall to play at Lego Land. We had to come up with free recreation these days. We couldn't even afford Mc-Donalds.

Now I threw the door open wide, eager to banish recurring images of cars spinning out of control and deliver hugs to my friends. Although I'd clung to the peace I felt from my decision to turn down the church job, I was about a quart low on encouragement and needed this night of prayer and study.

Sally was the first to arrive. She gave me a firm hug, then bustled past me, talking nonstop about a sale at Marshalls and a new lip liner she had tried. The topic was typical Sally, but her nervous energy set off my warning lights. She was up to something.

I didn't have time to probe because Doreen and Lori pulled up next. As we chattered on the front steps, Heather strolled up the block, leaving footprints in an early-April smudge of wet snow. She wore shorts and a hooded sweatshirt in honor of approaching spring, with big furry boots as a concession to the slush on the sidewalk. At my doorstep, she pulled off the boots revealing bare feet. When I stared, she raised her arms wide. "It's spring!"

"Yeah, but it's also Minnesota."

She looked at me in confusion. "That's why I wore boots."

Whenever I tried to convince Heather she was doing something weird, I ended up feeling like the crazy one. So I just shook my head and ushered her in.

When we had all settled in the living room, Sally bounced on her chair. "Look what came today." She held up a magazine but waved it so vigorously I couldn't see the cover.

Doreen snatched it away from her. "Oh, wow. Becky, why didn't you tell us?"

"What?" I reached across Lori and grabbed the magazine. My own smiling face looked up at me.

I gasped and the magazine rattled in my hands. Lori gathered it up and smoothed the pages. "This is a nice picture," she said.

I dared another peek at the cover. "Kevin took it at Micah's baptism. I don't know how they got it."

Sally giggled, doubled over, and hugged her stomach. "Kevin sent it to Stephanie. And I told him to watch the mail and hide your copy when it came so I could surprise you."

"What? But Kevin was supposed to tell them I couldn't do it." A sick dread was growing in my stomach in spite of Sally's high spirits. I had put the feature article out of my mind, relieved my failings wouldn't be printed for all the successful women of the Twin Cities to laugh at. I pulled the copy from Lori's hands. "Let me see that."

My hands felt clumsy as I tried to find the page with the article. Doreen marched over and pulled the magazine away from me. "Here, let me read it to the group."

"Don't you dare." Heat raced through my chest.

Lori patted my leg. "Becky, hush. We all want to hear it." She shot a quick glance at Sally. "Is it good?"

Sally beamed and gave a nod that sent her earrings jangling. "I think so."

Sweat beaded along my hairline. "Well, somebody hurry up and read it, then."

Doreen cleared her throat. " 'The Secret Life of Becky Miller, Ordinary Mom.' Oh, they have another cute picture. And look, here's one of you at the retreat." She held the magazine in front of her like a librarian at story time, and my friends oohed and aaahed. I chewed my bottom lip.

Sally preened again. "I sent them that one from the retreat. I bet you didn't even know I took it, did you?"

I shook my head, numb and terrified, and smarting a bit from the article's title. "Just read the blasted thing."

"All right. Let's see. 'I arrived at the Miller home with certain expectations. The friend who nominated her spoke of her involvement in her church and her vibrant faith, and our editorial staff felt it would be wise to represent a religious woman— given the high interest in spirituality these days. I admit I was prepared to find a somewhat smug, self-assured icon of the "right way to do things," full of conservative values and old-fashioned opinions.' "

For a moment all I heard in my head was Judy jeering, "Told you so, sis."

But Doreen plowed ahead. " 'Instead I found a woman who was a bit overwhelmed by the demands of her life and refreshingly bewildered—like most of the women I know. But this mom has a secret. While most of the women I interview pursue their goals with aggressive planning, Becky has a different approach.' "

I moaned. Here it comes. The description of my disjointed and unproductive life.

"'As I watched her in action and later interviewed her family and friends—'"

"What?" I yelped. "When was this?"

From her spot on the floor, Heather stretched her bare feet in front of her and wiggled her toes. "I think it was back when you were in the hospital."

Doreen nodded. "Yeah, that sounds about right." She turned to Lori. "Was that when she called you?"

Lori fingered the fine gold chain around her neck and adjusted the cross that rested at the hollow of her throat. "I think so. It was months ago." She gave me a reassuring smile.

I took several short breaths, fighting the impulse to hyperventilate. "And none of you bothered to mention this to me?"

Heather's smile was serene. "You had other things on your mind."

I jumped up and tried to snatch the magazine away from Doreen, but Lori pulled me back to the couch. "Shall we put her out of her misery?" Doreen asked.

Sally smirked. "If she promises to stop interrupting."

I crossed my arms and settled into the couch, throwing eye daggers at my so-called friends.

Doreen ignored me. "Okay, where was I? Here . . . 'Becky's secret approach to life can be summarized by one technique: rapid response. She might begin her day with plans in mind, but like a crack special ops team, her true mission is responding.

"'She drops everything for a sick child or a friend in distress. She dispenses kisses, Band-Aids, meals, hugs, and encouraging words—never knowing who might need them next. Her life is a frustrating mélange of interruptions. Yet everyone who knows her agrees that in the midst of these small choices, Becky makes a big difference.'"

Those words exploded into my heart. Doreen kept reading the article with quotes from various people about ways I'd impacted their lives. But the echoes of that one statement continued to ring in my head.

*I make a difference.*

Something wet splashed on my hand, and I realized tears were running down my cheeks. Sally handed me a tissue, and Lori squeezed my shoulder, but they refused to be distracted from their enjoyment of the article. Their laughter and comments swam around the room as Doreen read on.

"Her husband calls her 'the most courageous person I know.'

'She likes me to read my homework to her,' says seven-year-old Dylan, 'even the boring stuff.'

'Becky is the best friend to have in the tough times, because she doesn't lecture—she just listens and cares.'"

Warmth seeped into my heart as I absorbed scattered quotes and comments.

The last bit of disappointment I'd felt over surrendering the job at my church melted. Lingering resentment I felt toward God for slowing me down eased back. The frustration I felt for not solving Kevin's job situation, Doreen's marriage, and every other need in the universe disappeared.

*I make a difference.*

After some congratulations and good-hearted teasing, my friends set aside the magazine so we could get on with our Bible study. Still floating in a happy haze of confusion and affirmation, I didn't absorb much.

Soon everyone gathered up jackets and Bibles. Sally made me autograph her copy of *Women of Vision* and promised me that Kevin had a copy for me. I waved from the doorstep, then hobbled to the couch and collapsed. My hip throbbed its familiar pain in rhythm with my pulse, but I grinned until my cheeks ached.

The past six months had been an odd journey.

I had been careening through life, rounding curves, determined to pass my competition. But God had slowed me down. Invited me to pull off the racecourse and enjoy the scenery. And when life wasn't racing past in a blur of gasoline fumes and adrenaline, small moments did have value.

When Kevin and the kids tumbled in the door, I savored Kelsey's wild giggle as Kevin tossed her in the air. Dylan ran to give me a little-boy hug, and his mop of hair tickled my skin as he burrowed into my neck. Micah raced to catch up to his siblings with a tipsy toddling gait that barely missed the furniture.

Kevin stuck his head around the corner to gauge my mood.

I tried to frown at him, but it was a pitiful attempt. "I thought we weren't doing the whole keeping secrets thing anymore."

Innocent, wide eyes met mine. "Really? I must have missed the memo." He advanced into the room and eased down next to me on the couch. The teasing fled as he wrapped both arms around me. "I'm so proud of you."

"Did you think the article was good?"

"Not the article." He pressed his cheek against the top of my head. "You. You're an amazing woman, Becky Miller. I think I'll keep you."

I snorted and opened my mouth to remind him of all the ways I fell short. Then I closed my mouth and sighed, letting his words soak in.

Could I believe the magazine article? Had I made a difference? Did responding to detours count as my way to serve God?

It didn't fit my picture of how a heroic Christian life should look. I rarely felt as if I were winning any races. But as I snuggled in Kevin's arms I could almost imagine that my ordinary life of small moments was the Big Thing I could give God.

My heart purred like a Porsche on the straightaway.

# THIRTY·ONE

*Heavy humid air* pressed my skin. The
unique combination of jasmine and diesel fumes
kindled the pleasure of familiarity—of returning home. I had
missed Hong Kong.

I pushed my way aboard the tram, savoring the crush of people as
much as the languid air. Jumping off in the Wanchai neighborhood, I
darted across the congested streets, risking a quick glance over my shoulder. I'd been out of the field a long time. Would I still be able to spot a
tail?

My steps slowed as I ducked down a quiet alley. The clacking tiles
of dozens of men playing mah-jongg sounded like the beads of a giant
abacus colliding. I peeked in the window of the gaming hall as I passed.
Men hunched over the tables with desperate concentration. One block
down I passed the snake shop. An old man with a toothless grin banged
a large snake against the curb. He began the bloody process of skinning
it. A large caldron of snake soup bubbled in front of his store, sending
out enticing aromas. New skyscrapers scaffolded with bamboo rose up
from the ports, and half the people on the street chattered into cell
phones, yet old women with hunched backs carried buckets of broken
concrete away from construction sites. Full of contrasts. Rich with sensory
overload. Deep down, Hong Kong hadn't changed.

But I had. Until the urgent call came from an old colleague in the
CIA, I thought I'd never get back in the game. Now I carried vital
information that our contact refused to accept from anyone but me.

Certain that no one had followed me, I ducked down another street *toward the pier and melted into the crowd boarding the Star Ferry.*

*I stood by the rail and watched the water slip past. With each choppy surge of the boat, I felt my excitement mount. My contact would be waiting in Kowloon.*

*I could admit it now. I'd missed this. As the ferry docked, I leaned over the rail, scanning the faces.*

There he was. My heart climbed toward my throat with excitement. Kevin strode up the sidewalk from the bus stop. My skin tingled with electrical current, but I firmly set aside the conversation I'd just had and the information I was so eager to share. Kevin was back from his job interview, and I wanted to focus on him.

Kevin's keys rattled, and I limped to the door to throw it open before he had to unlock it. The grin that split his face stopped the question on my lips.

He raced inside, bringing along the wet scent of melting snow and the promise of spring. His bear hug lifted me off my feet.

"You got the job?" I squeaked.

He set me down, buffed his nails on his lapel, and tugged his tie. "You're looking at the latest agent in charge of new client development for Personal Life and Health Care Systems."

I shrieked and stumbled back into him for another hug. "I'm so proud of you! You've worked so hard all winter, and you never gave up, and now God's opened a door for you, and you never stopped trusting Him—well, almost never—and I bet this will end up being an even better job than the old one, and—"

He cut me off with a kiss that left me breathless. When he lifted his head, he stroked my cheek. "I couldn't have made it through this without you."

Tears stung my eyes, but before things could get too mushy, he broke away and started pacing. "Of course, it's a new company, so I'll be hunting for clients on my own for a while. Not an easy position. But I've made a lot of contacts in the past months, so that should help. The pay isn't great, but the potential to move up is super, so in a few months we should be able to start catching up on bills. And they promised me a commission on each new account." The competitive gleam in his eye made me laugh. "So I'm making a list this weekend."

I watched him glow with a new level of confidence and energy. Joy trilled like a piccolo chorus in my heart. And beneath my happiness for him, a marching band of eagerness and awe joined in rhythm. "Kev?"

He rubbed his hand over his newly shorn scalp, and the rich dark bristles fluttered like a field of grain. "Hmm?"

"I'm thrilled for you, but it's almost time to get Kelsey, and I need to talk to you about something."

"Sure, hon." He flopped onto a kitchen chair and shoved one in my direction with his foot. "What's up?"

The words from my recent phone conversation swirled through my mind. Unexpected, yet somehow completely right. "I'm not sure what you'll think of this. I'm kind of in shock myself. And maybe this isn't very good timing. It's just, well . . ."

His adrenaline was pumping way to high to endure my roundabout beginning. He leaned forward, elbows resting on his thighs. "Spit it out. What happened?"

I took two breaths. "Teresa Vogt called. She said she spent a lot of time learning about our church when she was considering the position." My fingers bounced a rhythm on the kitchen table. "She was so impressed with the program I developed at our church that when Faith Community decided to develop a women's program, she thought of me."

Kevin's head was bobbing cheerfully as he listened, not catching on.

"I mean, she thought of me to head their new program. On staff."

My husband's reaction was everything I could have hoped for. Openmouthed surprise, sputtering, and a whoop of pure excitement for me.

I laughed. "It's part-time, not full-time like the job at our church would have been. So I think I can handle it. And it's really a 'ground up' kind of thing. They have a strong general adult ministry program but need a new focus for their women. They want me to do a lot of what I did at our church—as far as developing resources for women in different stages of life, small groups, big events." I stopped waving my hands around with my description and grabbed Kevin's arm. "And the funny thing is, as soon as Teresa asked me, I had this sense—this *rightness* in my heart—that this was something God was asking me to do. What do you think?"

He stood and pulled me to my feet. Holding my shoulders he peered into my face with a look of total support. "We should pray about it. But it sounds to me that this might be what God was preparing for you all this time."

What a guy. He didn't show a bit of reserve or a dot of resentment for my news stepping on his own big moment. Instead, we hugged, absorbing the joy of both our new doorways together.

I eased back. "Oh, and I forgot. They have a preschool and day care, so Kelsey can go to the Faith preschool for free, and I can work a half day with Micah in their program."

He kissed my nose. "God's even thinking about the kids, isn't He? It sounds perfect."

That night, when we shared the good news with the kids, we explained that God had answered our prayers. We cuddled on the couch, Kelsey on Kevin's lap, Micah using me as a jungle gym, and Dylan sandwiched between us. With somber awe, I related the news of two wonderful jobs. A gift from God.

Kelsey nodded. Her bangs had grown back in and tickled her

eyelashes. Her curls bounced. "Yep, He's nice."

Dylan shrugged. "I told you He'd take care of it. Hey, can we get a puppy now?"

I didn't think of the wrinkle until later that night. The kids were tucked in, and I was fluffing my pillow and trying to get comfortable. Joy had pushed my pain aside most of the evening, but my leg was starting to resume its familiar ache. "I can't wait to tell Heather and Lori. And the other gals."

Kevin pulled the quilt up and murmured something, his mind probably already on actuary charts and client lists.

I gasped and sat up.

Kevin whirled toward me and grabbed for his heart. "What? What's wrong?"

"I just realized." I gaped at him in horror. "We'll have to join Faith Church if I'm on staff."

He shrugged. "That's okay. I like the people I've met over there."

"No, I mean, what about my Thursday night Bible study? What will happen to us?"

He yawned. "Ask them about it on Thursday." And he rolled over, leaving me to worry.

I restrained myself from e-mailing or calling my friends. This was news to deliver in person. Thursday night I drove to Doreen's house, pulled my walker from the front seat, and hobbled up her sweeping driveway. I was grateful the last of the slush had melted so I could maneuver more easily. My doctor had promised I'd be graduating to a cane soon. It couldn't be soon enough for me. Spring was taking hold, complete with daffodils and tulips. A *For Sale* sign dangled in the midst of Doreen's manicured garden. She seemed distracted when she opened the door. Inside, her house looked a bit frayed around the edges. I actually saw a few toys left out and a smudge mark on her expensive wooden coffee table.

Heather wafted in soon after. She had a woven chain of clover blossoms in her hair. I bit my lip to fight off a giggle. I hadn't made one of those since I was seven. Her twins raced upstairs to find Doreen's kids. They had come equipped with big pads of newsprint and a bucket of crayons, glue, and glitter.

When Lori arrived, she sat next to me on the couch and filled me in on how the Moms' Time Out program had been going. "We miss you. Are you going to start running things again? At least until they find a staff person?"

I was saved from having to answer by Sally's arrival. Rosy cheeked, and huffing a bit from hurrying in from her car, she wriggled into a chair and flipped open her bulging day planner. "Prayer requests?"

We launched into a flurry of catching up, offering advice, and tangents. I waited for the right moment to share my news, worried about how it might impact our group.

After a few minutes, Doreen cleared her throat. "I don't know how to say this."

Worry took my thoughts away from rehearsing my announcement. We all looked at her, wondering if she'd had more bad news.

"First of all, thanks for your prayers. I got the job I was hoping for, and with moving to a smaller house, we're going to be okay. It'll be hard being a single mom, but I found a great nanny."

We cheered and congratulated her, while acknowledging she still had a tough road ahead. Another surge of resentment toward Jim welled up in me, but I fought it down. If she was determined to forgive him, I'd try to follow her lead.

She tossed her head, and her sleek hair shifted and settled perfectly back into place. "But I've made a tough decision. I really need the support of other women going through this experience right now."

We nodded. We all cared about her, but none of us truly understood how it felt to have a husband cheat, then blithely cut you out of his life with barely a backward glance.

"So I've decided to join Open Arms Church." Doreen's spine showed some of its old strength. "I've been going to their divorce recovery group and started visiting their church services." She stared at us, daring us to argue. "I really feel like I belong there."

Stunned silence held the room. Then I started to giggle. The gals looked at me as if I were crazy.

"No, it's not funny. It's just . . ." I tried to catch my breath. "I was so worried about telling you. I'm leaving our church, too."

Sally and Lori jolted their heads from side to side, staring at Doreen and me in shock.

I filled them in on the job offer, and they were as excited as I was about God's leading in this new direction.

Once the excitement died down, we all looked at Lori.

"Well." She hugged her Bible to her chest. "Lots of things to thank God for. Lots of changes." Then she dared to address the question we'd all been worrying over. "So what are we going to do about our group? We're officially part of the small-groups program at our church."

My shoulders slumped. This was the bitter cost of moving to a new church. I couldn't imagine my life without this weekly time together.

Sally crossed her arms. "Well, I guess we'll just have to be *unofficial,* then. I don't care what churches we belong to. God put us together."

Doreen nodded eagerly. "I feel the same way."

Lori nodded slowly. "And with Becky and Doreen at new

churches, they can bring some different perspectives to our group."

"Perspectives are good," Heather said, shoving back her mop of hair and dislodging some of the clover. Doreen frowned at the leaves and petals that dropped to her carpet.

"Friendship is good." Sally dabbed a streak of mascara from her cheek.

Lori looked around the room with a shimmer of tears in her eyes. "*God* is good. I don't know what I'd do without each of you."

Our prayer time that night stretched long into our Bible study time, but we didn't worry about it at all.

Driving home, the warmth I carried helped me stop flinching at every intersection. Since the accident, I was still edgy on the road.

But tonight I felt wonderful. I had a mission again. A new challenge to face. My past experience was exactly what Faith Community Church needed. Better yet, I wasn't going to charge in with both guns blazing. I'd learned that saving the world wasn't on my shoulders. If God wanted to do some Big Things, I'd be happy to come along. But it wasn't up to me to figure out how to make everything happen. Whatever assignments waited for me, I knew there would be intrigue and adventure along the way.

I grinned. Secret agent Becky was back in the field.

# EPILOGUE

**The shriek of** a bird deep in the bamboo
forest seemed to mock me. I held off the attacking
ninjas but knew the inevitable end of this scene. I dodged
more whirling razor stars and flipped past an attempt to trip me
with a kendo stick. One attacker lay on the ground, disabled by a lucky
slice from my blade.

But the other three men circled me, swords flashing in the moon-
light. I'd gladly give my life to protect the emperor and the treasure. But
if I fell now, these enemies would race past me and win anyway.

Sweat slicked my grip and burned my eyes. A slight narrowing of
the eyes of one of the men was my only clue that he planned to move in
first.

I blocked and swung my leg around, snapping the other to his stomach while my blade held his out of the way. He staggered back, but the
next ninja had already moved in behind me.

The whistle of his blade warned me, and I ducked in time to save
my head, using the momentum to roll and spring back to my feet.

The night erupted into an orchestra of clashing metal, grunts, and
thuds. The muscles in my legs quivered with fatigue, and still I fought
on. My arm shook, pushing back blow after blow.

Suddenly, the tallest of the men walloped my blade with a down-
ward swing.

I watched in horror as my sword flew from my hands and spun far
out of reach.

I had trained for unarmed combat. I could disarm attackers with my bare hands. I leapt over fierce swipes, flipped past lightning-fast swings, and snuck in blows against sword arms, hoping to even the odds.

But I was exhausted, and they fought with a wicked energy that wore me down. A blow from behind drove me to my knees.

It was over.

In the last fraction of life that was mine, I looked up at the moon. My last vision of earth would contain beauty. I clung to that gift as clouds moved away, revealing the blue-white glow.

A fierce yell interrupted my dying moment.

I watched in confusion as other emperor's guards leapt from the windows of the palace.

In the moment of accepting my inevitable loss, I couldn't understand the rush of movement around me or gather my wits enough to get out of the way.

Voices shrieked in attack and victory. Swords clashed briefly but then silenced.

Before I could remember to breathe, the ninjas were being hauled into the palace. Two had to be carried, while the others hobbled under the grip of strong warriors.

My shoulders shook convulsively as I gasped in air and tried to convince myself I was actually alive.

Embroidered slippers stepped into my line of vision, gold threads glinting against the brick of the courtyard. Shame at my poor showing begged me to keep staring at the ground, but honor compelled me to look up and acknowledge my failure.

The emperor stood before me, red and golden robes falling from his strong shoulders. His face was grim, implacable. He held my gaze for a long moment.

"I'm sorry," I gasped, still struggling to regain my breath.

"You've honored me with your service." His voice was quiet, mixed with a murmur of wind escaping from the surrounding forest.

I dropped my head. "I failed you." My sword lay forgotten a few feet away. I had ended my battle so close to where it had fallen and hadn't known. I reached for it and held it up to the emperor.

A sound that could have been a low chuckle sounded above me. "You held your ground. You offered your life for my benefit."

When he didn't take my sword, I laid it at his feet. "My life has always been yours. I wanted to conquer for you." Tears not befitting a warrior clogged my throat. His silence made me uneasy. "I didn't get a stroke in once I was knocked down. They defeated me."

Just take my life now. Let this shame be over.

My night to stand guard. My role to defend the palace. My life's aspiration. And I had failed.

Hands grasped my shoulders and urged me to my feet. He waited until I lifted my gaze. A smile, both wise and gentle, played on his face. "Your job was not to guard the treasure alone. You served me faithfully in this battle."

His foot flicked forward, catching the edge of my sword and tossing it lightly into the air between us. I sensed it spin over our heads. Without moving his eyes from mine, he caught it, flipped it, and tilted the blade's hilt in my direction.

He still wanted my service? After my poor showing? I searched his eyes, barely able to believe the truth of his invitation. Joy and determination burned away the pain of bruises and humiliation, but I was still shy to move.

He pressed the handle of my sword into my hand. "Take it. You'll need it again." His smile grew.

I grasped the weapon, finally believing his sincerity.

He turned to walk back into the palace and I hurried to follow, my feet almost floating over the stone of the courtyard. More adventures. Another chance to serve him. Excitement sparkled through me like starlight on my sword. I couldn't wait.

# AUTHOR BIO

SHARON HINCK is a wife and mother of four children who generously provide her with material for her books. She has an M.A. in communications from Regent University and has served as the artistic director of a Christian performing arts group, a church youth worker, and a professional choreographer. She lives in Minnesota with her family. To learn more about her writing visit her Web site at *www.sharonhinck.com*.

For *The Secret Life of Becky Miller* Reading Group Guide, visit *www.bethanyhouse.com/secretlifeofbeckymiller*.

# ACKNOWLEDGMENTS

Becky Miller loves to dream, and so do I. So I feel immense gratitude to those friends who have encouraged me to write, even when the idea seemed like a grandiose fantasy. Special thanks to . . .

Word Servants—the best writing group in the world and a safe sandbox where I can play. Margaret Montreuil, Bill and Cheryl Bader, Carol Oyanagi, Nancy Brown, Jonathan Friesen, Kathy Wichterman, and Lisa Erlers. My writing has been enriched by each of you.

Randy Ingermanson—for shepherding me through the bewilderment of my entry into a new world. Thanks, coach!

Karen Hancock—for your mentoring and amazing example of keeping Christ at the center through all the angst of the writing life.

Jan Dennis—your enthusiasm and support provided me energy to keep writing. I've treasured each of our chats.

Steve Laube—for taking a chance on me, coming alongside, and adding your level head and wisdom to my giddy inexperience.

Sherri Sand, Kelli Standish, Camy Tang, Jill Nelson, and Cindy Thomson—amazing critique partners and sisters in writing.

All my dear family, friends, and prayer partners, and the test-readers who have circulated various manuscripts—especially my dear mom, Flossie Marxen, who reads every word.

The gifted writers of Minnesota Christian Writers Guild, Mount Hermon, and Writing Chambers—who have taught me so much.

The St. Michael's Family Fellowship—a place to be real.

The Thursday morning Bible study gals: Vicki, Marijo, Sue B., Sue H., Becky, and Marci—dearer friends could not be found. The best aspects of Becky Miller are shaped by all of you.

James Thurber—whose classic short story *The Secret Life of Walter Mitty* inspired the format of the book.

The amazing folk at Bethany House—who made me feel like part of the family from day one, especially Charlene Patterson, Ann Parrish, and Karen Schurrer.

Joel, Jennelle, Kaeti, Josh, and Jenni—for loving me even when I'm a weird mom (and mother-in-law) who writes stuff. You are each a marvel.

Ted—my soul mate, my safe place to fall, my solid ground.

My precious Savior—thank you for inviting me on this grand adventure.